D0407181

Books by AUBREY MENEN

THE RAMAYANA

DEAD MAN IN THE SILVER MARKET

THE DUKE OF GALLODORO

THE BACKWARD BRIDE

THE STUMBLING STONE

THE PREVALENCE OF WITCHES

Charles Scribner's Sons

the
Ramayana

the
Ramayana

AS TOLD
BY

AUBREY MENEN

CHARLES SCRIBNER'S SONS, NEW YORK

1954

FOR PHILIP DALLAS

contents

book i the palace of lies

book ii the tales of valmiki

Contents

BOOK III the siege of lanka

introduction

introduction

This is the story of Rama, a prince of India,
who lived his life according to the best advice. He reverenced
his intellectual betters, who were called Brahmins, and did what
they told him to do. He took his morals from the best moralists,
and his politics from the most experienced politicians. As a
result he was ruined, exiled, and disinherited: his wife was stolen
from him and when he got her back he very nearly had to
burn her alive from the highest of motives. In the teeth of the
soundest and most reliable guidance from his moral and mental
superiors, he finally recovered his country, his throne, and his
common sense. He lived more than two thousand five hundred
years ago but everybody will recognise his experiences.

Twenty-five centuries is a long time ago, but the Indians
were in many ways as civilised as we are today. There were great
cities with immense bazaars in which the shopkeeper cheated
his customers and was in turn cheated by the merchants. The
merchants were robbed by a vast civil service, and the civil
servants kissed the big toes of the politicians, who were known
as courtiers. The courtiers were Brahmins, and the Brahmins
were the top dogs. They made the laws, taught the ignorant,
dictated morals, controlled the temples, and terrified the king.
In those far-off days they had not yet become a rigid and hereditary caste. Any man could become a Brahmin provided he set
himself up to know better than his fellow men, and was sharp
enough to get away with it. But a Brahmin was usually the son

3

of a Brahmin, because the tricks of the trade took a long time to
learn, and a man could not start too early.

Besides the Brahmins, there were men of genius. These were
usually thought brainy but a danger to society and they were
customarily driven to live in the wilderness, another sign that
this ancient civilisation was not much below our own. One such
man of genius was Valmiki, who wrote the story that I am
going to re-tell.

It is said that the tale of Rama's adventures is the first story
ever put together. I do not know that this is true: but it is
certain that Valmiki was the first human being to be recognised
as a literary genius. He was therefore penniless and much disliked. He lived in a thatched hut and had to grow his own food.
He could move among his fellow men only if he were heavily
disguised, and then at the risk of his life. He was an outlaw.

The Brahmins said (and their views have survived down to
our own times) that he was a brigand in his youth, and in his
maturity he became an assassin. This may mean that when he
was young he stole other people's property and, when he was
older, killed someone. On the other hand it may mean only that
his verses scanned better than anything the Brahmins could
write themselves. We have no sure means of knowing which
interpretation is the true one, but it should be noted that some
of Valmiki's poetry is extremely good.

The Brahmins said that the man he killed was one of their
fraternity. The killing of a Brahmin was the most heinous crime
that the Brahmins could think of: but subsequently, millions
of Indians who are not Brahmins have not taken too gloomy a
view of it. His crime, if he did commit a crime, has not dimin-
ished his fame and has added, for some, to his personal charm.
He has obstinately remained the greatest of Indian authors.
Unfortunately, generations of Brahmins have re-written his poem

so that in parts it says the opposite of what Valmiki plainly intended. While restoring his tale I shall not attempt to revive his language: I shall aim at reviving his attitude of mind.

This will mean rejecting whole sections of the work that the Brahmins have written into it, and inventing much that they destroyed: a drastic course, but then I am not, myself, a Brahmin.

note

the
indian
enlightenment

The *Ramayana* is a poem of twenty-four thousand couplets. The first version, now quite buried, was very much shorter. It was written during a wave of philosophic scepticism which is sufficiently remarkable to be called the Indian Enlightenment, a movement which threw doubt on the very foundations of society.

The better to understand how extraordinary this was, let us imagine such a revolt happening in our own times. First we must see what the sceptics would disbelieve; what particular pillars of our own beliefs they would shake; in what way they would scandalise even such intelligent, broad-minded persons as the reader and myself.

To do that we must first determine which things in our own civilisation we take for granted because we believe them to be good. I can best arrive at this by describing a man I met in Corsica.

A few years ago I had retreated for the purpose of quiet reflection to a small village on the warmer side of Corsica. This was the village of Cargèse, which has one hotel and this hotel has only two bedrooms. In the dining room of this hotel I met a Scandinavian. His name meant nothing to me but he was clearly a man of remarkable capacities. I had been living among a backward tribe in India and we struck up a conversation on the subject of primitive peoples. The Scandinavian was most interested to know if my tribe ate maize. I was able to assure him they did not, at which he lost interest in them. But he kindly expounded for me his own theory about the migration of tribes in the Pacific, in the earlier periods of human history. I was interested by his theory but astounded at his proof. He maintained that the inhabitants of the Pacific islands had colonised them from South America by floating across the ocean on a balsa raft. He had built a raft and floated across himself.

Like most brave men Mr. Thor Heyerdahl is serious and practical. While he left me to guess the perils of sailing a raft across the Pacific, he told me of the meticulous organisation behind his adventure. This had begun (if I remember correctly) years before with the help of learned societies. It had involved the transportation of his crew by airplane: it called for cinematography and for radio telegraphy: it demanded official contacts with more than one department of more than one government: and it naturally had ties with the major news journals of the world. The danger, the vision, the courage, and the glory were those of one man and his chosen companions; but his vision brought into play a vast social apparatus: and not the least striking thing about the Kon-Tiki expedition was that this apparatus had been turned for the first time after many years of war to the peaceful services of civilisation at its finest. It did not surprise me to learn from Mr. Heyerdahl that he had found this side of his enterprise the most exhausting.

Now if we are proud of anything in our times, I think this is what we most take pride in—this community of civilised men that any of us can call upon, either to assist us to send a letter to a friend in the next town or, if we have Mr. Thor Heyerdahl's imagination, tenacity, and powers of organisation, to cross the Pacific on a balsa raft. When we think of Mr. Heyerdahl and his fellow navigators, we are moved by the picture of a few men in the middle of a limitless sea. But we must not forget that Mr. Heyerdahl's object was not to prove the trip a difficult one, but to show that it was easy enough to have been done first by savages, and in that, he maintains, he has succeeded. What, then, distinguishes Mr. Heyerdahl from the original savage? In point of courage, nothing. In point of culture, everything. The savage did little more than shift his body from one point to another; Mr. Heyerdahl moved half the world, in every sense. He used the skills and the brains of uncounted men who make films, operate radio, print newspapers, follow the progress of ethnology, chart currents, own libraries, pilot airplanes, bank money, and reward brave men. Nothing, of course, can detract from the pioneering merit of his feat; but it is significant of our times that when this highly individual scientist kindly left me his address, I found that it was "The Explorers *Club*, New York."

We have organised the world. Even if we aim, in the end, to blow the world to pieces, that will still call for a greater organisation than history has ever seen, and we shall no doubt be capable of it.

Now suppose some sceptical thinkers arose amongst us and said: "The whole elaborate organisation is, in our opinion, preposterous nonsense. You are all mistaken. It must be scrapped and we must start again on different lines." Would we have a parallel to the Indian Enlightenment? By no means. We should have merely a few cranks.

Suppose, on the other hand, these sceptics spoke rather differently. Suppose they said: "We have nothing against the elaborate toy which you call civilisation. It is very pretty, especially when all the parts are in working order. We do not suggest for a moment that you pull it to pieces and start anew. We do not suggest that you improve it. We do not suggest you do anything at all. So far as we are concerned our only wish is, with the greatest good will, never to see your face again. If you are curious to know what we propose to do, we shall endeavour to explain, but not very often. We intend to set about the proper business of a human being, which is the improvement of his own soul. In this you cannot join us because you cannot call your souls your own. Since you depend every minute of your existence on everybody, you yourself are nobody. However, we will agree, in parting, that you are a jolly good fellow."

This is a true parallel. It will occur at once to the reader that there is another one. The first Christian monks turned their backs on the greatest civilisation the world had seen in the same way except that I could not quote the language that many of them used in doing it because it is not fit to print. They, too, considered Roman civilisation preposterous; they also had no desire to alter it; and they too did not encourage earnest seekers after the light to follow them. St. Jerome, writing to a female admirer, who wished to make a pilgrimage, told her sourly that a visit to Bethlehem was not an absolute essential for holiness, Bethlehem being, at the time of writing, his place of residence.

What is it that caused thinking men at two apices of civilisation, that of Brahminical India and that of Imperial Rome, to dismiss the whole conglomeration from their minds as trash, and *to leave it*. It needs no effort of the imagination to see a man wanting to put civilisation right. We all do. This is called *Progress*. It is more difficult to understand how a man can hold that the civilisation of which he is a member is so unimportant that it is not worth his trouble to put right even if he knew how it should be done. We cannot even dismiss them as saints. Saints generally aim with holy determination to put things right. If I say, "He is a saint: he does not give a click of his beads whether you or even his own mother burns in hell or not," does it not conjure up a somewhat confusing picture? So these people are not what you ordinarily call saints, whatever your religion: unless, of course, you are a Hindu, when you will not find it confusing at all.

The best way to avoid confusion in thinking about the ways of human beings is to remember that the number of the ideas that have really moved mankind is very small and most of this small number of ideas are very simple. The difficulty is that you and I have room in our heads for only one or two of these simple ideas at the same time.

For instance: one of the most powerful notions in the history of thought is that of the Devil. Another powerful idea is that of Nature obeying fixed laws. If you believe in Nature obeying fixed laws and I believe in black magic, and if we both want to obtain a nugget of gold, you will go prospecting in some place which your study of the laws of geological action has led you to believe has auriferous rocks. I will put a lump of lead in a basin, and sacrifice a cock at midnight on a bare mountain. You will think me an unsavoury charlatan; I will think you an uninspired fool. Nowadays our friends would expect you to find the gold: in the Middle Ages they would (privately) have put their money on me. Because I cannot see your simple idea and you cannot see mine we shall not only differ in our ways of getting gold, we shall differ about nearly everything under the sun. Since you believe that if you know how Nature works she will do as you bid her, you will be confident that if things are left to you and your co-workers, everything can be made bigger and better and everybody made happier. I, on the other hand, believe in the power of evil and I shall say that men are wicked and nothing will make them better and the fact had best be faced. Your idea may lead you to discover antibiotics or nerve gas: mine can make me a great leader of men. But the two ideas that are the base of our differences can be explained to an intelligent child.

The simple idea that led the first monks to turn their backs on civilisation was Heaven. Heaven was a place much better than Rome. It was obvious that everybody was not going there, but it seemed to the monks that those who did not try with all their might and main were as lacking common sense as a man who owned a palace but lived in the basement because he could not take the trouble to climb upstairs to bed. Like all men who have made up their minds and have no intention of altering them, their greatest plague was well-meaning admirers who would neither take their advice nor stop asking for it. They therefore retired to remote spots to get to Heaven by fasting, praying, and hoping in peace and quiet. Yet Heaven is such a simple idea that nobody has troubled to explain what it is, except Dante, who in spite of his majestic poetry does not convince a single reader that he has been there.

The simple idea which arose in India centuries ago and which has shaken Indians, and many who are not, ever since is that of moral obesity.

If, by the action of some malicious genie, I found that instead of being at my writing table I was clinging to a trapeze forty feet above an audience at a circus, I would be helpless until I was carried down the ladder by attendants. If the same genie transported the trapeze artist at the same time to my writing desk and invited him to write about the doctrines of *karma, dharma, maya,* and *moksha* as I am doing, he would also be at a loss. We both lack the necessary practice. Nobody thinks this remarkable. It is accepted as obvious that some years spent daily at a writing desk will have given me a knowledge of the elements of self-expression: while some years spent in rehearsals will have given him a knowledge of what, from ignorance of the right technical terms, I shall call the ropes. We are both set in our ways and cannot easily change our rôles.

Now suppose that the genie, having restored us to our desk and circus, decides to have more sport. This time he transports us together into the middle of Africa and presents us with two guns, a faithful servant, and a rhinoceros. The rhinoceros charges. I fling down my gun and run for the nearest tree and I am too busy climbing it inexpertly to notice that the faithful servant is under the rhinoceros' feet. The trapeze artist, on the other hand, leaps gracefully aside and with admirable coolness raises his rifle and, unable to miss at such short, if terrifying, range, shoots the animal dead and rescues the servant. Everybody would think this most remarkable. The trapeze artist would have shown bravery and I the white feather. If I pleaded that swinging from a trapeze teaches a man to face danger with steady nerves while writing books is a dangerous occupation only under a totalitarian regime, where authors are taken very seriously, it will be accepted as an excuse. But I shall still be thought a coward. Yet what has caused this difference in our moral natures if it is not the same thing as that which causes the difference in our skills; namely, what we had practised in the years before?

Since the genie is concerned to prove that it is indeed the same thing he now transports us both to a Buddhist monastery.

By this he makes his point and saves my self-respect. After a few days I find a cloistered life perfectly acceptable; the trapeze artist finds it worse than incarceration in an asylum. I do not mind spending most of my day in a cell, since writing is a solitary act. The obligatory prayers, which consist of the same sentiments endlessly repeated in different words, I find a good substitute for the daily newspaper. I do not miss my wife because I am a bachelor. The trapeze artist finds the company of monks strikingly less warm than the company of trapeze artists: he does not know what to do with himself when he is alone except handsprings, which are not encouraged. He is desperate for his wife and his growing and acrobatic family. I am given the saffron robe. He is expelled. He goes back to the circus and I proceed upwards to Nirvana.

At this point the genie has established that both myself and the acrobat are a sort of addition sum of the things we have done before. But the trapeze artist denies this hotly, and so do I. He maintains that he is much more than a performer on a trapeze. He is a good father, a faithful husband, a member of the association of trapezists, a Republican, an Elk, an admirer of Ernest Hemingway's "Death in the Afternoon," and a taxpayer. I have an equally long list, which I may sum up by saying that to describe me as an author would satisfy nobody but a passport official.

However, we have not proved the genie wrong. All the things which we cite as describing ourselves are again things we have done in the past, and again the genie may say that we are both the mere sum of such actions.

If the trapeze artist and myself are not this—and we are sure that we are something more—then what are we? We are of course two separate arrangements of muscles, veins, flesh and bones, his being more efficiently arranged than mine. But that is not what we mean. The question is better put as "*Who* are we?" Or, to include the reader, "Who are *you?*"

One possible answer to this last question is: "I know exactly who I am. I am John (or Judith) Doe of Acacia Avenue in such-and-such a city in such-and-such a state. Moreover I have no taste for Oriental hairsplitting."

This answer has saved a great deal of the world's time, and it is practical in the way that it is practical to put a dog's name and address on its collar if you do not want it to get lost. However, the answer is false. The dog is not Pete: you are not John Doe. Both are names given by people who are not dogs or not you.

To proceed to try to find a true answer to the question is to take the first step in entering the world of the Indian mind. The Indian mind was formed by the sceptical thinkers who, twenty-five centuries ago, decided that the answer to the question was that you are originally something utterly different from anything you are called, or anything you do. However, everything you do is added to what you originally are. After a lifetime of doing you are not yourself at all; you have lost yourself. That is, you have lost your soul; that is, you are damned.

This is the explanation that these thinkers gave of their extraordinary answer:

When a man eats, some particles of the food he takes remain behind in his body. If he eats too much the food becomes particles of fat and he swells so that he can barely recognise himself as the same man. In the same way, of each act that a man does, part remains with him. If he acts in accordance with his own soul, then he is like the man who eats enough. He will remain himself. But if he acts more than he needs, and more than his soul requires—above all if he acts not from his own soul but because of the desires or passions or prejudices of others—

then his soul becomes covered with the deposit of his acts and grows obese. In the end, it may be smothered and die.

The men who put forward this theory offered a proof of it. The proof is metaphysical. The trouble with a metaphysician, then and now, is that either he explains everything or he explains nothing. He can have no half-measures. The Indian metaphysicians proved their theory by explaining the nature and origin of the Universe. Their arguments have been discussed by metaphysicians down to our own times. But speculation about the Universe can be as idle an occupation as chewing a straw. Much of Indian (and any other) metaphysics is little more than an ingenious postponement of the stage when the philosopher has to admit that he does not know what he is talking about: and since what he is talking about is God Almighty, this admission is never altogether a surprise.

Having demonstrated the nature of the Universe, the metaphysicians among the sceptics went on to prove their theory of the soul by describing the substance of the soul. Since neither they nor anybody since has discovered what the soul is made of, we need not stay to follow their reasoning. The best argument for their theory of moral obesity was that numbers of thoughtful people felt that it hit the truth.

They felt this largely because the sceptics were courageous. Had they said that wicked acts influence the soul forever afterwards they would have been saying no more than nursemaids do in training children. Instead they argued that all actions corrupt and stifle our spirits, and in the word "all" they necessarily included good acts as well. This is what many people had been long suspecting. They listened to the sceptics with a new respect and when the philosophers were driven into exile by an outraged orthodoxy, they followed them in large numbers. The revolution in thinking had begun, and it is still not finished.

I think that it is still not finished because it seems that there comes a time in the history of every civilisation when, for the sake of human dignity, men turn their backs on it.

Let us see why this is so.

When Rama was a prince in Ayoda, the life of all the inhabitants from the King downwards was governed by a series of minutely detailed rules. Some of the rules were backed by the law: all of them had the sanction of everybody's sense of good citizenship, and this was more powerful than the law. The lives of any group of human beings can be governed entirely by written laws: but you must first build a prison and lock them up in it. Should you be able to persuade them, however, to want to be good fellows, decent citizens, and respected by all, they will build the prison for themselves. In the first great civilisation of history, of which Rama's story tells, men and women had such a respect for the opinion of their community that they even obeyed a set of rules when privately excreting. This would be incredible if later the rules had not been written down in a code which can still be read; and this, in its turn, would be comic, if those rules were not still obeyed by millions of respectable Hindus today, which makes it melancholy.

"Bright shining faces, and all in our places"; this was the common aim of Rama's contemporaries, as it must be of any civilised body of men. So far as their places were concerned, they all knew them perfectly. Each person was born into a caste, and this caste had its duties and its privileges. Of these, its duties were the saddest: they employed all the most generous impulses of the human spirit, and regimented them. Compassion became almsgiving: courage became military service:

religion a drill; and independent thinking became bad manners. From the moment a man rose from his bed till the time he disengaged himself from the systematised embraces of his wife and fell asleep again, his acts were prescribed by a committee, part visibly composed of his neighbours, part invisible and made up of the watching dead. He could do only what others did, what his forebears had done, or what his spiritual advisors thought might please the gods. The only way in which he could be sure that he was acting from his own free will was to commit a crime.

If you feel, reading this, that such a state of affairs is a shame, but it happened in a very distant past, then you will find it interesting to ask yourself the question that the Indian sceptics asked two thousand five hundred years ago: "If I wished at this moment to do one good deed that was quite my own—that had not been taught me by schoolmasters, or parents, or priests, or books, and which did not spring from my social conscience, what would that good deed be?"

The answer that the sceptics gave was a paradox—but then Indians have never flinched from paradoxes. They said that the only thing you could do was to go off to some place where you could be quite alone, sit down, and then do nothing at all.

Their answer brought every respectable element of society about their ears.

The Brahmins, who were responsible for the government of society, asked if these self-styled philosophers were not aware that the gods decreed that man was a social animal and that he could not live alone?

To this they tranquilly replied:

"Our forefathers lived beyond the Hindu Kush where they lived in tents of goats' hair and drank the milk of asses. They were also without the benefit of a highly educated caste of Brahmins to provide them with information about the decrees of the gods. We, their descendants, have progressed. Are we not to progress further? Suppose that we, having learned how to live in peace with at least our nearest neighbours, must now, according to the will of the gods, go on to learn how to live at peace with ourselves."

Prince Rama, being a young man of good education, deplored these heretical ideas before his exile, but they were in the air of the century. Another prince, heir to a kingdom as Rama was, but perhaps less well educated, was struck one day by the sight of a dead body at the very gates of his palace. Realising that he, too, was mortal, he determined to understand more about himself while he had time to do it. Following the precepts of the sceptical thinkers he withdrew from his kingdom, leaving his wife and family behind him, and went to live in a forest.

Here he decided that whatever he was, he was certainly not a bundle of appetites for food, warmth, and sexual pleasure, all of which, to be properly supplied, meant that he would be bound once more to his fellows and again enclosed in the prison of social circumstance from which he had escaped.

He therefore practised the most severe austerities, denying himself all but the minimum of food and sleep, sitting motionless for days on end, praying incessantly and fighting down fearsome rebellions of the flesh. At the end of six years of this life he found that he knew what he was not—he was not a creature of impulse—but he was no nearer knowing who he was.

He lightened his penances and reduced them to thinking while he sat cross-legged under a tree. Here, after long meditations, he found a way of knowing his own soul and a series of

ways by which it could be freed from any contamination by
worldly things.

The only contamination which remained with him seems
to have been a desire to pass on his discoveries to others. He
rapidly gathered a devoted if not very intelligent following, and
he expounded his methods of securing detachment from the
world. It is not easy to see how he could have preserved his own
soul uncontaminated when he, by choice, spent the next forty-
three years knocking sublime truths into the heads of disciples
and admirers. But his notions were profoundly new and exciting: he was an admirable teacher and, it must not be forgotten,
a member of the nobility. He was greatly in demand all over
the country. Soon his following grew so great that he was forced
to organise it. He set up monasteries in which seekers after release from the world could live, meantime, in a world of their
own. In spite of the protests of the Brahmins, these monasteries
were filled to overflowing as soon as they were set up. It was no
doubt a paradox that people should seek to release their ties with
men by binding themselves to live cheek by jowl with them in
cramped quarters, but again, it was a paradox which disturbed
few Indians of the time, or subsequently.

The founder of these monasteries was now, by the nature of
things, leading as busy and full a life as a modern bishop. His
fame continued to grow until, surrounded by weeping disciples,
he died. He has been known to history ever since as Gautama
Buddha. He was eighty years old at the time of his release from
this world and he died from eating too much pork.

The reader may now feel that he is on more familiar ground.
Buddha is well known in the West although it is often forgotten
that he was as much a typical Indian as Mohandas Gandhi.

But from the point of view of the sceptics, Buddha was

something of a disaster. No sooner had he died than an ortho-doxy only slightly less absurd than that of the Brahmins was erected over his teachings. The Brahmins found little difficulty in regaining their hold on men's minds and they maintained it down to modern times.

It was during this second hegemony that they altered Val-miki's poem to suit their purposes. Valmiki was not a philoso-pher: but it is clear from the bare bones of the story of Rama that he was a sceptical realist. With that in mind, I have retold the story, replacing the Brahminical moralising with some tales of my own.

BOOK ONE

the
palace
of
lies

CHAPTER ONE

the olò story,
maòe new,
begins

The traveller to Ayoda, having crossed a pass between flat-topped hills and descended to the plains, came first upon a road lined with tombs. These were rounded structures, like the top half of an egg, with carved bands telling stories of the gods. They were surrounded by a thick railing, sometimes of wood, sometimes of stone, but always rich with sculpture. Under the egg was a small chamber and in this, resting on a shelf, an urn holding the dead man's ashes. This avenue might well have been a gloomy approach had there been any sign of mourning on the tombs. There was, however, none. They gave, as they were intended to give, the impression that the dead man had been comfortable and respected here on earth and was confident of being treated in the same manner beyond.

The gate of the city lay at the end of this avenue. It was a low affair with two towers. It had heavy teak doors, folded back during the day, and closed during the night. A few minutes before it closed a great thumping and roaring would break out from a small chamber immediately above the arch. This was the ceremonial drum, an affair of oxhide some eight feet across and beaten by four men with heavy drumsticks. On the nearby battlements other men would blow into the pointed end of large

conch shells, that made a mournful sound, half animal in
quality, but of a power to carry across the whole city, a matter,
perhaps, of a mile.

The road underneath the gateway was the only paved road in
Ayoda, which it bisected. It was marked on either side by two
deep grooves made by carts and chariots. Once a cart entered
the gateway and its wheels fell into those grooves it was com-
pelled to follow them. There was no way of getting out of the
ruts made by its predecessors. The inhabitants made no objection to this because it was the principle on which they ran
their own lives.

The single street was lined with the houses of the rich:
behind them in a tangle of mud alleys were the huts of the
poor. The houses of the rich had plain walls facing the street
with a stone symbol to indicate the owner placed near a tall
doorway. When the doors stood open the traveller could see
into a courtyard, open to the sky and surrounded by a colon-
nade. In the middle of this courtyard stood a stone altar. Here
the head of the house made his sacrifices to the gods. Since respectability required that he do this at least six times a day, the
traveller would stand an excellent chance of seeing him at his
devotions.

He would usually be a man of good stature, pale brown or
even ivory in the colour of his skin, a great deal of which would
be visible since his only garment during these religious moments was a loin-cloth of fine material reaching below the knees.
He would be surrounded by his family, the women swathed in
coloured saris, which they held together over their faces while
looking through a fold.

Other sacrifices would be constantly in progress at the main
temple of the town, a large structure which lay in a piazza mid-
way along the street. It was a pyramid of stone, all carved, and

entered by a doorway writhing with allegorical figures. The piazza in front of it would be filled with people at most hours of the day and during the first part of the night. One type of person was immediately distinguishable from the rest. These people were much darker in complexion than the rest and appeared to avoid any direct contact with their paler co-citizens. These black men were princes, sons of the blood royal, dukes, landowners, and knights. They owned the land on which Ayoda stood, but they had had the misfortune of having it taken away from them by armed robbers in the past, the robbers being the ancestors of the more fair, and Aryan, inhabitants. The early Aryans, since they knew that the black men were the true owners of the soil, were forced by the nature of the case to decree that the black men were particularly disliked by God, who specifically wished them to lead unattractive lives. The Aryans, thus fortified, gave the black men, among other similar duties, the sole right to clean out the city's latrines. This made the black men as important in the life of society as they had been when they were landowners, but they were less well rewarded.

The next class above these were the merchants, whose shops and warehouses made busy the long stretch of the road that led from the main square to the gates of the palace. In the palace lived the king (who was a noble descendant of the original conquerors) and his government, which was made up of Brahmins, who were the highest caste of all. At the time of this story the king was called Dasa-ratha.

King Dasa-ratha, Rama's father, was loved by all his subjects and he loved certain of them in return, especially if they were women. His one wish for his people was that they should, every one of them, enjoy all the good things of life, and he sincerely hoped that they would find some way of doing it. Meantime, he set them an example by enjoying the good things of life himself.

One of these good things was his vast palace, in which the King pursued happiness with the same ardour as some men pursue moral perfection, making himself equally miserable in the process. The palace occupied a quarter of the whole area of the city, of which only a fraction was devoted to the King's debaucheries. The rest was composed of great courtyards, surrounded by porticoes and columns, each courtyard having at one end a large hall, the roof of which was held up by pillars carved in the shape of a lotus, or a rearing horse, or four elephant heads or warriors back to back. These halls were named according to their intended function.

The most splendid of these courts was the Hall of Audiences. Here the King received his subjects. The humblest inhabitant had the right of access to his monarch, provided, out of respect for his King, he covered himself with the official robe of audience, which was edged with gold braid and could be purchased from the Master of the Robes at a price fitting to the dignity of the occasion. The fortunate person then approached his lord by edging himself forward with his elbows, flat on his belly.

One of the reasons for King Dasa-ratha's immense popularity with all classes was that, while holding audience one day early in his reign, he observed that some of the more elderly of his subjects were caused pain by the unevenness of the floor in front of his footstool. He had immediately given orders that it be re-laid with the smoothest marble.

A leather merchant who remarked in public that it would have been simpler for the King to have ordered that his subjects approach him on two feet, like men, instead of on their bellies like snakes was given the mild punishment of being beaten with one of his own straps in front of his jeering neighbours.

He had not received more than five hundred strokes before he admitted in a loud voice that crawling on one's belly was a highly suitable posture for a citizen when faced with the power of the state in person, upon which (by a kindly forethought of the King himself) he was released.

The next most splendid hall was the Hall of Justice. The system of justice in Ayoda was the wonder of the Indian world. Every man was equal before the law. If a dispute arose between a rich man and a poor one, and if the latter was too poor to hire a lawyer, the Court would appoint him one from out of the waiting Brahmins (all lawyers were members of this distinguished caste) who was not allowed to accept money, and who must forthwith plead his penniless client's cause. This he would do to the utmost of his ability; much depended for him on the way he conducted the case. Many of the most wealthy advocates had won their spurs in such poor man's cases, since it was not easy to plead a case at an instant's notice and make a showing against a lawyer who had been studying his richer client's case perhaps for months.

Not only was every man thus given an equal chance before the judges, the judges themselves were impartial. They were always appointed from amongst the most successful and experienced pleaders, it being an established principle that the man most likely to arrive at the truth in a legal matter was the man who had spent the greater part of his life doing his best to conceal it. However strange this rule may appear at first sight, it should be noted that no better has yet been discovered.

Nor is this surprising, for the major discoveries in the method of governing mankind had been hit upon very early,

for without them men could not be governed at all. Thus the
next hall was called the Hall of the Exchequer, and although
the accounts were kept in a primitive manner by notching sticks
and flicking the beads of an abacus, the method underlying the
collection and the assessment of taxes was as sound as any used
since and in principle much the same. The Controller of the
Exchequer taxed the people as much as he thought they would
bear without violent protest: and when he was wrong the King
declared a necessary war. These wars were called necessary both
because they were useful in defending the frontiers and because
they made it possible to levy double taxes. Occasionally the
King did not have to declare a necessary war. A neighbouring
kingdom did it for him. When the armies of the enemy approached the frontiers it was usually found that the Royal Arm-
oury (a part of the palace that we shall not trouble to describe)
had far too few bows for the archers, and a perplexing deficiency
of arrows; the pikes were rusty and half of the spears were
stolen; and not one quarter of the chariots of war would be
found fit to take the road. Only the elephants would be found
to be in fighting condition since these were taken out twice
a year in public on the occasion of religious processions.
Neither the King nor his Controller troubled to excuse these
deficiencies. But when the public dismay was at its height, they
would execute a general. This always restored public confidence,
though how, and in what, it would be difficult to say.

Behind the Exchequer were the women's quarters, and here,
owing to the proclivities of the King, was the real centre of government.

If the morals of the Exchequer are familiar, the morals of
the Bedchamber are not. By law and by divine sanction the
King was allowed as many wives as he could keep: that is to say,

as many as the public would pay for, and the public was very indulgent.

This was because the priests explained that the custom made sure of the succession to the throne, and the unthinking members of the public accepted this explanation as satisfactory. The citizens who looked more deeply into the matter saw clearly enough that it did nothing of the sort: since the King produced a great number of sons, the succession was very much a lottery, and often a bloody one. But even these thoughtful people approved of a plurality of queens, because it gave the King something to divert his mind from ruling his subjects: and if subjects are ever to live a quiet life, this is an essential facet of political organisation.

The King, like all men of wealth and leisure, also kept concubines, and King Dasa-ratha kept them in profusion. But here again the system of having more than one official wife had its advantages, for the wives kept the concubines in their place, which nobody else could do. It is notoriously beyond the capacity of one single wife, acting alone and in embarrassing circumstances. But several wives shared both the shame and the vigilance, and succeeded.

To judge from the bustling life of the overcrowded harem, Dasa-ratha might be thought to have been an attractive and passionate man. He was, in fact, neither. He was a round man with short legs and short arms, with a forehead, nose, and chin that together followed the curving contours of half a melon. As for his passion, he was frequently in bed, but finicky, and in seeking to prove himself a stalwart male, showed himself to be something of an old woman. He planned his debauches beforehand in great detail and if ecstasy were to be achieved, like genius, by taking pains, his life would have been blissful though possibly short. The atmosphere he produced, however, was less that of romance than of a pernickity review of a regiment consisting of one imperfectly trained recruit. But he thought himself a great voluptuary, and that was a matter in which his own opinion was the only one that counted.

His eldest son, Rama, was in his twenty-fourth year when he gave the King a parrot. He did this because he was warm-hearted, generous, and a loving son.

But he was many other things which it is not wise to be at court. He was handsome and the King was not; he was fonder of the hunt than the women's quarters, while the King hunted for the same reason he ate gold leaf, namely because his anxious physicians told him it was an aphrodisiac. Rama's conversation was sober and manly; the King was a gossip. Rama's wife, Sita, was devoted to him; the King was devoted to his wives, a very different thing.

Rama was therefore by no means the King's favourite son, but the King was touched when he gave him the parrot. He had a cage of silver wire made and had it set with semi-precious stones. He would point it out to his courtiers saying: "That is the first thing I have been given for twenty years without the giver expecting anything in return." The third time that he said this, the Lord Chamberlain thought of a reply.

"Majesty, what should he expect from you?" he said. "When you die everything you have will be his. God grant that he has to wait a hundred years."

From that moment the King was satisfied that Rama plotted his death. The Lord Chamberlain was granted the revenues of three temples for his vigilance in warning the King of a conspiracy which he had invented in a moment of spleen. From the moment of his being rewarded with the revenues of the temples, he ceased to be a courtier and became a statesman. That is to say, he invented and suppressed three more conspiracies in the next two years and was regarded as the saviour of the state.

One day Rama's parrot bit the King's finger.

Dasa-ratha conceived the idea that the parrot's beak had been poisoned. He consulted his Lord Chamberlain, who answered that it was quite possible to poison the beak of a bird and that three hundred years ago a certain king of the Western Marches had been assassinated (it was said) by this very means. The King's suspicions were thus confirmed and he ordered his personal servant to wring the bird's neck and leave the body on Rama's couch.

But the servant despised the King, and being privy to all his excesses, was sure that he would soon die. He had no wish, therefore, to embroil himself with the King's successor. He lied to the King, told him that the bird was dead and placed on Rama's couch, but in fact he had given it away to a young woman of the court. The parrot bit the young woman, who in turn gave it to a concubine, who kept it, for she was the one person that the bird did not bite.

CHAPTER TWO

the ups
and downs
of
a concubine

The concubine almost immediately fell out
of favour with the King (for talking after the lights were out,
a thing he could not abide) and she was relegated, both she and
her parrot, to the back quarters. Her maiden beauty ripened
with the years at much the same pace as the King's taste. Three
years after her fall she caught the King's eye as he was touring
the palace with his master mason and she was restored to favour.
A sentimental woman, she wished to leave the King a memento
of her second honeymoon with him, and she gave him the
parrot.

Her second fall was dizzier and deeper than her first. The
King recognised the parrot and its cage, and the concubine was
thrown into prison. At his next meal the King summoned Rama,
and when the dishes had been taken away, he sent for the parrot and had its cage placed in front of the low stool on which
Rama sat.

He then asked Rama to give it a piece of sweetmeat. Rama
obeyed. The bird snatched the food, but did not bite the King's
son. This ruse having failed, the King sought another, for he
was now obsessed with the need of testing whether the parrot's
beak was envenomed or not. The Lord Chamberlain, reading
his mind, cast his thoughts round the palace for a person who
was sufficiently obscure for the test. His powerful mind had

already seen that the stability of his personal government and hence the future of the state depended on his seeing to it that the test succeeded.

"The bird, Majesty," said the Lord Chamberlain, "reminds me of an old nurse who looked after your second wife's son, the Prince Barat. What was her name?" he went on, meditatively, "Ma, Me, Mi, Man, Mun . . ."

"Mantara!" said the King, with delight, immediately seeing the resemblance.

"Your Majesty's memory is astonishing," said the Lord Chamberlain, without flattery, for the Lord Chamberlain never ceased to marvel at the way the King's mind retained the smallest detail connected with the women's quarters, while unable to hold anything else. The Lord Chamberlain thanked the gods for the King's memory daily since it enabled him to govern the kingdom without interference. "Why not send the bird to her?"

"Send the bird to her?" said the King. "Why? Oh yes. Yes. I see. A splendid idea. A splendid idea. Send it to the nurse Mantara with my compliments and say it will save her the need for a mirror."

The courtiers who were dining with the King chuckled at the royal jest. The courtiers who were standing behind the dining courtiers laughed loudly to draw attention to themselves; the courtiers who were watching the scene of the banquet from the end of the room roared with mirth till they cried although they had not heard the joke; and the courtiers who had not been invited into the banquet hall at all but were listening under the windows slapped their thighs, wiped their eyes, choked and gasped for breath, asking one another if they had ever known the King to be in such a jolly mood.

The bird was taken away by the Lord Chamberlain, its beak instantly anointed with poison, and it was despatched to Mantara. The King's physician was warned to be in readiness, the

Chamberlain's assistants were told not to leave the palace, and the Chamberlain's supporters among the rest of the Brahmins were warned that something was brewing. The Chamberlain permitted himself a small brass jar of fermented palm-tree juice, and relaxed until it was time to save the nation.

This Mantara was an ugly woman of some fifty years. Since Dasa-ratha in his search for delight produced a great number of children, the women's quarters swarmed with nurses. They were important to their charges while the children were still young, but to nobody else. They were engaged by the High Steward, who selected them rigidly according to the size of the bribe that he was offered. When Dasa-ratha's second wife produced a boy called Barat, this nurse was appointed to look after him. This she did well enough, but not in a way to attract any attention.

Barat grew up, and Mantara grew ugly. She was pensioned off with a room and something to eat daily from the scraps of the royal banquet. Her room was one of the very few that were higher than the single storey of the main palace, and was in fact no more than the hollow inside of a carved, pyramidical turret that had been added as an architectural fancy. Mantara was so forgotten that no one in the palace knew for certain where she lived, except the kitchen hand who brought her food.

One day, with her food, the man brought her a bird in a cage. The bird was a very old parrot with tattered plumage and a bad temper. It rattled savagely at the bars of its cage with a scarred and peeling beak as the servitor, planting the cage down beside the dish of food, told Mantara the astonishing news that the bird was a present from the King.

"The King himself?" asked Mantara, getting up from where she was squatting on the floor.

Yes," said the serving man. "They say he's drunk now but I

don't think he was drunk when he sent this. I kept it by me while I did the sweetmeats. Nobody else could bring it 'cause nobody knew who you were."

"Except the King," said the ugly woman sharply. "Except the King: was there a message?"

"Not that I know of."

"There must have been a message!"

"There wasn't."

The nurse stamped her foot and screamed: "You've forgotten it, you idle fool. Go and find out what it is! Go at once, you greasy good-for-nothing!" Saying this she aimed a box at his ears which he only avoided in part.

He turned on his heel and stamping down the narrow stairs that led to the turret he swore loudly by the more obscene of the popular gods that he would never set foot in the nurse's room again.

The poison was excellent. It would have killed Mantara with terrible agony within an hour, had the parrot bitten her. It killed, however, the bird instead. When this news was brought to the Lord Chamberlain he hesitated for a while between dismissing the whole matter, or announcing with suitable alarums that a parrot which had been given the King had been found dead with poison on its beak. There were two things against the latter course. The first was that everybody would suspect that he had put the poison on the bird's beak: whereas with a dead old woman being carried out of her room feet first and horribly swollen, nobody would have thought him capable of such a monstrosity; secondly, it was the plain truth, even if not all of it, and although he was prepared to admit that telling the truth was not always harmful, he had never, in twenty years of politics seen much good come of it.

So he did nothing. He told the King that there was no evidence of a conspiracy at the moment, and to the people he issued a proclamation declaring a public holiday in celebration of the King's continued safety. He had made an irretrievable blunder. He had annoyed the King; while the people were convinced that he was fobbing them off. The adherents to his party, whom he had warned that something was about to happen, began to talk openly of his losing his grip. When he contracted a cold in the nose, it was rumoured that he suffered from a malignant disease in a disgraceful part. The Lord Chamberlain was too good a politician either to miss these signs or to discount them.

He cast about to find means of preserving his reputation for being the man the country turned to in a crisis, but the stars in their courses fought against him. There was a bumper crop, there were no disastrous droughts, nobody (it seemed to him) had either the brains or the courage even to think of sedition: and to crown matters, the rainy season was approaching and he could not start a war.

In this last matter, however, he did his best. He sent an insulting embassy to a touchy neighbour state, but it did him no good whatever. The Lord Chamberlain of the insulted state, himself a Brahmin and a statesman, privately asked the ambassadors if their master did not know that elephants, when in mud, invariably got stuck and that this brought derision on even the most Necessary War. When this remark was hesitatingly conveyed to him by his abashed envoys, he began to consider whether, for the sake of his place in history, he would not have to poison the King himself.

Thus oppressed by contrary events, he decided to question the concubine. In a cooler moment he would have seen that this course might well lead to further embarrassments, and since the concubine could not possibly know anything, he would not have had her tortured in order to think of lies which he could better concoct himself. He was not a cruel man. He was, however, in a hurry.

The concubine was therefore taken to another room in the jail and jerked up and down on a rope which hung from the ceiling. The rope was fastened to her wrists and these in turn were disposed behind her back, in a position best calculated to stimulate her thoughts on constitutional problems. She was spitting blood before she was told what her torturers were aiming to find out. They then let her down, and giving her a cup of water, asked her:

"Did you conspire to kill the King?"

She should, according to previous experience, have muttered incomprehensibly in answer to this, from which mutterings, with the renewed aid of the rope, a connected answer could have been built up.

But the concubine was neither a frightened chit of a girl nor a weak old woman. She was in the prime of a none too easy life. Twice she had emerged from obscurity into the light and warmth of success, both occasions being those in which she had received the favours of the King. She clung to these triumphs with the determination of a woman who knows she cannot have many more such in front of her. She massaged her arms, brushed her hair from out of her eyes, and asked that the question be repeated.

They said: "Did you conspire to kill the King?"

She answered, in unblushing vernacular: "I slept with His Majesty six days ago. I don't know anything about killing the King. All I know is that I thought he would kill me."

The answer was all round the palace in an hour. The Brahmins who had the hereditary honour of waiting outside the King's privy shouted it through the door. The King was delighted. He denied having heard the remark twenty times in the course of the morning in order to have the pleasure of hearing this simple but impressive evidence of his prowess repeated again and again. Shortly before going into his midday meal he swore that he would give the concubine the privileges and apartments due to a royal wife. By the time he had finished eating, the forthright woman had been washed, scented, given a cordial, and handsomely robed, and her two torturers had kissed her toenails and begged to be recommended to the King for their devotion to duty.

The Lord Chamberlain met the King for the first time that day as the King retired for his siesta. He read his fate in the King's eyes. By the time that the King and the royal guard were well set in their afternoon sleep, the Lord Chamberlain was on his way to the frontier. By night time he was across it and in a matter of hours was being received with every mark of distinction by the other Lord Chamberlain who had been so disturbed by his apparent lack of knowledge of warfare and elephants. He told his story to sympathetic ears since he had brought a camel loaded with a portion of the year's recently collected taxes.

In a short time he was presented to a courteous monarch and a wildly cheering populace as the man who, at the risk of his life and the cost of his career, had dissuaded the King of Ayoda from following up his notorious ultimatum by bloody and aggressive war. Henceforth he was popularly known as the Peacemaker and plays no further part in our story.

The concubine accepted her honours with grace and dignity. She recommended the torturers to the King, and thereby made friends of the two best-informed men in the palace. This rendered her position impregnable, and she died, years later, much respected.

CHAPTER THREE

a
procession
is
postponed

The dead parrot, merely as a decomposing bird, was fit to feed a few maggots and enrich a few inches of soil. By the alchemy of human folly it was enabled to ruin a career, change the government of the country, and elevate an old woman to fortune and power. The old woman was the nurse Mantara. She achieved her position not because she was clever, industrious, talented, or gifted but because she was half mad. The recipes for worldly success are greatly varied.

Mantara had the dead bird stuffed. She put it back in its silver cage and waited. She waited with great confidence, even though she was driven to fetch her own food—the servitor refusing to wait upon her any more. Then she was utterly alone but she was sure it would not be for long. She was convinced that the King had sent her the parrot as a sign of some special favour that was to come her way.

Nothing at all happened. She dusted the bird, and raised her hopes.

Now it was customary for the kings of Ayoda to hold a festival on their fiftieth birthday, should they attain it, in which they proceeded in state down the principal road of the city, seated in an elephant howdah with their eldest son beside them. The kings were traditionally required to make this journey lean-

ing their right hands symbolically on their sons' shoulders. This
served to declare that the succession was secure. It was also the
tradition that, on this day and for some days previously, every
building in the city should be decorated with flags. Some
months after the flight of the Lord Chamberlain the King
achieved his fiftieth year, the loyal populace hung out its flags,
and the King swore that he would see the royal elephant trample
Rama to death before he would ride by his son's side and declare
him heir.

The Brahmins closest to the King shook their heads. The
tradition was a deep one, they said. If the King broke it, the
people would take it as a sign that good luck would desert them
and the crops would fail. The King replied that this was superstition, at which one Brahmin arose and said that he agreed
with the King and that the best way to fight superstition was
by scientific thinking. Most of the young Brahmins and, of
course, the King, greeted this argument with approval. The
Brahmin then went on to suggest to His Majesty that the royal
astrologer be asked to make the most stringent observations of
the stars to see if, by chance, it should be written there that the
procession should be abandoned owing to the unfavourable conjunction of (for example) Venus and Saturn. The King was
pleased, the other Brahmins were impressed, and the man with
the idea was elevated to the vacant post of Lord Chamberlain.

The Royal Observatory was a wide platform at the top of a
flight of steps from each of which calculated observations could
be taken with the cross-staff. At the top, on the platform, were
stone quadrants with spy holes in which stars appeared at certain
fixed times. With the aid of these the royal astrologer had been
able to predict eclipses of the sun for the next fifty years. These
and other predictions were considered as being of vital importance to the state, especially in time of war, when a true knowl-

edge of the movement of the heavens was a great advantage over the enemy. The royal astrologer enjoyed the protection of the King. He had full freedom to pursue his researches: but since they were so important it was decreed, as a precaution, that if he should tell them to any person other than the King or his appointed minister, or even if there were grounds to suspect him of telling, then he should have his tongue torn out by the roots. While the royal astrologer could predict what would happen to the sun in the next half-century, he was quite unable to predict, therefore, what would happen to himself in the next half-hour. He was an obliging but apprehensive man.

Nervously mounting the steps of the Royal Observatory that night to make the crucial observation required by the King, he saw that he was being followed by two men. He turned to ask who they were, and they said that they had been sent by the King to help the astrologer make his observations. They also said that the King hoped very much that the stars would be found to advise against a procession, but that he did not want to interfere with the learned man's methods. The astrologer bowed, the two men bowed, and then threw back their hoods. By the light of the lamp which he carried, the astrologer could see that they were the King's torturers.

"Shall we go on up?" said one of the torturers.

"Gentlemen," said the astrologer, "I think we can all save our breath. We may dispense with the climb. The stars, like everybody else, are only to anxious to please His Majesty."

"Our orders," said the other torturer, "were to help you. His Majesty was very particular that you should do all the squinting that you wanted. No violence, no interference, were his very words. Help; that's what we were to do.

"Gentlemen," said the astrologer again, trembling from head to foot, "I know my job and I am well aware that you know yours. If I start my squinting, as you so accurately call it, I shall only confuse myself. The stars, I feel tolerably certain, are very adverse to the holding of a procession, since the relevant planets were in a most unfavourable conjunction the last time I observed them."

"You hear that?" said the first torturer to the second.

"I do," said the second.

"You know what he means?" asked the first.

"I don't," said the second.

"My friend don't know what you mean," said the first torturer. "Would you tell him?" he asked the astrologer politely.

"I mean the procession's off," said the astrologer, his teeth chattering.

"There you are," said the first torturer. "It's all settled."

"I shall," said the astrologer, gathering a little courage to uphold his professional dignity, "have to make a few calculations and checks. I can give the King a positive answer tomorrow or the next—"

"Our orders—" began the second torturer, but his companion interrupted him.

"Look at it this way," he said, "if we had this learned gentleman here tied up with weights on his feet and you did you know what and I turned the little so-and-so and he said, 'The procession's off,' would we let him down?"

He had accompanied the supposed prisoner's words with a scream of agony that was most realistic. It echoed round the stone observatory and inside the astrologer's head.

"Well," said the second, "yes, we would."

"Then there you are," said the first. "We've done our duty."

"Yes," said the second, "but we haven't tied him up yet."

"And I say," said the first, "that's all to the good. We don't like hurting people. We take a pride in it, yes. But we don't *like* doing it. It's just that we are ready to serve our country, same as soldiers. Do you see?"

"Yes," said the other. "I always do when you explain things. I sometimes wonder why you don't go in for politics."

"I do," said the first, and both laughed so heartily at this jest that the astrologer had to sit down on one of the observation steps, his knees having turned to water.

When he recovered his breath he explained that he had just done all the necessary calculations in his head.

"What a brain!" said the second torturer admiringly.

"What talent!" said the first. "His Majesty would like to hear of this straight away I'll be bound. He's waiting for the verdict in the Royal Wardrobe."

Next morning the great state drums in the chamber over the gateway roared a summons to the people. A few minutes later the iron-studded doors were hauled open and a cavalcade ablaze with the royal colours of orange and white came out, their horses prancing, and rode at a dashing pace to the central square.

They took up a position in line facing the crowd with their backs to the carved stone pyramid of the principal temple, and a young man in a sash of gold embroidered with rubies and moonstones held up his hand. The horsemen at the two ends of the line swung the mouthpieces of their trumpets to their lips and blew. The stems of the trumpets curved round their bodies and rose over their heads. From their bronze mouths embossed with hemispheres, one lacquered orange and the next white, came an inspiriting roar of sound.

The young man said loudly:

"In the name of the King!"

The trumpeters blew another blast and all the horsemen

lifted their lances, from which hung oblong pennants of the
holy colour of saffron.

The men in the crowd bowed their heads and touched their
foreheads. The women drew their saris more closely over their
faces, and peered through the folds at the young men.

The principal horseman moved his horse with infinite grace
of carriage until he stood in front of the others. He then made
his proclamation, saying it first in the stilted Sanskrit that only
the Brahmins used and only the Brahmins could properly
understand, following this by an explanation in the vernacular
which he delivered with great vigour. He showed the whites of
his eyes as he rolled his glance over the crowd and he was greatly
admired by everybody.

He announced that owing to the findings of the great astrologer (and here followed a long reminder of the great astrologer's
previous scientific triumphs, including the prediction of eclipses)
the King would have to forego the pleasure and honour of
receiving the felicitations of his loyal subjects on the occasion of
his fiftieth birthday, and also to forego the privilege of present-
ing them with their future ruler (and here the expected name
of Rama was omitted). The King, said the proclamation, had
been warned by the astrologer that the direst consequences to
his beloved people might follow were he to flout the message
of the heavens. Since the well-being of his subjects, whom he
looked upon as a father looks upon his children, was always first
in the King's mind and always nearest his heart, there would be
no procession. They could take down the decorations.

The horseman backed his horse with consummate skill into
the rank behind him, the trumpets bellowed again, and then
broke into the royal anthem, a simple melody (the trumpets had
only seven notes) but very stirring. With pennants waving and
many dashing looks to the left and right, which the women in

the crowd received as special tributes to their figures, the cavalcade rode back to the palace; the drums over the main gate
throbbed again, the horsemen clattered inside, and the gates
were closed.

In the main square in front of the principal temple com-
ment was divided. There were those who had been moved by
the handsome display and who had felt a constriction of the
throat when they heard the anthem. These said that it was a
bitter shame but that it was typical of King Dasa-ratha to put
the good of his subjects before his own pleasure and that it was
a wonderful thing to be a citizen of Ayoda. Where else, they
asked one another, could a man of learning go straight up to a
king, bold as brass, and tell him to his royal face that he could
not have a birthday procession? In the Kingdom of Vamsa he
would have been boiled in a cauldron of oil; in the Kingdom of
Magada he would have been sewn up into the raw skin of a
wild beast and put in the sun till he was squeezed to death; in
the Kingdom of Avanti he would have been sent to labour in
the rock-salt mines. Only in Ayoda was he free to tell the
truth.

On the other hand, there were those who deliberately restrained their emotions in front of the display, since they were
people with a reputation for independence of mind. These said
that it was certainly a pity that there would be no procession,
but they doubted if the King had much say in the matter. It was
probably an intrigue of the Brahmins who held the poor devil
(they dwelt upon this bold description of Dasa-ratha) in the
hollow of their hands. If anybody asked them, they said, then
their opinion, for what it was worth, was that it was all some
jiggery-pokery on the part of the new Lord Chamberlain. But
others pointed out to these doubters that, Lord Chamberlain or
no, the astronomical facts were there, the stars could not lie,

not at least in a land where there was freedom of expression. With this argument the doubters were happy to agree.

The crowd dispersed, unanimous in the opinion that being a king was no bed of roses. Even the beggar in the street (they said) had the right to celebrate his own birthday.

the
paRROt
is
explaineδ

Mantara in her top room had seen the flags; she had heard the trumpets and she had seen the flags come down. But it did not concern her. Her thoughts were filled with the hard and bolt-eyed shell of a bird in its regal cage, and with her good fortune. This she had already begun to enjoy. That is to say, she was in rags, she ate scraps from the kitchen, and she was still ignored, but she now loitered in the various courtyards of the palace observing the courtiers as they went about their business or idled during the interminable waits that made up most of their waking hours.

She marked them down. This one turned his head away when she passed. That one did not move his legs as he leaned against the wall of a corridor, and she was forced to step over his feet. This one was urinating in a flower plot and did not trouble to conceal himself as she passed. That one pushed her in the back when she was in his way. When she came to power, the man who turned his head away would lose it or pay to keep it with a bag of gold; the man who would not move his feet would move them fast enough under the bastinado; the urinating courtier would spend a year looking after the royal buflaloes, where he would be among manners as simple as is own; and the courtier who pushed her would be ruined and disgraced, to teach him not to be in such a hurry in going about his business that he forgot the respect due to an elderly lady. She memorised their faces carefully.

But she still did not know just how she would come into her own. The King was still silent about the meaning of her gift. She talked to no one and nobody came to visit her. Yet she had faith that all would be revealed in good time, and so it was.

The two principal royal cooks in the royal kitchen were an ill-matched pair. One was broad and jolly as a cook should be. He cooked the main dishes: he was adept at grinding spices together to make a sharp curry. The other cook was lean and cynical; he looked as though he ate nothing but the other cook's curry powders. He made the sweetmeats. His skill was unbounded; special boats, straw-covered against the sun's rays, brought snow by river once a day from the mountains in order that this gloomy artist could chill the froths of milk, sugar, the whites of eggs, and ingredients more mysterious that it was the King's delight to eat after his meal. Possibly because the products of his labour were so insubstantial he was devoted, in argument (and the two cooks argued incessantly about everything), to demanding the solid facts. The happy cook took things as he found them (except kitchen boys) and did not find them insupportably bad.

On the day of the proclamation Mantara went down to the kitchen about three o'clock in the afternoon with one of her few possessions, a large wooden bowl in which to put her scraps. The broad and jolly cook was beginning to prepare the evening meal, and the thin cynic was squatting on the floor, surrounded by a basket of two dozen eggs, a heap of sugar on a fig leaf, and an open box of powders that were his own secret. He was looking at these with distaste since he was an artist and like all artists had a profound disinclination to begin his work.

The fires in the low charcoal stoves were drawn, but the kitchen was hot from the morning's cooking. The two cooks were in a desultory argument, the large curry cook squatting over a black stone, on which he was grinding spices with a stone roller. This cook nodded to Mantara in a friendly fashion and indicated a bronze cauldron full of leavings. The thin sweetmeat cook looked at her with such disapproval that she might have been a stick of cinnamon that he proposed to use in the evening's masterpiece. Mantara ignored him, for she had long ago settled upon his punishment. He was to be put in a dungeon and fed on nothing but sweetmeats until he was as round-bellied as a spoiled poodle. She filled her bowl slowly and listened to their conversation.

"What's really going on, that's what I would like to know," the sweetmeat cook was saying.

"It's all in the proclamation," said the other.

"*Proclamation!*" said the sweetmeat cook, in a tone of deep contempt. "You believe anything they say in a proclamation, don't you? I suppose if one of them fancy young men spat in his trumpet a bit and announced that the King's cook was henceforward and from now on as with effect from today really a woman and not a man you'd give up shaving."

"Wish I could," said the other cook equably, "what with getting up for early market and all, but the superintendent likes things looking neat and clean. Not that anybody ever wants to see *me*. I could grow a beard long enough to clean a saucepan with before anybody would notice. I haven't seen a member of the royal family closer nor you are to me come, oo, now, it must be five years. Still, it suits me. 'Tisn't my beauty what makes my curries taste, its me turmeric, is what I always say."

"I have," said the thin cook.

"You've what?"

"Seen them."

"Seen who?"

"The royal family. One of them, at any rate. I was sent for," said the thin cook meaningfully.

"Was you? Why was you?" said the other with genuine pleasure.

"My mango syrup. That's what she *said*."

"She, eh?"

"That's what I said. Trust a woman," remarked the thin cook in a tone which showed that one should trust her only to do unspeakable villainies.

"Who was it? The Queen?"

"She behaves as if she was," said the other. "No. It was Her Highness, Her Mightiness, Her Who-are-you-and-Spit-in-your-Eye Sita."

"Well, she will be queen one day when Rama gets his turn. They do say they're a happy couple."

"She isn't queen yet."

"No. You're right there, of course," said the other rolling his spices. "But she seemed a quiet sort of a girl to me."

"Ho?" said the sweetmeat cook sarcastically. "That was when she asked you up to chew over a little *halva* in the boudoir and have a nice chat, was it?"

The other man laughed. "You're the one what moves in high society," he said. "What did she say to you?"

"It wasn't what she said, it was the way she put it. Asked me where I was born and if my mother had taught me how to cook. Then she asked me if the Queen liked my mango syrup and how much she ate of it and what else the Queen ate and could she have some like it and would I make her lots of it when she was queen because when she was queen she was going to do what she liked which now she couldn't being a stranger and not liking to give orders and thank you she would remember me and here was a couple of pieces of silver so's I would remember *her*."

"Yes, and what did you say to all that?"

"I thanked her for her money but I give it back to her," said the thin cook with fierce dignity; "I told her I was happy to know she liked my mango but as for what the Queen said and as for what the Queen ate that was court business. Oh yes, I forgot."

"You forgot what?"

"She asked about Master Barat."

Hearing the name of the prince that she had nursed, Mantara made an excuse to stay. She asked if she might heat her food a little, and being given permission willingly by the curry cook, she stayed, poking and blowing at the charcoal, and she listened.

"Well, now," said the curry cook, turning back to his companion, "what did she say about Barat?"

"She asked if he liked sweets. She asked what he was like when he was a boy and what her husband was like. Then she said: 'The King must have spoiled him, I'll be bound. He's always been the favourite, has Barat, hasn't he?' "

"She's right there," said the curry cook. "I suppose you told her so."

"I told her that as far as I was aware His Majesty the King had no preferences as betwixt and between the heirs presumptuous and aperient," said the cook, and he closed his lips in a hard line like an ambassador refusing to give information that was not covered by his instructions.

There was silence in the kitchen.

"You can see what she was getting at?" said the sweetmeat cook.

"No. I can truly say I don't," said the other, leaning on his roller.

"Think," said the thin cook impatiently. "What about the proclamation?"

"Ah, yes," said the other, anxious to oblige. "Of course." But after grinding in a clove or two he shook his head and said, "I can't remember anything in it about mango syrup."

"*Syrup!* Who's talking about syrup?"

"I thought the Princess Sita was."

"Syrup, huh," replied the other. "She was spreading plenty under my feet but I didn't get stuck. Can't you see what she was driving at? Everybody knows that the King and Rama has had words from time to time. What over I don't know, but I can guess it's over that foreign wife he's brought back. And I wouldn't mind betting my year's wages that the King's made up his mind that rather than have a woman like her as queen he'll make Barat the heir. He can, you know, if he takes it into his mind. So she's starting up a party to support her and she thought—she *thought*—she'd get me mixed up in it. *That's* why there'll be no procession. Wheels, is what I say. Wheels within wheels."

Mantara took her food off the fire, put it in her bowl, and left without speaking a word. The sign had come. She knew why the King had sent her the parrot.

Without stopping to eat, Mantara went straight to the royal quarters of Barat's mother and demanded admission from the eunuch at the door. He gave her a single glance, held out his pink palm, and when it was not instantly soothed with the touch of money, he rubbed this thumb and forefinger together under Mantara's nose to indicate what he wanted.

Mantara had no money. But she did not argue and she did

not hesitate. She was sure her moment had come: had the eunuch demanded her bloodshot right eye she would have given it to him. So now she waddled as fast as she could go back to her own turret and took the dead parrot out of its cage. She blew the dust off it, stroked it, and apologised.

"When I have done my work," she told it, "I shall give you a cage of gold wire with a perch of lapis lazuli and two servants to look after you forever. Just now I must give your cage to the eunuch because I must see Barat's mother."

She put the parrot carefully among the rags which made her bed, where it lay with its head on a greasy cushion, its beak gone scaly and green from the poison with which it had once been anointed.

The eunuch examined the cage in detail, breathing through his nose and letting his fat lips fall open. At length he nodded and walked away from the door, his bribe swinging from his finger. He disappeared down a corridor leading to the eunuchs' quarters, and Mantara, left alone, pushed open the door and went in to see her old mistress.

The Junior Queen was lying on a round bed that stood a few inches above the floor and had a fence of pierced silver to hold in the cushions. She was forty, with what remained of her youthful and fragile beauty after years of irritable bad temper. She lolled on the bed with the utter weariness of a person who has done nothing whatever for a lifetime.

She looked up petulantly as Mantara entered. She recognised her immediately although she had not seen her for more than a year. She had a capacious memory for people against whom she could complain.

"Mantara," she said and fidgeted with her bangles. She nodded permission for the woman to speak.

"Your Majesty," said Mantara, and creaking down to her

knees, she touched the Junior Queen's painted toenails as they lay curled in the cushions. "I have come . . ."

"You have taken your time."

"Your Majesty did not summon me."

"Am I a magistrate?" asked the Queen. "Must I send the guards to everyone I want to see? Can nobody come to see me because they are fond of me?"

Mantara bowed her head and holding the lobes of her ears shook her head slowly from side to side, in the immemorial Indian gesture of contrition.

"I have been ill," she lied.

In this palace of lies, illness was the customary one, and passed for an apology. The lie was necessary. The Junior Queen had begun her life as the pretty daughter of a small country nobleman. She had early shown that she had two fixed aims in her life: she wished everyone to love her, and she would do nothing whatever to make them do so. When she was twelve her mother explained to her that this attitude had no sense; at sixteen she was told angrily by her father that it would lead to her ruin. At seventeen she was taken to court. When the King became fully aware of the depths of her feminine selfishness, he fell at her feet, and after grovelling there for some time, married her. She became Junior Queen, and neither her mother nor her father nor anybody else criticised her behaviour again.

"Well, then," said the Junior Queen to Mantara, "so you have been ill and now you are well so what do you want?"

"I want to save Your Majesty."

"From what?"

"From being ruined and despised and sent to live in the backroom of these quarters."

"Despised?" said the Junior Queen. "I think I shall slap your face. People do not use that word to me."

"Not now, Majesty. But when the King dies and Rama rules, his wife, Sita, will be queen and you will merely be the mother of Barat, a younger son."

"The Princess Sita is an honourable woman. She will know how to behave towards me."

"Yes: she's already plotting it."

"Plotting? With whom?"

"The pastrycook."

The Junior Queen laughed very heartily at this. But she listened to what Mantara had to say intently.

Mantara lowered her voice, but after she had been speaking for some while the Junior Queen feared that even her muttering might be heard. She drew her into a corner and bolted the door. The two women huddled closer.

"But my brooch is not a parrot," protested the Queen, after some time.

"Your Majesty must be mistaken."

"No, I'm not," said the Junior Queen. "It is a hawk. I remember the King telling me so when he gave it me."

"Then your Majesty is quite right to say it is a hawk, but it is the King who was wrong," persisted Mantara.

"Well, let us look at it," said the Junior Queen.

Hearing a noise outside the door, she opened it slightly and sent the eunuch away on a long errand. Then she went to her jewel box, which stood on four small wooden antelopes in a corner. She searched, rattling the jewels until she produced a small brooch.

It was shaped like a hawk.

"There," said Mantara. "It's a parrot."

"How *can* it be?" said the Junior Queen, pointing to the bird's head.

"It must be," said Mantara, "or else the King would not

have sent me a parrot; he would have sent me a hawk. He wanted me to remind you that he had given you the brooch."

The Junior Queen giggled as she looked at the hawk.

"I've never told anyone why he gave me it."

"You told me," said Mantara.

"Did I?" said the Junior Queen. She giggled once more, and Mantara did the same until a fit of coughing overtook her.

King Dasa-ratha, they recalled with looks and winks, had given the Junior Queen the brooch after her wedding night because their embraces had been disastrous. The King, for once, had become impotent. He had made a royal gesture to cover his confusion.

"Anything I wanted, I could have, he said," the Junior Queen whispered. "I'd only to show him the brooch."

"Then show him it and ask for Rama to be thrown over and your son made heir. He won't refuse," said Mantara. "It's what he wants, don't you see? He wants an excuse. Barat's always been his favourite."

The Junior Queen hesitated.

"But suppose," she said, "suppose—it's a long time ago—that he doesn't agree—suppose he won't keep his promise—suppose . . ."

"Then let him know," Mantara answered, "that you'll tell everyone in the court the story of why he gave you the brooch."

The Junior Queen thought for a while. Then she giggled once more. She said:

"Yes. *That* will do it."

CHAPTER FIVE

ΙΝΤRΙGUE
anδ
ΙΝΝΟCΕΝCΕ

The assembly was of the utmost splendour; the King was positively seen to weep; Rama turned a pale ivory; and all the Brahmins agreed that his behaviour subsequently was a credit to his education. It was, in a word, a historic occasion.

Having summoned Rama to the Audience Hall, King Dasaratha received him with every mark of affection. He seated him on a stool on his right hand, next to the low throne on which he himself sat cross-legged. He put his arm round his son's shoulders and asked tenderly after his health, and while Rama answered, the King, plainly with his thoughts on the sad duty to come, shook his head that looked like half a melon from side to side.

Then an usher, his long hair richly oiled and a garland of flowers round his neck, waddled to the entrance of the hall. He came back shepherding a man and a woman both dressed in Brahminical white but poorly. The usher prodded them officiously with his ivory stick of office until they were exactly opposite Rama and the King. He then gave the man a sharp tap on the shoulder and the two poor Brahmins fell prostrate at the King's feet. That they omitted the usual crawling on the marble, and that the usher permitted them to do so, showed that they were no usual suppliants.

The King rose. Rama rose. The King held up his hand. The two Brahmins got to their feet and Rama could see that they were an elderly man and woman, both of a mild aspect, and both frightened. The King began to speak, and as custom demanded, Rama listened to his father with bowed head.

"Son," said the King, "dearly beloved and inheritor of my sceptre, your father humbly begs your forgiveness." At this the King bowed his own head towards his son, and stood holding his ears in contrition. Generous tears started to Rama's eyes and he protestingly murmured that a son could not forgive his father but only obey him: but if a son could, then it was done.

"I am grateful," said the King, "and now I may speak freely." He turned away from his son, not without showing some signs of relief, and, while addressing him in his form of words, in his posture addressed the court, in particular the scribes who, sitting cross-legged against a pillar, made notes for the court historians who would later work up the King's words into the Chronicle of the Deeds of the King.

"Dearly beloved son, you know that in my youth I went hunting, one ill-omened day, and I was led away from my companions by a deer of exquisite beauty. I chased it for many hours and even when the sun had set I followed it, contrary to the prescriptions of our holy Brahmins who say that we should put aside worldly concerns at the onset of night, and pray."

Here there was a murmur of approval from the court Brahmins and the King proceeded:

"I followed this animal along the banks of a river and I would not give up the chase even when it was almost night. Then I heard it, as I thought, stop to drink. I loosed off an arrow through the reeds, blindly, shooting at the place from where the sound had come. I heard a great cry of pain. But it was not the cry of an animal. It was the anguished voice of a boy."

Here a profound silence fell on the Hall of Audience, although everyone present knew the story well. The man and the woman bowed their heads. The woman put her hands to her face and it could be seen that she was weeping. If the silence of the courtiers was a mere politeness, no one could doubt the genuineness of the woman's grief.

"I had shot a young lad," said the King in a lower voice. "A fine boy of fourteen years lay in the water that was reddening with his blood. He was the son of this simple and holy man and this simple and holy woman. I took him back to their modest house which he, with his last strength, pointed out to me. He died in his father's arms within the hour."

The King lowered his eyes and bent his head. His scant curls, artificially lengthened, swung forward and hid his cheeks. He looked up. The curls returned in disarray and underlined the King's unhappy knack of appearing an aging woman.

"Is this true that I have said?" the King asked the father. He did not answer, but a sharp tap of the usher's rod brought him to his senses.

"Majesty, it is true."

The King turned his rounded nose and receding chin upon Rama and looked on him with his exhausted eyes.

"I told them that I was a king. I swore that I would make any reparation which they asked of me, short of my kingdom or my life, which were given me by the gods themselves. The father asked only one thing: that as I had taken away their eldest son whom they had cherished fourteen years, my eldest son should be taken away from me for the same time: and that it should be done when I stood, as he did, on the threshold of old age. I had

no son. I consented. I am now fifty years old. They are here to
claim the fulfillment of my royal and sacred oath."

In the spandrels of the arches that rested upon the columns
of the Hall of Audience were grilles of stone, from which the
ladies of the court and their women could watch in decent seclu-
sion the ceremonial below. The Junior Queen leaned her face
against one of these: a few feet away Mantara peered through
another. Now, as King Dasa-ratha repeated the vow he claimed
to have made, the Junior Queen stretched out her hand, tugged
Mantara's sari, and then tapped the jewelled hawk, winking and
grimacing.

Below, Rama, white with dismay, was protesting that he had
always thought that the King had vowed a temple in reparation
and that he had built it and that . . .

"You were not born for two years more," said the King, his
irritability showing through his stately manner. "I wished to
make some gesture of my grief that would be immediate. But
the vow stands. And they claim it now. That is true?" he said
turning to the man.

The gentle old man raised his eyes and looked at the King
in terror. He licked his lips.

"Yes," he said.

The King nodded his half-melon of a head briskly. "Dearly
beloved son," he said, and now his impatience was plain. "You
will want me to break my oath. Say so now, with the greatest
Brahmins in the land as witnesses, and in front of this old
woman and this old man, so that they may go away and trouble
me no more, and so that I may go to my death and face the
penalties which the gods will inflict upon me for my murder and
my broken word. Speak!"

But Rama, folding his hands in front of his face in a gesture of respect, bowing his head towards his father, repeated the lesson he had been taught since his childhood.

"The word of a King may not be broken. The duty of a son is to obey."

With that he fell silent, but bowed still deeper. The King said nothing, and Rama, his voice trembling, asked the King's permission to withdraw.

The King unwillingly agreed, first glancing across at the Lord Chamberlain, who nodded his head in approval of Rama's request.

Rama descended to the floor of the Hall of Audience, paused, did reverence to the parents of the boy who had been killed, and then, his head still bowed and his face bloodless, he left the audience chamber.

Rama first asked advice of his tutor, a small Brahmin with a schoolmaster's mind, who had taught him to read, and to be a good boy.

The tutor was a man of the highest ideals who lived in constant fear of being without employment. He loved his pupil Rama but he was aware that a man of twenty-seven does not need a schoolmaster. Rama had no children: the King had more than he could count.

He advised Rama that a father's oath was sacred to son and father alike; he sang several Sanskrit texts to prove it, not failing to point out the interesting points in the grammatical structure of the sentiments as he did so. He suggested that Rama spend fourteen years in China, studying.

Next, Rama asked advice of his personal priest, the Brahmin, who tended his altar fire. The Brahmin had accepted the post in the hope that he would be in the centre of court intrigue and thus secure his advancement. Rama never intrigued and the

Brahmin despised him. He told Rama that a man who caused
his father to commit a crime would be tormented by devils for all
eternity in hell. He advised Rama to go to Magada and throw
himself on the mercy of its ruler. By playing his cards well, said
the Brahmin, he might collect an army and return with something to say for himself.

Next Rama asked the advice of the Lord Chamberlain. The
Lord Chamberlain was privy to the plot and had already made
good his post with Barat. He told Rama that he thought no
young man should be loaded with his father's mistakes. However—and here he lowered his voice and spoke in a very round-
about fashion—however, the King's weakness for ladies had got
the monarchy into bad odour in the city. If it were known that
the royal family condoned the killing of a Brahmin and broke
its sacred word, the reputation of the monarchy would suffer still
further. The monarchy should set an example to lesser men. A
prince had certain advantages—certain responsibilities, as well.
For the safety of the state he advised Rama to leave the kingdom. "Try a trip to Malabar," he said; "the scenery, I am told,
is superb and the hunting in the Nilgiris is not to be equalled."
He overreached himself here, for Rama, uneasily suspecting that
the Lord Chamberlain was treating him not as a man with a
moral problem (as he felt himself to be) but as an idle-minded
boy, protested:

"I cannot spend fourteen years hunting."

The Lord Chamberlain recovered himself.

"Fourteen years, Your Highness? That is a very long time. In
the life of a great prince like yourself, *one* year is a long time.
Who knows? The King may die—the gods forbid, of course—or
I, even, may see some way—who knows—some reason—of state,
naturally—to accede to a popular demonstration, shall we say,
demanding your return—ah, hum, a *spontaneous* demonstration,
of course."

"Do you think that they will?"

"I am practically certain they will," said the Lord Chamberlain. "I only regret that it's impossible, for political reasons, to organise a spontaneous demonstration this very night. But—well, you understand these matters even better than I do."

Rama understood nothing, but he nodded sagely. He should not be blamed. The middle-aged flatter the young for no purposes save their own—but only the middle-aged know it.

The Lord Chamberlain thought of taking his leave, but stayed to ask one question.

"And what does Your Highness mean to do tonight?"

"I shall sacrifice on my altar," said Rama, "and I shall supplicate the gods to guide me."

"Good," said the Lord Chamberlain solemnly. "Very good." He was reassured, for he knew that a man of action offers thanksgivings, but never supplications. He was now convinced that Rama would give him no trouble. He said, in an off-hand way:

"His Majesty asked me if I thought you would be able to give an answer by morning tomorrow and I said that I thought that a true nobleman like yourself with your great intelligence wouldn't need as much time as that to do his duty."

"Of course, of course," said Rama unsteadily. "Tomorrow morning then. Duty, yes. That's simple, as you say. But it raises questions: so many questions . . ."

The Lord Chamberlain, satisfied, settled himself down to what he shrewdly estimated would be about ninety minutes' listening. He did so amiably. He was a man who did not believe in hurry unless there was something to be got for himself: and he had got all he wanted.

Now Rama was a young man of fashion, and the fashion among young men of his (and less distant) days was to roll notions round their minds and to ask tremendous questions about life: a proper thing to do because the history of mankind is moulded by their ideas and a fine spectacle it is.

Rama wanted to know what his purpose was here below: to do his duty by the gods? to do his duty by himself? or to be free? He wanted to know if as a prince he should do what he thought would be good for his subjects, or what they thought would be good for themselves; or something of each; or to build heaven on earth? He wanted to know if his destiny was more powerful than his free will, if he should control his appetites, or educate them, or suppress them, or indulge them without stint? He wanted to know if he ought to strive to be a great man, a humble man, a practical man, or a saint? Was the world real? Or an illusion? What was man doing here? Should he rejoice? Or despair? Was he damned? Could he be saved? How? Was the way of renunciation (which was attracting so many of the best minds of the day) the right way? Should he seize this chance to give up the world?

All of these were good questions and only a cynic would say that they have never been answered. But it might be said that they were difficult to answer between supper and breakfast.

When the Lord Chamberlain rose to go, he said:

"I am out of my depth with a brilliant mind like yours. But I leave you with this thought: Renunciation, say all the sages, is the path to liberty. And if a prince becomes a hermit he is sure of being famous throughout the land."

The Lord Chamberlain bowed and left. He had made up his mind that Rama was generous, warmhearted, loyal, well-meaning, intellectually brilliant, idealistic, and a damned fool. In this he summed up the general opinion and this was only to be expected, for that is the major art of being, as he was, a successful politician.

CHAPTER SIX

sita

There were two people in the palace who did not think Prince Rama a fool. One was his brother Luxmun and the other was Sita, his wife.

Sita was a young woman with an oval face, long eyes shaped like almonds, a slender figure (but she was rather short), and a graceful carriage when she walked. She was otherwise quite unremarkable. Because of this she presents an insoluble problem for anyone re-telling the ancient story of Rama.

Whether we take the story as altered by millennia of Brahminical forgery, or whether we take the bare bones of the tale, which is all that we can be sure is original, there is no doubt that Sita is the heroine.

But Sita was not heroic. She was perfectly satisfied with loving her husband, and this, with a husband as handsome as the young Rama, did not call for heroism. She was never torn with anguish—she was too busy looking to Rama's comfort. She was never seized with the desire to revolt from the bonds of marriage—she would have considered it as silly as revolting from being, as she was, just under five feet high. She was not determined to make her husband a famous man—she looked upon all other men as unfortunate failures beside him. She was not passionate; she merely enjoyed being in bed with her husband. She was faithful, but not dogmatically so, as we shall see. She was not proud, except of her husband; she was not imperious, except with her dressmaker; she was not mystical, except when doing arithmetic. She had none of the qualities of an Indian, or any other, heroine. She was a good woman, a good wife, and a simple soul. We must put up with her.

Luxmun, Rama's younger brother, can best be described as a good companion for her. He was strong in body, and wore large moustachios. His moustaches and his brother were the things he loved most in the world. Next, he liked a good fight, but a fair one. He thought of himself as a soldier and had been through a campaign or two, in which he had shown courage. He was brave, honest, straightforward and, again, a simple soul. His unsophisticated face behind his unsmart moustaches appears in the background of all Rama's adventures. We must be content, therefore, with two good and uncomplicated people.

They sat together now outside the room in which Rama was meditating his decision.

Luxmun put his hand on Sita's. She smiled up at him briefly and then returned to her watch upon the door which she had maintained for two hours.

Then a servant came in with a cup of hot syrup. Sita took it, and tapping gently at the door, went in to her husband.

Luxmun waited, pacing the room with a military stride and biting his moustaches. Once he yawned (for he was young and the night seemed endless) but he rebuked himself and bit at his moustaches more savagely to keep himself awake.

After a long quarter of an hour Sita came out. She set the empty cup down on a small table.

"Well?" said Luxmun, keeping his voice low lest his brother should be disturbed. "Has he decided?"

Sita nodded. She smiled at him again, but uncertainly. "It

seems," she said, pulling the headpiece of her sari forward, "that we are going to renounce the world."

"When?"

"Tomorrow morning."

"Does he know that we mean to go with him, whatever happens?"

"I told him so."

"Did he forbid it?"

Sita paused. She sighed.

"I think, brother-in-law," she said, "that my husband is in such a wonderfully elevated mood that he won't notice whether we are with him or not."

"Oh," said Luxmun, "well, good, then."

"Yes," said Sita. "I suppose it is. Well, I must go and put a few things in a bundle."

"Bundle?" said Luxmun. "Well, I don't know about that. Never seen one of these fellows who's renounced the world with a bundle. A stick, yes. And a bowl. But they never carry a bundle."

"Oh," said Sita. "I've never noticed much myself. But I'm sure you're right. Well, then, I must go and pack it."

"The bundle, you mean, Sita?"

"Yes, Luxmun."

"But Sita, as I said, they don't carry one."

"Never mind," said Sita, "I shall carry it."

"Yes, of course. Or I could," said Luxmun.

"You'll have your bow and your spear. He'll need protecting. And I don't care whether the others do or not. You'll have to take care of my husband."

"I shall, most certainly."

Sita looked at the door reflectively.

"It's strange. To think that he'll be a great saint."

"Always knew he'd be a great *man*," said Luxmun, also looking at the door. "I'd rather hoped he'd be a great king."

"To renounce the world," said Sita firmly, "is a far finer thing than being a king."

"Yes, of course," said Luxmun.

"Well," said Sita. "I'm going. Aren't you going to bed?"

"I think I'll wait a little."

"Then, good night, Luxmun."

"Good night, Sita. The gods keep you."

Thus, unheroically, they parted.

the
noble
gesture
of
prince rama

The news that Rama was going into exile to
fulfill a sacred pledge of his father's stirred the whole town.
People wept openly in the streets. Everybody felt uplifted.
They all felt that they, too, were really capable of such a noble
deed if it were not for their wives, their children, their debts,
their mistresses, their businesses, or their rheumatism. The early-
morning beggars did very well; a merchant informed a customer
that he had paid too much by mistake; men going home from
the brothel quarter and hearing the news in the hot-drink shops
determined to rescue at least one woman from her life of shame.
It was as though an angel had passed through Ayoda, brushing
the inhabitants with the tips of its wings.

"They'll be looting the shops by ten o'clock," said the Lord
Chamberlain to his barber as his spies briefly reported the morning gossip of the town. The next hour showed signs that he was
right.

The sentiments of the people changed. From feeling that
they all could do so noble a thing they turned—as the press of
daily affairs grew worse—to saying that not even Rama should
be asked to do it. They were being robbed of a future king and
a king such as history had never witnessed. All knew the story

of the dead boy: nobody until now had heard of the oath. Those who had wept in the streets dried their eyes in the hot-drink shops and took a realistic look at the matter. While praising Rama as a saint they had to agree that he was a simpleton. Something, they said, was going on behind the poor boy's back, and it boded no good for the people. There was a woman in it, they'd be bound. That was where the taxes went, on women.

The sun rose higher and so did the indignation of the people. The beggars got no more money, a loss which they accepted with philosophy: in common with priests they had every reason to know that religions fervour changes men's lives, but not usually for very long.

Sweating deliciously from their spiced hot drinks, the more fiery members of the crowd began to make for the tax-collectors' booths. The tax-collectors having prudently put up their shutters, the crowd wrote RAMA across them and then, somewhat inconsequentially, smashed them up. They were shouting outside a rice store when the Lord Chamberlain strode to Rama's quarters, bowed to the ground, and begged him to save the situation.

Rama was in a state of exaltation, partly from lack of sleep and partly because of his decision. He was quite unable to follow why his resolve to take the saffron robe (the mark of renunciation) should lead to the sacking of food stores. The Lord Chamberlain fervently assured him that there was an explanation but the time consumed in making it would cost the town at least two rows of shops. He begged Rama, out of the nobility of his spirit, to show himself to the people dressed for the hunt, and so reassure them that he was not leaving.

Rama replied reasonably that since he had made up his mind to go he did not see any purpose in leaving disorders behind him.

But a question occurred to him, and this time it was not one to do with the universe or his soul. He said:

"Last night you spoke of demonstrations in my favour. This is one, then?"

The Lord Chamberlain had forgotten what he had said the night before, a habit which he had cultivated. As a rising politician he had hoped that what he said would always be memorable: as a mature one he depended on its being the reverse.

"That," he said, "was different." And then recalling with an effort what he had said, he went on triumphantly, "These are hooligans."

"I understand," said Rama. But he did not understand, and for the first time in his life he knew that he did not. It was the beginning of his education in living.

The world had never looked so difficult to renounce as it did that morning. By the Lord Chamberlain's guileful forethought, Rama's chariot was ready for him, and it was in this that he drove to the confines of the city. Crowds gathered round his horse: women threw flowers: old men called blessings and some younger ones shouted remarks against the King.

But the soberer heads among the citizens, those who could stand back and take a steady look at things, pointed out that there was one clear proof that the rumour of the Prince's exile must be false: nobody would go on a long journey into the countryside by chariot. With the roads what they were he would have to abandon his chariot in the first five miles. Plainly Rama was going hunting in the woods outside the walls. These sensible citizens joined in the cheering good-humouredly, and then quietly went home, advising everybody else to follow their example.

The shouting died away, the cheering subsided, and there were no more flowers. Rama drove through the city gates, surprised at finding how pleasant the tribute had been, and surprised, too, at himself that he should think so.

Half a mile beyond the gates of the city the road passed through a wood and there Rama found his wife and brother waiting for him.

Now came his most testing moment; now he must send back the charioteer and his horse and chariot; now he must renounce the pleasures and power of the world.

The cheering still sounded in his ears: he could still smell the scent of the flowers as they had been crushed beneath the hooves of his horse.

He reflected as he patted his horse's neck that nobody had ever taken that amount of notice of him before. He reflected again, as he gave the charioteer a ring from his finger as a keepsake, that they had only noticed him because he decided to uphold the honour of his father and to show himself a dutiful son, and because a father's honour and an obedient son were the foundation (so said the Brahmins) of all society and all religion. He had roused the city by his noble gesture. He would not betray it. He dismissed the charioteer.

But Sita and Luxmun noticed that he watched his horse until it could be seen no more, and that when he turned to them and said that he was ready, he was crying.

He walked ahead. The others fell in behind.

"Shall I tell him," whispered Sita, "that I've got his hermit's dress in the bundle?"

"No," whispered Luxmun. "Not now."

So Rama began his exile dressed in the trappings of a princely hunter, seeking, not game, but answers to his questions.

The hermit's saffron robe remained in Sita's bundle through the spring, the hot season, the rains, and the cool weather—the better part of a year of wandering.

This did not happen because Rama was unwilling to become a holy man, but rather because of the reverse. Rama had conceived the notion of having the robe put on him by some saint who, having answered his questions, would welcome him into the community of the elect.

In the course of his travels he met several saints who were very ready to welcome him but who were not so warm towards his questions.

The three journeyed from holy place to holy place, not only for piety but also for shelter, there being no other places in which to rest in the countryside. Their approach to a holy place would be heralded by gossiping peasants who had met them on the road or had seen them at their last halting place.

The holy men would come out to greet them with garlands and edifying hymns and invite them to a meal. The holy men were all Brahmins of the most orthodox variety, and in the Brahminical version of Rama's history that remains to us, great space is given to describing them. Their holiness is extolled, their courtesy magnified, and their edifying hymns included word for word. After the meal, the three pilgrims would retire to rest. In the morning Rama would respectfully ask his host to instruct him in the path of renunciation, after which he would beg leave to ask a few questions. In a matter of days the three voyagers would be travelling again with the most urgent and pressing introductions from their host to the next holy man along the road: who, having withstood the questioning as long as he could, would resort to the same device.

In this manner Rama, Sita, and Luxmun arrived at a riverside holy place where the saint had just died. Having assisted the villagers at his cremation, they were at a loss where to go. The headman of the village, awed by the plain signs that his visitors were high-born, knelt and touched their feet. With great hesitation he told them that some few miles along the bank of the river there was a hermitage. When pressed by Rama to say whether any holy men lived there, he begged to be excused from answering. It was called, he said, the Hermitage of the Gluttons.

Rama, Sita, and Luxmun set out with many misgivings, hoping to find some more promising halt on the way. But the road, although beautiful, was deserted, and all day they passed no sign of habitation. Towards four o'clock they came within sight of the Gluttons' Hermitage, and Rama, cautiously exploring it, met the man who was to make his name and his adventures famous—the exiled poet Valmiki.

BOOK TWO

the tales
of
valmiki

the
heritage
of the
gluttons

Valmiki was the first author in all history to bring himself into his own compositions. This was a remarkable thing to do. If you take pleasure in reading books, whatever your race, you should do honour to the memory of Valmiki. In the sunrise of writing he established the fact that a book is written by an author and not by a committee of accurate grammarians. Valmiki insisted that he was somebody, although in fact he was a nobody. The least important Brahmin who screwed taxes out of the peasants who sold onions in the market place was more important than this disgraceful scribbler who was not even allowed to live in decent society. But Valmiki did not think so, and he put himself into his story, as bold as brass. I think that he even began the story with himself, although in the texts that we have the Brahmins have written in a few preliminary chapters to make things more respectable. But they did not suppress Valmiki. They left him in the story, merely altering his opinions.

But civilised mankind, in its morning hours, had more than one Valmiki. There was a whole sect of men who, disgusted with Brahminical subtleties, Brahminical tyranny, and the Brahminical love of philosophical argument—by which they proved that everything they did was right because God said so—had gone off into the forest and set up a hermitage. They called their sect the Gluttons, because (they said) a man lives by eating: or, rather

81

(they argued), by observation they had established the fact that
when a man does not eat he dies. Whatever gods there be, one
of them must be in a man's belly, and they sacrificed to him
three times a day—or, in the case of the more devout members
of the community, four times. They were soon joined by other
sceptical people who had fallen foul of the Brahmins, and among
them, it would seem, was Valmiki. There is no evidence that he
was an official Glutton, but he evidently found their company
congenial, because he put one of them into his book.

While Valmiki was living in this hermitage Prince Rama
arrived there and the author gave him shelter. It was then that
the idea of writing the life of this unfortunate prince arose in
Valmiki's mind.

The hermitages at which Rama and his companions had previously stayed had been uncomfortable and squalid. This was because the hermits who lived in them wished to be holy. When
Rama and his companions came upon the Hermitage of the
Gluttons they found it neat and clean and pleasantly disposed
between a half-circle of hills and the bank of a considerable
river. This was because these hermits did not wish to be holy;
they merely did not want to be wicked. People so lacking in
warmth and enthusiasm must be content with their own company, and the Gluttons, having quarrelled with the Brahmins,
had set up the hermitage to make this possible in a convenient
and inexpensive manner.

The houses stood well apart in a half-circle that followed the
sweep of the enclosing hills. They were made of clay and
thatched with the dried leaves of palms. The ground rose gently
behind each of them, and it was terraced. On the terraces grew
fruit trees, flowers, and vegetables. The space in front of each
house was sanded and paths led from each sand patch to a

banyan tree that grew near the river. Its wide-spreading branches and the roots that grew down from them in thick columns made a meeting place. There was nothing else. No house was bigger than the others: all had one storey. The men lived in perfect equality, none was jealous. Since there was no jealousy, there was no rivalry. Since there was no rivalry, everybody did much the same as everybody else. The community was harmonious, since nobody would have cared a rap if it had broken up the very next day.

Valmiki had been the last to join them and his house was therefore on the tip of the half-circle. Thus, Rama, coming into the settlement, approached this house first.

He signalled to his two companions to remain behind, and he himself strode into the middle of the sanded place in front of the door and he rested upon his great bow.

This weapon was six feet long and rose just above Rama's shining black hair. It had two sinuous curves, and in the middle a handgrip of silver, chased with designs of antelopes. It was a bow that could be drawn only by a man of great strength; it was a bow that could be controlled only by a man whose strength was disciplined; and such was Rama, after his months of pilgrimage. His skin was a golden brown and gleamed with the movements of the muscles beneath. His torso, naked save for the strap that bore his quiver, was heavy-shouldered and greatly narrowed at the waist, in the manner most admired among Indians. The pleated cloth around his hips curved over buttocks that were something womanish, a sign in his race of high breeding. It fell halfway down his thighs, which were strong and spare. His feet were now shod with country sandals, made of the hide of a deer. He wore no ornaments, so that nothing beguiled the eye from the astonishing beauty of his face.

Down the centuries the face of Rama has never been for-

gotten. Sculptors have handed on the memory from generation
to generation, and from a thousand statues each differing a little
we can derive his true portrait. He had long eyes. His nose was
thin and flaring: his lips rich: his chin that of a boy. There was
nothing arrogant in his expression, but the carriage of his head
was very noble. He moved with grace and spoke with the voice
of a man who is accustomed to being heard with attention.
Apart from the sum of all these attributes there was something
more—an air of freshness, a clarity, a directness, as of a young
man coming in from a fine hunt on a glorious morning. At the
time when he met Valmiki he was twenty-eight years old and
still rather simple for his age.

As a sign of peace, he unstrung his great bow with an expert gesture. He then looked around him for the owner of the
house and found him at work on the terrace above, pruning a
tree.

"Reverend father," called Rama.

The man looked round. Then the man nodded, and hitching
up his loose robe, came down some stone steps that joined the
terraces, alternately looking at Rama and at where he placed his
feet, so that he stumbled a little and made anything but an
impressive descent.

When he had reached the sanded area and come nearer,
Rama could see that his hair was greying, although he was not
in any way infirm. He was well built, but bowed in his shoulders,
and had no repose in his movements. He gave Rama a friendly
but very keen glance.

Rama saluted him by raising his joined hands and bowing
his head.

"Reverend father," said Rama, "I ask you to grant me and
my companions shelter. We are strangers."

"Yes, yes, certainly," said the owner of the house quickly.

"Strangers are always welcome. It's my old friends who aren't. They come here and lecture me on my bad habits and go away with a basketful of my best artichokes."

As he said this he grinned. This grin was the most remarkable affair, and it was largely responsible for his having innumerable enemies. It was so striking that anybody watching the two—the stalwart Rama and the round-shouldered poet—and observing the grin would immediately forget Rama, his deep chest, his great bow, his correct buttocks, and his strong legs; all would be shadowed—if a grin can throw a shadow—by this phenomenal expression of the face of the older man.

The setting for the grin, Valmiki's face, would have commanded respect but not interest, and certainly not hostility, if it had been devoid of this feature. In repose Valmiki could be seen to have a high forehead, a narrow face, and a long nose dividing large eyes that were full of intelligence. These eyes were heralds of the grin. They shone, glittered, and appeared to change colour. Then the poet would smile; the smile would make two deep creases from his nose to his jawbone and a myriad smaller ones at the corners of his eyelids; and the smile would expand and blossom into a grin, and this was so redolent of comedy, of satire, of amusement and suppressed laughter, that the watcher found himself smiling, or laughing aloud, as though the world had become a clearer and enlightened place, as though much that was dark had been mysteriously explained and a great many fears had been shown to be bogies: that is to say, if the watcher were young. If he was older than forty he felt, usually, as comfortable as a thief in the beam of a lantern.

"May I call my companions?" Rama asked.

"By all means. And who are they?"

"My wife, and my brother."

Valmiki, grinning once more, said:

"Well, then, who are you? But you are, of course, Prince Rama, the famous young man who has been thrown out of Ayoda for his crimes."

"I am a pilgrim seeking the path of renunciation," said Rama. "I was not thrown out of Ayoda, I was—" He paused and searched for the right words; he found it difficult to find them under the scintillating gaze of Valmiki. "I was asked to leave," he said, a phrase which, he could not help feeling, was unsatisfactory. "In any case, I, at least, am innocent of any crime."

"Except," said Valmiki, "that of being handsome, generous, and a loving son, and of having a devoted wife and a faithful brother. I wonder that they let you escape with your life."

"Then you know Ayoda?" said Rama, and once again felt that there were better replies.

"Yes," said the other. "I am also an exile from your city. My name is Valmiki. I, on the other hand, committed four thousand crimes, each of them without a single professional flaw. Go and fetch the lady, your wife, and His Highness your brother. I will go in and make the house ready to receive you."

Rama bowed hastily, full of the gravest doubts. He returned to the road that led to the hermitage. He found his wife sitting in a dispirited manner on the root of a tree and his younger brother leaning wearily on a spear. As Rama approached, his brother straightened; he gave his sister-in-law an encouraging pat and his own large moustaches an upward twist. "Here he comes," he said to the woman. "We shall soon be able to rest ourselves." But when he asked his brother if he had found shelter Rama shook his head.

"No, Luxmun," he said. "I do not think so." He looked at his wife with great gravity.

"Has he turned us away?" she said, and she pushed the hood of her sari from her forehead and sighed. The sun, although it was late afternoon, was still very hot and they had walked many miles that day.

"That is the difficulty, Sita," said Rama. "He has made us very welcome. As for me, I wouldn't mind taking the risk and spending a night there."

"Risk, eh?" said Luxmun eagerly. He shifted his grip on his spear.

"But I cannot allow you to do so."

Sita lowered her head in obedience; such, the Brahmins taught, was her duty as a wife. She also determined that, come what may, she would sleep in the hermitage that night. This was her duty to herself as a woman, about which the Brahmins taught nothing because they knew nothing.

"The man's name," said Rama, "is Valmiki. I remember being told by one of my instructors that he was a murderer."

Sita raised her face in alarm at this, and even Luxmun showed uneasiness.

"Yes," said Rama, "I was told that he killed a Brahmin."

"Oh," said Sita, calm again. "That is a very terrible thing to do, of course."

"Of course," said Luxmun, once more resting easily on his spear. "But then none of us is a Brahmin."

"And I have very sore feet," added Sita.

"He says," went on Rama, "that he has committed four thousand other crimes."

"That is a *very* large number," said Sita. "The surprising thing is that he has been able to keep count of them. I think I should be more frightened of a man who had committed one crime than of a man who says he has done four thousand."

"Besides," said Luxmun, "they are probably old woman's

crimes, like not finishing his prayers. These hermits grow very odd in their ways."

"And," said Sita, "I do not think I could walk any further, unless you ordered me to do so."

"Perhaps we could try some of the other houses," said Lux-mun, "but since I can see him waiting at the door, he might be offended if we did and lay a curse on us. In fact, I think he will curse us in any case if we keep him waiting much longer."

"And I was always told," said Sita, "that a hermit's curse was a very awful thing. So perhaps we had better say a prayer for the Brahmin he killed and hope he soon gets out of hell— although of course being a Brahmin he wouldn't be in hell—and go at once."

Rama, who as the eldest of the party felt his responsibility for them, hesitated.

"I think," he said, "I remember being told by a Brahmin that this Valmiki was a poet."

"Very well," said Sita, "if he starts talking poetry I shall get up and leave the room."

"And I shall hit him once or twice with the blunt end of my spear," said Luxmun. "So that is all settled. Brother, please lead the way."

Rama did so, and Luxmun followed one pace behind and Sita five paces, according to the rules of propriety that their Brahminical tutors had impressed upon them when they were little children. According to these rules, no one could walk side by side with a prince, unless he were a Brahmin.

They eyed Valmiki cautiously as he made them welcome, but for a criminal he was very well-mannered. He led them to a clean bare room where a boy waited with bowls of water, and when they were seated on mats of dried palm leaves, the boy washed their feet, not keeping his eyes on the ground while he tended them as he should have done (being, according to the Brahmins, an inferior being) but looking them in their faces, and even speaking to them.

The impertinent boy then served the meal, which was a simple preparation of fruits and vegetables. This, at least, was proper for a hermit, and they began to eat freely. Valmiki's way of saying grace was, however, very much his own. The grace that the Brahmins said for Rama in his palace before joining him in his meals was long, sonorous, and thanked a battery of gods by name for their favours. Valmiki said:

"Gods in your heaven grant that we eat this meal remembering that we may die this very night and never taste such good things again. Sweet gods, fatten the pumpkins. I've done all I know and just look at them. So be it."

Nothing very much was said during the meal. Valmiki's attempts at conversation were turned aside by his guests. It was not etiquette for a prince to speak at mealtimes and the habit of silence had become too strong for any of them to break it, even in exile. The etiquette of the court had been drawn up during the reign of a king who not only did not speak at mealtimes but spoke hardly ever between them, for the reason that he had nothing whatever to say. The Chancellor, who had governed the kingdom and amassed an enormous fortune in doing so, established this taciturnity as a court rule. The rule had been maintained and now the custom that had been designed to cover the ignorance of one king was held to be essential to the dignity of his successors. Since it is as difficult to stop making rules as it is to stop eating almonds, once having started, the King and the royal family were soon surrounded by so many ceremonies that a theory was necessary to account for it. Several learned Brahmins set to work at it, and thus arose the doctrine that monarchy was a divine institution. This was satisfactory and reasonable, since the gods, by definition, are capable of anything. The meal, then, proceeded in silence.

When the lamps were brought in, this silence was broken by the sound of music. The music came from outside the house. Rama looked up from the banana leaf on which were the remains of his meal, and his face showed astonishment and displeasure. This was because the musicians outside were playing the wrong tune for the time of day.

Music, of course, started with people singing, and in more barbarous days people had sung when and what they pleased. With the progress of civilisation they had been put in order and the principles of good taste had been established. A celebrated Brahmin analysed all the melodies which he heard people sing and found that there were exactly twenty-four, a number which was later revised by an equally celebrated Brahmin, who found that there were exactly forty-eight. It was found, also, that the commonest cowherd knew all twenty-four (or forty-eight), often as well and sometimes better than the most learned musicologist. Plainly there was a flaw in this, and it was soon brought to light. The first of the celebrated Brahmins found that where the cowherd differed from the Brahmin was that he sang as his vulgar spirit moved him. More cultivated people, however, ought to sing the tune most suitable for the mood of the hour. From this it was only a step—or, better, a happy skip— to drawing up a list of the twenty-four tunes arranged according to the twenty-four hours. (The second Brahmin later arranged the tunes for the half-hours, but agreed with his predecessor in his fundamental principles).

This settled, the way was clear to make a rule that people of good taste should sing or listen to the prescribed tune at the prescribed hour and to nothing else. This being the most extravagant absurdity, it followed inevitably that the gods were called upon to support it, which (according to the Brahmins) they did. The gods announced that they were only pleased by certain sorts of music and that all other music offended them. The sorts nobody was to learn were listed by the Brahmins. Very soon a literature grew up round the subject and then another literature explaining the first. Among men of taste and fashion it was considered essential to have a nodding acquaintance with this immense compilation of criticism, and the habit of listening to a good tune and enjoying it died out. Instead a musical performance became a desperate business in which both the listeners and performers tried to display their erudition. The resulting music was offensively bad, but since nobody expected to enjoy it, nobody was disappointed. The sounds that Rama now heard were tuneful, happy, and wrong.

At this point a peasant woman came into the room, and after saluting Valmiki, she took Sita away to help her prepare for the night. Sita touched her husband's sandals, as good manners prescribed, and left silently, as became a woman. But all this took time and the music outside changed before Rama could protest. This new melody was not one of the forty-eight—a thing which was strictly speaking impossible. Rama said so, as they moved out to sit on the porch of the house to feel the cool air of the evening.

Valmiki said nothing in reply to this, but sat for a while listening to the music. Some of the hermits had gathered under the tree, squatting by the grey columns of the aerial roots and looking towards two of their company who sat with their backs against the bole. One of these two men had a zither with a great number of strings which he plucked rapidly, making a humming music, the melody of which was subtle and long, its shape emerging from the deeper notes and then retreating again, like an iridescent snake glimpsed in long grass. The other man was singing. To follow such a melody demanded prolonged control of the breath, and this he achieved by moving his hands and arms, expanding and deflating his chest as he did so, but unobtrusively, since he matched his gestures to the meaning of the words, pointing the phrases, and illustrating the meaning in a ceaseless weaving of his bare arms and his brown hands. Behind him the river lay silver in the last short light of the evening, and black canoes, slowed by their paddling crews to catch something of the song, passed behind him and so out of sight round the bend of the river, where Rama could see the paddles rise, drip, and plunge again, in rhythm with the singing. On the river's far bank, the forest was already dark, and fireflies had begun to dance in pyramids above some of the trees.

Then the last light faded from the sky and in a matter of minutes it was quite dark, with the sudden soft darkness of the tropics. The singer and the zither-player ended their song, whether because they had reached its end or because of the darkness it was difficult to say, for the melody found no resolution, the last note thinly aspiring like the finial of a tree, promising growth but for the moment, the last. A servant walked towards the tree carrying a tray of earthen lamps, which the listeners placed in a semi-circle at the feet of the singers. Rama used this pause to say:

"I am surprised that a poet—an artist—like yourself should not find such music objectionable. I mean, at this time of day—or, for that matter, at any time. I don't recognise the tune at all."

Valmiki's boy came onto the porch, carrying a tray with four lit lamps which he placed in brackets on the wall of the hut. Valmiki watched him do this before he answered Rama, and Rama saw by the light of the lamp that Valmiki's face was creased in his disconcerting grin.

"It is strange," thought Rama to himself, "that I, a prince of the blood royal, should sit here in the forest talking about music to a man who has murdered a Brahmin—although it is difficult to imagine him doing it—and who admits to four thousand other crimes. But it is the will of the gods."

Luxmun, for his part, thought: "I am glad he's brought the lights. A man can see what he's at if any trouble blows up. There is my spear leaning in the corner, the left hand corner. Although I must say this fellow seems amiable enough. Still, my brother says he is a dangerous man and what my brother says is right."

The boy turned to go, but Valmiki said: "Wait." The boy obeyed, standing in an unembarrassed way, looking at his master. Valmiki said to Rama:

"Have you ever seen the sea?"

"The sea?" said Rama and felt with some resentment that this dubious man had a knack of suddenly making him feel young just when he thought himself most mature. "No. You mean the Great Water? No, I have not seen it. But of course my tutors have fully described it to me. It resembles green glass. It is inhabited by a race of men and women whose lower bodies are fishes' tails, a punishment for their having refused to give a Brahmin the best piece of fish when he was eating with them in some previous life."

The shadows in the lines beside Valmiki's mouth grew deeper.

"I have seen it," he said. "Before I came here I wandered over most of our land and I spent some time among fishermen in a village by the sea. No doubt if the Brahmins say so, then the sea must be inhabited by men with tails. I never saw one. But I saw something which struck me as much more marvellous."

"What was that?" said Rama and Luxman together.

"Look," said Valmiki and pointed to the waiting boy. "Do you see what he wears in his ear?"

The boy smiled at the Prince in a manner which would have earned him prison for insolence in Ayoda, and turned his head so that they could see two pieces of curiously shaped pink stone that hung in the lobes of his ears.

the
conspiracy
revealed

"That stone," said Valmiki, "is made by an insect no bigger than the smallest gnat. It lives in the sea. It builds itself a small, crooked house, and other insects build houses on top of it. They go on building, year after year, in shapes more and more fantastic, until they have built a hill. They go on building upon the hill until they have built a cliff. Then they build on the cliff until it rises out of the sea, and the water which once had been smooth—not as smooth, perhaps, as green glass—but still, smooth, now breaks into white foam that roars continuously against the innumerable pink houses of the little insects."

"I think I remember hearing something of the sort," Rama began, but Luxmun, round-eyed, better expressed his brother's feelings.

"How extraordinary," he said. "A cliff? How long does it take?"

"I have no means of knowing," said Valmiki. "I was not there long enough to see a house built. I went on my travels again and I saw many other things perhaps just as curious. I saw a judge order one man to be fined a silver rupee and another man to be mercilessly flogged, both for the same offence. And what was marvellous was that everybody, including the flogged man, thought it was just. It was the law of the land that a man

of darker skin should be punished more severely than a man
more pale than he. This, they proved, was bound up with the
origins of the world. It is an interesting proof, but I shall not
repeat it for the first part of the exposition alone takes two
hours.

"Then I went on a journey into the western lands where
the men are all pale and of extreme refinement. I found a vast
building inhabited by men who had castrated themselves in
honour of a goddess who lived, they said, in a black stone which
smelt abominably of the rancid oil which they poured on it
every hour of the day and night. They accompanied their wor-
ship with hymns which they sang in high, cracked voices. In one
part of the building was a long room in which twenty men
worked at desks continuously inscribing diatribes against men
who were physically complete and made use of their advantage
in the customary manner. Nobody in the kingdom could aspire
to being considered a learned man unless he was willing to make
the same sacrifice as these devotees. One man, who claimed to
have invented a method of measuring the area of curved sur-
faces—I cannot say if he had really done it or not—was refused
a hearing on the grounds that he had raised a family of five
children and was therefore no scholar. They showed me a cata-
logue of their writings, which already runs to a roomful of
scrolls. It is not complete and never will be, for dissertations are
produced more quickly than they can be listed, since the cata-
loguers are themselves writing dissertations on the proper principles of listing dissertations.

"My mind began to ache after a short sojourn among these
people and I passed on to a country which lies beyond the
Hindu Kush. There I talked across a small boundary stream to
an old man who was voluble in the praises of his native land,
in which he had not set foot for thirty-seven years. The little

stream over which we talked was the boundary of the country. Thirty-seven years before he had gone across it on a journey. While he was away, an enemy laid information against him, and his return was forbidden until the magistrates had decided upon his case. The enemy had said that the absent man had once disagreed when someone had declared in his presence that the King's second daughter was the most beautiful woman in the world. The unfortunate man, through his representatives, denied that he had ever said it, or, if he had, then it was not sufficient ground to separate him from his home, his friends, and such fortune as he might have after paying his legal expenses. The case became celebrated. Each magistrate upheld a different opinion and in a few years candidates for the office of justice were required to produce opinions of their own. Meantime the man was ruined, his wife died from vexation at having to live in a hut on a riverbank, and the princess who had been the cause of the matter at the age of twenty-two became a mature woman. When I saw her she was beak-nosed, rheumy-eyed, and had developed a formidable and hairy wart on her right cheek. For all that, the man himself and everybody that I met were immensely proud of the way things had been done. It proved, they all said, how careful their government was to protect the freedom of the subject. The scrolls recording the various opinions were of the finest vellum, tied up with red tassels, and a copy of each one was always sent to the man across the river, who, having heaped them conveniently, sat on them, since he had sold all his furniture to fight his case.

"Now," said Valmiki, "when I returned from my travels in other countries and I settled here to think about them, it seemed to me that I had made one discovery. I had found that clever men greatly resemble the insect that made the earrings in my servant's ear. They will elaborate vast structures of thoughts from their very nature. They cannot stop, even though the thing they are building is senseless. They must go on. And we must live in the nooks and crannies of their aimless building, and sometimes be imprisoned in it, as they work, endlessly, surrounding us, closing our escapes, until we live and die a part of the gigantic folly, as blind and in as deep a darkness as its frantic builders."

While he had been speaking, lights had appeared in many of the other huts, while the lamps under the tree where the musicians sat shone more brightly. The sound of talking and laughter came through the still air, with the echo that is not an echo but an underlining, an enrichment of the sound, that marks the tropical night.

Prince Rama had listened to Valmiki with great attention. He had been thought an admirable student in his youth; that is to say, he had developed the habit of listening with the appearance of pleasure to long speeches from elderly men, whom he never interrupted. As Valmiki had progressed, Rama grew more and more at a loss to discover what he meant, but the less Rama understood the more profound grew his attention. He was therefore caught quite defenceless when Valmiki turned to him at the end of his speech and said:

"So you see that a man with ideas like mine might very well have killed a Brahmin and eaten a hearty meal to top it off."

Rama blushed and the carriage of his handsome head lost a little of its nobility. He had been thinking this very thing.

"Did—did you kill him?" asked Luxmun.

"What would be the use of killing one Brahmin?" asked Valmiki in return.

Luxmun, to Rama's surprise, and not a little to Valmiki's, said:

"Yes. I quite see what you mean." He nodded his head sagely and stroked his moustache, a sign that his mind was running on his military career. "When I was just about to engage the King of Magada's forces on the morning of the Battle of Tamralipti I was on the end of the line and we opened the engagement—not that we didn't have to finish it as well for Raja Bhuma—he was in charge of the elephants—lost his head completely and charged off the field in the wrong direction just when we had them in the hollow of our hands—blaming it *of course* on the elephants, though I said then and I say now an elephant's toenail knows more about fighting than Bhuma's will ever learn—so he left it to us, as I was saying—what *was* I saying? Oh, yes. In the morning when we were just about to engage I said to myself, 'Suppose I kill one man, or two, or three, or four this morning, what difference will it make to that trampling herd'—the enemy I meant. Fright, you see. Pure fright. When they sounded the conch shell, in I went, still frightened out of my wits and then—*clang*—I got my mace on one of their helmets and down he went, then—*clang*—I got another and then, well, I laid out eight before I got my second wind and that was just the beginning. But that's what I mean, you see, you've just got to make a beginning and what I always say is—correct me if I'm wrong—but you begin with number one and let number two, three, four, and so on take care of themselves. It's like that with your Brahmin, or," he said, catching his elder brother's eye, "perhaps it isn't."

"No," said Valmiki, smiling at him, "I am afraid that it isn't. You see, I have not even started with number one."

"Then you did not kill a Brahmin?" said Rama.

"On the contrary," said Valmiki, "I have committed a much worse sin. I have made, I fancy, one or two of them immortal."

The zither-player sounded a new melody and this was greeted

with murmurs of approval from his small audience. One or two of them could be seen to turn towards Valmiki's house as the zither played. Valmiki said:

"Now, if you are not too tired, I would like you to hear some. of my four thousand other crimes. I fear that they must be very good or I would not be sitting here in the middle of the jungle as I am."

Rama, quite mystified, was about to ask him to explain, when the singer began the *Song of the Parrot*. It did not tell of the conspiracy in all its details—Valmiki did not know them all till many years later, when he put them in and, later still, the Brahmins cut them out—but it told enough to bring Luxmun to his feet in anger before half the song was done. Sita, hearing the song through the thin walls of the hut, came to a window and listened. She, too, grew angry, especially at that part which told of the pastry cook: for their conversation was an invention of his: she had done no more than thank him and give him money.

As for Rama, he listened unmoving, but as the narrative drew to its close, he took his gaze away from the singers and looked fixedly at the ground.

When the song was done, he said in the silence that followed:

"That is a most ingenious invention. I congratulate you."

"I wish it were an invention," said Valmiki. "I would think myself ever cleverer than I do."

"Then it's all true?" said Luxmun.

"As far as it goes," Valmiki replied. "Yes, it is true."

"You are very well informed," said Rama, "considering you are an exile."

Valmiki said: "Very."

Then he called a name and two people came towards the hut from the banyan tree. The other hermits fell silent and watched them. When they came up to the place where Rama was seated, they slowly kneeled and then touched the ground with their foreheads. By the light of the lamps Rama saw that they were the old man and his wife whose son the King his father had killed.

"You know who they are?" said Valmiki.

"Yes."

"Then you must forgive them. They have been very unfortunate and they cannot be blamed. On the night before the King held his audience, they were taken, by his orders, by two torturers and . . ."

Rama got up. For all his simplicity he had the authority of a prince when he chose to show it, as he did now. Valmiki fell silent.

Rama went to the old man and the old woman and raised them gently, saluting each of them, the first in the fashion of a son saluting his father, the second with the reverence of a son greeting his mother.

"You were made to lie?" he asked them.

The old man said, his voice shaking: "They did not hurt us. They showed us their ropes and whips. They showed us the blood on the floor and told us it was from a servant who had just received an hour's punishment for disobeying the King. We are very old. We were very frightened. My wife vomited. So we lied as we were told."

"Then you never bound the King to a vow?"

The woman said: "We have never done a cruel thing in our life. I do not know why people are so cruel to us. We forgave the King that night and we were happy when he built a temple. He left us in peace for years until one day we were dragged to his court because he wanted—" Her old voice was rising in anger, but her husband bade her be quiet.

"We ran away when Your Highness left," he said, "and they chased us through the woods and shot arrows. But we escaped and His Reverence here, Valmiki, gave us shelter. We were frightened when we saw you speaking to him, but he sent a message to us in the evening that you were a good man—may Your Highness excuse the phrase—and we were not to be afraid."

Rama stood for a moment quite still. Then he stooped swiftly and lightly touched the feet of first the man and then the woman.

"Forgive me," he said. "I am not a good man. But I think I am a very great fool."

He walked quickly away into the darkness. After a while Luxmun took his spear and followed him, pausing to whisper a word to Sita as she stood at her window.

Valmiki sent the two old people away with a kind good night. He then sat staring into the darkness until the hermits had gone back to their huts and the singers were asleep. The boy, sleepily looking to the lamps an hour later, saw that he had not moved: and that he was not smiling.

the tale
of the
passionate ascetic
and the
hidden wife

When Rama set out for his night's walk in the surrounding jungle he had intended to review his life, but he discovered like most young men that he had never taken any notice of it. He had lived happily, but inattentively. He had known that the court was full of intrigue: he had seen men rise and fall and be destroyed because of it. But he had never considered that intrigue could have anything to do with himself, because he could not imagine anybody disliking him in so marked a fashion.

As he walked he reflected that he had always aimed to win golden opinions from his elders and betters. He leaned against a teak tree and recalled that he had always got them. He sat down and decided that that must have been the cause of the trouble. He rose, very considerably wiser than when he had sat down.

Meanwhile Luxmun from a discreet distance kept a watch for beasts of prey.

Some two hours later he had walked out of the forest into a small plantation. It was three o'clock in the morning and Rama felt deeply sorry for himself. He sat down again, and putting his face in his hands, wept for his folly.

Luxmun, in a discreet voice, offered him some mangoes. Rama ate one and sighed. Luxmun peeled another with his hunting-knife and Rama ate it, absent-mindedly. Luxmun peeled yet another, intending to eat it himself, but Rama took it, thanked him, and consumed it. They ate about a dozen and the moon rose. Rama attempted to resume the thread of his melancholy thoughts, but Luxmun was cracking the great mango pips to find if they had beetles in them. This is an idle Indian pastime, the interest lying in the fact that the weevil is found only in a small proportion of the fruit (which it enters in the blossom stage) and one can lay bets. Rama laid bets, won, and felt much inspirited.

However, when the first light of morning began to turn the river pale, he reminded himself that the new day would be very different from those that had gone before. He had been stripped of many illusions and one of them was that he had cut a fine figure by going into exile.

When the sun was just about to rise, Rama looked at the world of men and found it distasteful. He walked somewhat apart from Luxmun and after a while he came to his decision.

He would finally renounce the world, and, as a mark of his new-found maturity, he would ask Valmiki, the heretical exile and despiser of Brahmins, to invest him with the saffron robe. Thus, he felt, he would regain his self-respect and the respect of the world, which (he reminded himself) was nevertheless a despicable one.

He said to Luxmun:

"Let us go back."

He woke Sita, who was dozing fitfully beside the window. He said:

"Where is the hermit's robe?"

She dutifully repressed her joy at seeing him return safe and sound, and stifling a yawn said:

"In the bundle."

She produced it and a few minutes later she and Luxmun heard with utter dismay that Rama was going to send them back to Ayoda.

In the hour that remained before Rama fell asleep from weariness, he explained to them that chastity was the first requisite of the true renouncer of the world. In this matter he would brook no argument, but quoted, in a melodious voice, several stanzas of a celebrated work on self-restraint and its spiritual joys. He felt, and looked, very much his old self.

He told his wife that although she disliked leaving him now, she would not later on, when she came to reflect on the austerities he would practice and how difficult they would have made her life with him. The indignant Luxmun he tried to soothe by explaining that someone would have to take Sita back to civilisation. That done, he did not object to Luxmun returning, but he thought the life not one for a soldier.

Then, overcome, he lay on Sita's bed and fell into a dreamless sleep.

Valmiki was looking sadly at his meagre pumpkins, a thing he did on rising every morning, when Luxmun and Sita climbed onto his terrace and saluted him. He showed them his garden and listened to their story. Sita felt that he was more interested in his seedlings than her troubles, and in competition with them, spoke out more than she had ever dared in her life.

When, in the still hour that follows eleven o'clock, Rama came to Valmiki with his hermit's robe on his arm and without his hunter's quiver, he found the poet sitting on the root of a carob tree. Valmiki invited Rama to sit beside him and directed his attention to the magnificence of the view that lay spread out at their feet. Rama looked at the river, the forest, and the

peaceful hermitage and said, to open the conversation which
Valmiki was giving him no opportunity to begin:
"For myself I shall choose a hermitage which is more
austere."
"Which would you prefer," said Valmiki, "the desert? That
is extremely trying, I believe. Or perhaps snow and ice?"
"Snow and ice," said Rama sharply, because he had seen the
smile deepen on Valmiki's face.
"A good choice. They are very cooling to the fleshly passions, I am told." And here he began to quote verses from the
poem in praise of chastity that Rama had recited the night
before.
"I greatly admire the author of those verses," said Rama,
and he shook out the folds of his gown and cleared his throat.
"His real name was Kumar," said Valmiki. "I suppose that
you never knew him. No, you would have been too young. But
if you like—and there is nothing else to do at this hour, which
is very inauspicious for beginning any important action—I will
tell you about him."
"Do," said Rama. "I shall be glad to hear anything about so
virtuous a man." So, moving his seat a little so as to be in the
shade of the thickest branch of the carob tree, Valmiki began:

In his prime (said Valmiki) as a preacher, Kumar was the
best-known spellbinder north of the Vindhya Mountains. He
travelled the whole country calling upon the population to renounce the vanities of this life and to live in holy simplicity.
Kumar himself was not very holy and he was the reverse of
simple. But he did sincerely think that a life of renunciation
would be better for everybody, including himself: and, to do
credit to his honesty, he never said that a life of self-denial was
easy.

Most hermits live hard lives in their hermitages and taste the fleshpots of the world only when they come out of them. Kumar reversed this. He lived rather comfortably in his hermitage, where nobody saw him, and he lived with gaunt austerity in places where he was more under observation. By this means he managed to be publicly edifying and personally sound in wind and limb. If his tall, half-naked figure showed rather fewer bones than it ought, it did not matter. His fascination lay in his eyes, which were large, black, and always burning.

It was these eyes which won him his principal admirer. This was Govinda, by far the richest cloth merchant of Ayoda, who had in the way of wealth and terrestial comforts more to renounce than any other member of his caste. He had grown in girth and weight step by step with his business; by the time he met Kumar his warehouse and his cummerbund were the most impressive sights in Ayoda after the royal palace and the main temple.

Hearing Kumar preach one day on the temple steps (for the Brahmins would not allow him to preach inside) the cloth merchant was converted the moment that Kumar ran his burning eyes first over Govinda's belly and then over his face. He asked Kumar to take a meal with him and when Kumar had eaten it he told the ascetic that he had made up his mind to give all his worldly wealth to the poor and to join Kumar in his hermitage.

Kumar surveyed the remains of the sumptuous meal with his burning eyes, dabbled his fingers in a silver bowl of rosewater, and picked his teeth with a jewelled toothpick that had a most amusing little set of minature gold bells attached to it so that it tinkled as it was used. Kumar produced a lengthy tinkling before he answered.

Then he said this:

"Good. God be praised. Honour and glory to Shiva, lord of ascetics, for another saved soul. But, my friend, I must warn you that the path is far from easy."

"No, I don't suppose that it is," said Govinda, "but I am used to doing difficult things. Still, I suppose it will at least be easier to give away my fortune to my poorer neighbours than it was to make it."

Kumar thought of all the good things around him disappearing, as, so to speak, he set them to his lips, like a fairy feast. His heart jumped, his palate went dry, and he took a long draught of sherbet from a bronze cup with silver inlay work. He thought quickly. He looked at his host over the brim of the cup. The men who lead us upward to higher things share one gift with those who lead us downward. They are good judges of character.

"There are harder things to give up than money," he said.

"Name them, master."

"For one," said Kumar, "women."

"At my age," said Govinda, "such pleasures are not important."

Kumar shook his head.

"Nobody can make that remark truthfully," he said in his best oracular manner, "over the age of fourteen."

Govinda smiled. "I don't deny that it has had its attractions for me," he said. He gave a reminiscent belch. "But with your example in front of me, I shall rise above it."

Kumar politely echoed his host's belch. It was noncommittal.

"You are married, of course?" he asked.

Govinda clapped his hands. He was a very respectable merchant and in his circle wives did not eat with their husbands but stayed in the kitchen or near it to supervise the dishes.

He instructed a bowing servant to call his wife into his presence.

She came. She was swathed in a sari of lustrous Chinese silk tinted with a soft Phoenician dye. It was bordered six inches deep with a pattern of gold thread and the wing-cases of iridescent beetles. She held the headfold of her sari closely across her face and kept her head bowed and her feet together as she stood before her husband. She was the very picture of a good wife of a substantial merchant.

Kumar greeted her. She did not reply until her husband said: "This is a learned holy man who is a master of wisdom. His name is Kumar. May it be always pronounced with reverence in this household. You may show your face."

She did, and the master of wisdom instantly succumbed to her charms.

"For a long time," said Govinda to his wife, "I have thought that life held something bigger and finer than selling pieces of cloth. Master Kumar has shown me what it is. Do you understand?"

His wife lowered her eyelids respectfully. She inclined her head obediently. She parted her classically full lips to show her perfect teeth.

"No," she said.

"It is difficult to explain to a woman," said Govinda.

"Nevertheless we should try," said Kumar. "Women, although a grave temptation, are God's creatures." And Kumar thanked God in his heart that He had made this one. "It may be," he went on, "that I shall experience a sudden revulsion against everything human and stay in my hermitage for some ten years or so. I feel that it might happen. But if it does not, and I come again to Ayoda, I should consider it my duty to instruct your wife in the principles of holy living."

"Do so," said Govinda, "and I shall be doubly in your debt. Cover your face and go." This last was to his wife. She covered her face slowly, her features disappearing one by one, each indelibly printed on Kumar's memory. She bowed deeply to her husband, revealing the magnificence of her haunches, and she left.

For Govinda to have mentioned his wife again would have been impolite and for Kumar it would have been incautious. It was taken for granted between the two men that Govinda's wife would do as he wanted, and the conversation turned back to the path of renunciation and its pitfalls. When at last they rose and bid each other good night (for Kumar had agreed to sleep under Govinda's roof instead of under the open sky as he would have preferred—he said—to do) Kumar delivered a final argument against any hasty action on Govinda's part.

"Now you said that you intend to give away your money."

"I did," said Govinda.

"To the local poor, I understand," said Kumar.

"With your approval," said Govinda.

"Of course it has my approval," said Kumar impatiently, "of course, of course, of course. It is naturally pleasing to the gods that you should give to the poor. You will earn merit."

"So I had hoped," said Govinda, and since they had reached the guest chamber, he added: "There are four lambskin rugs from Bokhara on the bed and two quilts of swans-down. You will want these removed, of course, master?"

"Don't trouble," said Kumar. "If I sleep at all, I shall sleep on the floor. You may leave them in place."

"As you wish, master."

"As I was saying," resumed Kumar, as the two men held hands in wishing each other good night, "to give to the poor will gain you merit. Now it follows that to give more to the poor will gain you more merit. It follows, again, that if you delay your action, as I advise, on spiritual grounds, you will go on making more money in the meanwhile, and so you will have more to give away when the time comes. More haste, less merit. Does my reasoning satisfy you?"

"Eminently, master," said Govinda. Both men at that moment breaking into a simultaneous yawn, they parted. Kumar, having ascertained that it would be a moment's work in the morning to put the coverlets straight, flung himself down on the Bokharas and dreamed of his host's wife.

Kumar returned to his hermitage the next day, greatly impressing Govinda with his self-abnegation. His disgust with humanity lasted seventy-two hours and, to Govinda's great delight, he once more appeared in Ayoda, preached, and was borne off to Govinda's house. When they had finished an even more sumptuous meal than the first and when it was done and both men were tinkling their toothpicks in the most companionable manner, Govinda said Kumar had been away much too long. Kumar heartily agreed but prudently refrained from saying so. Govinda complained that without Kumar's elevating conversation daily life was a grey monotony. If at the end of day he had accumuated twenty pieces of gold ("Twenty?" said Kumar. "I don't mean markct days," said Govinda), well, what were twenty pieces of gold? Twenty was a small number compared with the infinite; and gold did not shine so bright as the hermit's begging bowl.

With these sentiments Kumar sagely agreed, since they had been copied word for word from his morning's sermon. He waited for Govinda to come to the point. He was well satisfied when Govinda did.

"You mentioned that one of the difficulties in the way of

renunciation was women," said Govinda, "and you were, as inevitably you must be, right. My wife will not hear of the idea."

"Let me talk to her," said Kumar more quickly than he could have wished. A new brilliance came into his already burning eyes. Govinda noticed it with awe.

"I see that you anticipated my wife's stupidity," said Govinda. Kumar anticipated a good deal more, but he nodded his head.

"I saw when I first met her, that she needs instruction. Lengthy instruction, I am afraid. She has not got your own quick grasp of sublime truths."

"For that reason," said Govinda, smoothly accepting the compliment, "I had hoped that you would honour my house by making it your home for the rest of the hot-weather season. I fear for your health in that remote spot where you live, especially when the sand-wind is blowing. Thus if you condescend, we shall kill two birds with one stone."

Kumar accepted, and privately determined to kill three.

Govinda's wife received him at their first interview on the verandah of the women's quarters. But the heat increasing daily, Kumar suggested that they continue their instruction inside. Once inside he was able to get closer to both his theme and his pupil. His passions rose higher with every meeting, but if he had lost his heart, he kept his head. He realised that he had to do with a faithful, if not very loving, wife. He decided that it would be impossible to seduce her under his host's roof. He therefore put her under a vow of secrecy not to reveal to her husband what he was about to tell her, and this settled, he proceeded in the following manner:

"I have just explained, my dear, the *ksana-bhangarada* doctrine, which, as you know, says that nothing lasts longer than an instant. That, I suppose, is just about the time that my explanation stayed in your pretty head."

Govinda's wife lowered her darkened eyelids, parted her classically full lips, showed her faultless teeth and said:

"Yes."

"Very well," said Kumar, "now I will tell you something which will not be beyond your powers of understanding. But you must promise never to mention it to your husband. Do you promise?"

Govinda's wife nodded. The jewelled plaque which she wore on her forehead bounced in a way which Kumar found alluring.

"Your husband," he said, "is not really going to renounce anything. He is going to give his money to some trustworthy neighbours. Then he is going to desert you, dress as a hermit, and then he is going to Benares to live with another woman. Once everything has settled down, his neighbours are going to take the money to him and, in return for a consideration, give it back to him. He has told me that he cannot bear the sight of your face another moment. This other woman," said Kumar relentlessly, "is a Kashmiri whose complexion is like that of the tusk of an elephant reflecting the rosy dawn."

The part of this total lie which pleased Kumar best, as he thought over it in the next few days, was the Kashmiri woman with the good complexion. The business of the tusk and the dawn showed, he thought, a capacity for poetry in him which had been buried in the course of his practice as a rhetorician. Had he not had the wife of Govinda to love in the flesh, he would have been enamoured, he thought, of his own fiction.

Next, he admired the artistic flourish of asking Govinda's wife not to tell her husband. It was pure ornament. He knew quite well that she would tell him and he had already prepared his defences. This he had done quite simply by telling Govinda that his wife had conceived the silly notion that her husband's renunciation was a mere deceit to enable him to live with another woman in Benares. Govinda laughed heartily when he heard this story the first time (from Kumar) and even more heartily when he heard it the second, from his wife.

Kumar quickly pointed out to Govinda's wife that this was exactly what her husband might be expected to do. She put her face in her hands and cried. Her ornament bobbed more alluringly than ever.

Kumar's plans went well. Each time Govinda's wife spoke to her husband he declared that the day of his great renunciation was nearer. The actual moment awaited the decision of Kumar, who, Govinda told her, was a man she should listen to, respect, and obey. Each time Govinda's wife spoke to Kumar he drew a more detailed picture of the illicit household that was to be set up in Benares, and a more gloomy picture of the fate of Govinda's wife, deserted, despised, a widow without the chance to gain éclat by committing *suttee*. He also enlarged upon the charms of living in a hermitage: first, in any hermitage; later, in his own.

One night he came to the women's quarters in a feigned state of agitation and told her that she must decide. Her husband was pressing him to name the day of the renunciation and he could not delay any longer. If he refused to give a propitious time, Govinda would choose his own, and they would gain nothing. There was no alternative. Either she fled with him instantly (for he had already warned Govinda that he might leave for his hermitage to meditate his decision) and kept her self-respect, or she would be deserted and soon—when the true story was revealed by gossiping neighbours—disgraced.

She fled with him.

the tale of the hidden wife continued

For the first few days at the hermitage Kumar set his beautiful disciple a strict regimen of prayer, meditation, and the saying of hymns from the *Rig-Veda*. She obeyed enthusiastically but this did not worry him. He had begun in the same way when he had set up his hermitage and he knew she would soon tire of it. So she did, after a very few days, and Kumar rejoiced. He had restrained himself as a lover with a fortitude which he had never shown as a saint. He was glad that the trial was over, save for certain steps which he had had in mind from the very beginning.

Catching her yawning one day, he said:

"Are you thinking of your husband?"

She screwed up her pretty eyes and set her classic lips.

"No," she said, between her flawless teeth, for she was still extremely angry whenever his name was mentioned.

The next day, catching her yawning again while she was saying some prayers, he said:

"You have acquired great merit. You have renounced the world and you have renounced your husband. You are living a holy and chaste life. But you can acquire still more merit. Do you know how?"

She opened her correctly curved lips in a vaster yawn than ever and said:

"No."

"By renouncing the renunciation," said Kumar. "That is the path of ultimate perfection: that is the way of uttermost detachment. Now you are bound. By what are you bound? Do not trouble to answer yourself: I will do it for you. You are bound by your desire to live a life of renunciation. This is called spiritual pride. Do you understand? It does not matter if you do not. The next point in my argument is the important one. To gain the ultimate merit of renouncing the renunciation, you should do something which shows that you have a contempt for your own endeavour to be holy. For instance, you could renounce chastity. Or," he proceded with a show of open-mindedness, "any other austerity that you would prefer to renounce. Is there," he said, taking her hand and gazing at her with his burning eyes, "any other?"

She lowered her eyelids, now innocent of paint but not less beautiful. She pursed her mouth and looked between her lashes at Kumar's frame which was somewhat too sturdy for that of a holy man.

- "No," she said.

They retired to an inner room of the hermitage. Kumar, undressing, recited several verses of great beauty in praise of chastity. He added some of his own, extempore, which announced that this virtue was about to be abandoned by two devotees who wished to show their humility. With that he proceeded instantly to embrace her. The versified prelude to their enjoyment proved no worse than any of the other devices of lovers. The sacrifice, on both their parts, was whole-hearted. At Kumar's suggestion, to gain further merit and to make their humility beyond doubt, they repeated it.

At Kumar's suggestion, again, they sacrificed the following

afternoon and at Govinda's wife's prompting they observed the ritual again at night. Kumar was a man beside himself with joy.

In this mood he readily agreed to go to Ayoda and gather news of what had happened. Since he had already settled in his mind what the news should be, he went with a light heart and, as was his custom, an ingenious lie ready on his lips.

He found Govinda in his warehouse. Govinda hastened to greet him, but seemed in no hurry to mention his wife.

"You must forgive me for welcoming you here," he said, bowing deeply, "but a new parcel has arrived from China, of the most wonderful silks. I am disposing of them at a handsome price—in accordance with your wishes, of course, master. Have you," he said, and Kumar detected some hesitation in his manner, "settled on the propitious date for my taking up a holy life—beginning it, that is, of course. I do not suppose that the thing can be done in a day."

"Govinda," said Kumar with his most solemn voice, "I am the bringer of bad news."

"There is no propitious date?" said Govinda, running his eyes over his tight-packed shelves. "Well, well. One must be resigned to the will of the gods."

"Your wife," said Kumar, "is dead."

As Kumar had planned it, the rest of this lie was as tremendous as the beginning. But his plan went wrong and the best parts of the grand lie were never told. Kumar became quickly aware that Govinda was barely interested.

"Dead?" said Govinda. "May she avoid the noose of Yama," he said, a pious expression which meant that he hoped she would not be dragged down to the god of death's grey hell. "She ran away from me, you know." He flicked a bead of the abacus in front of him. "Or perhaps you do not know."

"I had heard," said Kumar with circumspection.

"She ran away on the night that you went back to your hermitage. She made fine fools of us both," he said. "Or perhaps it would be more respectful to say that at least she made a fool of me." Govinda flicked several beads along their wires with deliberation. "All the time that she was accusing me of having a plan to run off to another woman, she was planning to run off to another man."

· "How do you know she ran off to another man?" said Kumar.

"She was seen in the company of one at the town gates. The guard couldn't swear to the description of the man. He bribed them, I suppose. Well, now, dead, you say?"

"Alas, yes," said Kumar. "Her body was found by the holy bathing *ghat* in the Mother River near the place where it leaves this kingdom. The Brahmins there gave her the proper burning ceremony for a wife. I happened to be passing there, and they told me of it. They had this. I recognised it."

He held out the forehead ornament. Tears came to his eyes, partly by plan, but partly through the strain of searching Govinda's face for some clue to what he was really thinking. Govinda gave the ornament a casual glance.

"Make a present of it to the—Brahmins for their—trouble," he said, pausing between his words and emphasising some by a flick of his beads.

"You take your wife's death calmly," said Kumar.

"What is death but a blessed release?" he said, in the formal phrase. "Of course you will dine with me?"

Kumar accepted. The food was delectable but the banquet was not a success. They discussed philosophy, but languidly. Govinda went back to work during the night in his warehouse. He was affable: he was even happy; but Kumar could not make him out. Kumar left next morning for his hermitage. Govinda bade him a warm farewell; Govinda pressed him to come again; Govinda went off to his warehouse humming a tune; but for all that, Govinda remained a mystery.

Govinda's wife bit her classic lips with rage when Kumar, on his return to the hermitage (a day and a half's rough journey from Ayoda) broke the news to her that her husband had fled to Benares. She went for a long and angry walk in the surrounding forest, but the forest being thick, the weather hot, and the hermitage being not without its attractions, she returned in a good temper and suggested to Kumar that they once more renounce the renunciation.

Kumar was weary from his journey and would have preferred a bite to eat and a good sound sleep. But Govinda's wife was determined and for that reason more alluring than ever. They embraced several times with all the passion aroused by absence.

They embraced on the next day, at the suggestion each time of Govinda's wife, this time with all the ardour of propinquity.

They embraced on thirty succeeding days, and, so far as Kumar was concerned, on the thirtieth with no ardour at all.

Kumar wearily asked her, on the thirty-first day, whether she did not think that they had piled up sufficient proof that they had no spiritual pride in renunciation.

Govinda's wife set her impeccable lips, looked at Kumar through her curling eyelashes, and said:

"No."

She went further, which was most unusual for her. She said:

"As I see it we have to show that we can take it or that we can leave it: is that right?"

"Allowing for your limited choice of words, yes," said Kumar, holding his aching head.

"Then we must show that we can leave it."

"We must," agreed Kumar.

"But we can't do that unless we take it," said Govinda's wife. "Is that right?"

"Allowing for your limited . . ." said Kumar wearily, "oh, but never mind, never mind," he finished and allowed his head to sink dispiritedly on his chest.

"Good," said Govinda's wife and placing her arms round his neck she kissed him again and again with her irreproachable lips.

Months passed away in this fashion, and if Kumar found his hermit's life montonous, Govinda's wife did not. The nearest village was two miles away, but her fame as a holy woman soon reached there. The villagers flocked to kiss the feet of the beautiful hermitess and to have the privilege of speaking to her. Their language was simple and so was hers: their interests were limited but scarcely more so than those of Govinda's wife. She enjoyed their company and relished her prestige.

As for Kumar, his eyes no longer burned. On the one occasion when he resumed his preaching, at an obscure town some twenty miles way, his lacklustre glance, his enervated gestures, and the fact that he yawned in the middle of his sentence caused him to be chased down the street by the boys of the town as an impostor. He did not expose himself to further indignities. He many times determined to go privately to Ayoda but never summoned up the energy to face the long walk there and back. He spent his time composing a moral poem on the virtues of chastity by which he hoped the wreck of his hopes as a preacher might be redeemed. He threw great feeling into the verses.

Now one of the last vestiges of Kumar's old profession which he had retained was the blessing of the spring caravans. These set out from all over the country at the end of the cold weather to make the crossing of the snow mountains far to the north. Their road passed within an hour's gentle walk of the hermitage. In common with many other holy men on the long route to the passes, Kumar would sit by the side of the road in springtime, seated on a mat, his beads round his neck, his forehead painted with the vermilion signs of his calling, and read a devotional book. His begging bowl would be in front of him in a conspicuous position. The caravan's master would see him and stop for his blessing, if the owner were devout: and he usually was, for even the most hard-hearted man's thoughts turned to religion when facing the high passes of the northern barrier.

Two years or so from the day he had brought Govinda's wife to his hermitage, he was thus seated by the roadside, nodding and yawning over his book, when a caravan of exceptional magnificence began to approach him along the road.

First came a party of mounted soldiers with bows and swords, shouting and running little races on their squat horses, cursing, laughing, clanking their armour, and every so often taking swigs from leathern bottles which hung from their saddle bows. Their drunkenness proclaimed the generosity and wealth of the owner of the caravan. Next came a long string of camels, loaded high, so that the camel-drivers were forced to walk beside their complaining beasts, instead of riding, and constantly to adjust the ropes, whose knots joined in the protest of the animals. After some fifty camels all weighed down with merchandise came a company of mounted servants, gorgeously arrayed, and most with soft leather riding boots from Tibet, richly embroidered, and all wearing sashes of vermilion silk, the same colour as that which streamed from the lance of the horseman who rode immediately before their master's palanquin.

This was ingeniously slung between two white dromedaries, on the necks of which were seated camel-boys in dresses of fine cotton and small, tight turbans with an ornamenting of silver. They guided the dromedaries skillfully, making sure that the palanquin, a box of painted bamboo, swayed as little as the road would allow. The palanquin had silk curtains, and these, when the palanquin was exactly opposite Kumar, were sharply drawn back. The hand of the owner emerged, and with a snapping of thumb and finger, the palanquin was brought to a halt. Shouts were relayed to the horsemen in front, who reined in their mounts and swigged deeply again from their bottles as the dust clouds settled on the halted column.

The owner clapped his hands, the dromedaries groaned and knelt down. The owner got out of the palanquin. He came towards Kumar and bowing in the customary manner asked through the folds of his dust cloak for a blessing. "We go, master," he said, "to China for silk. Pray for our safe return."

Kumar raised his hand in benediction and the traveller piously unwrapped his cloak to bare his head.

"Govinda!" said Kumar, trembling with excitement.

"That is my name," said the traveller.

"And me—don't you recognise me?" said Kumar.

Govinda surveyed him carefully. Govinda's eyes lit. Govinda smiled, and his smile grew broader and broader.

"Kumar," he said at last. "How the—austerity—of your life has changed you. Why did you never come to see me since the day you brought me news of my wife's death?" Govinda shook his head in gentle reproach while his smile stretched, it seemed, from earring to earring.

Kumar summoned his last remaining energy. He was determined, cost what shame it may, to tell Govinda the truth and make him take back his insatiable wife.

"I have to tell you—" he began, but Govinda interrupted him:

"You have to tell me gems of priceless wisdom, I do not doubt. Can I ever forget how you laid your holy finger on my trouble at our very first meeting. I was so desperate that I contemplated giving up the world and all my possessions," he said, indicating the caravan with ringed fingers. "All this," he said, "or to be more precise, one half of this, as I have more than doubled my fortune since I have been able to put my whole mind to it. But you said that it would not be easy . . ."

"Yes, but . . ." said Kumar, and Govinda bore him down.

"And it was not. 'Women' you said were my trouble and you were right in every way except the number of your noun. My trouble was singular, not plural, and from the day you spoke to me I determined to rid myself of her."

"Your wife—" shouted Kumar, but his voice was not very loud.

"Had many good points, you would say," said Govinda. "That is of course very proper for a man with your charitable view of human beings. But the trouble between us was a matter between husband and wife, something," he said and snorted as though with suppressed laughter, "I would blush to even whisper in your sanctified ears. But she left me and she is dead. From the day that I was free from her, how fully I understood your sermon on the dangers of fleshly ties binding us to mundane things. Renunciation! That is the sublime doctrine." With this he wrapped his cloak about him, and flinging a chamois bag of money into Kumar's begging bowl, returned to his palanquin, clapped his hands, and was on his way in a great cloud of dust, shouts, cracking of whips, and bellowing of camels.

"Your wife is alive!" screamed Kumar but no one heard him.

He was not to be defeated. He knew that the road made a great curve to avoid the forest in which his hermitage stood and that the caravan would have to climb uphill for some of the way.

Compelling his tottering legs to break into a run, he set off for his hermitage. He stumbled as he ran and his breath hurt at each beat of his lungs. But despair drove him to do wonders and he reached the hermitage without collapsing.

Yet his appearance was so ghastly that when he seized the wrist of Govinda's wife and glared at her with eyes which now burned as they had done in the days of his preaching, she dared not resist him, but hearing his order, "Come, woman! Come with me!" she obeyed. As Kumar dragged her along the forest paths, she once or twice tried to find out what had happened. But Kumar had neither the wish nor the breath to reply. Thus running, panting, and tripping over the roots of the trees, they arrived at last at the road as the camels with their high bales were passing by.

The palanquin drew level with Kumar. Frantically waving his free arm (for he kept tight hold of Govinda's wife), Kumar shouted to Govinda to stop.

Govinda's hand emerged from the curtain of the palanquin. Govinda's fingers snapped, and the palanquin halted. Kumar dragged Govinda's wife towards it.

Govinda put out his head.

"Look," said Kumar, his voice cracking with triumph. "Your wife!"

Govinda looked at his wife for a long moment while she, setting her classic lips, muttered: "Elephant's tusk!" and searched with her lustrous eyes the interior of the palanquin to detect her husband's concubine.

At last Govinda turned his face to Kumar, and with an expression of profound admiration said:

"What power lies in true holiness! You are able to bring

back the dead. She is, I know, a phantom, held in her corporeal state for a brief moment by the power of your holy incantations, but how real she looks. How very real." And flinging yet a second bag of money at Kumar's feet he cried to Kumar: "Thank you a thousand times for this lesson in the power of virtue," and to the boys on the dromedaries: "Forward as fast as you can go." The boys shouted, whips cracked, the dromedaries bellowed, the horsemen shouted oaths, and the caravan moved on. When it had passed, Kumar and Govinda's wife were covered in white dust, through which, on Kumar's cheeks, tears were making dark channels.

His release from this chain of the flesh ("which, as you know," said Valmiki, "is metaphysically known as *moksha*") came six years later when Govinda's wife caught a fever and died. Kumar, once he had seen her well and truly burned to a cinder, flung himself into the work of completing his poem in praise of chastity. He made it a masterpiece. He himself gained a second fame, this time as an author of a morally improving work, until by the time of his holy death he was known throughout the land as the apostle of self-restraint; which shows (Valmiki ended) that the springs of Virtue lie very deep, and sometimes lie in unexpected places.

CHAPTER FIVE

ÐISCOVERIES

By one o'clock that day the saffron robe was back in Sita's bundle, but this can be attributed only in a small part to Valmiki's story. The tale disturbed Rama and retiring to the cool of Sita's room, Rama had a vision which at first he thought might be a heavenly admonition, but which he finally agreed was sunstroke.

Sita immediately put Rama to bed and the hermit's robe safely away. Luxmun returned hurriedly to the plantation and asked the owner for a basket of mangoes, which, most readily given, he squeezed into a brass jar and gave the juice to his brother to drink. Sita laid wet cloths over her husband's forehead and Valmiki, bustling about his hermitage to prepare light food and restoratives, blamed himself for not warning his guest to avoid sitting in the sun. Sunstroke is rarely a prolonged illness but with a determined wife, an attentive brother, and a co-operative host it can be spun out considerably. Rama was kept on his couch a week, during which he was forbidden to think about his spiritual condition. This prescription, together with a decoction of senna pods grown in Valmiki's garden, soon put roses in Rama's cheeks.

This mild illness was the first he had experienced since childhood, and like many other young men who have been tenderly cared for while unwell, he fell in love with his nurse. It did not matter that his nurse was Sita, his wife. He had never been in love with her before because their marriage had been, of course, arranged by their respective fathers. It is one of the advantages of an arranged marriage that it sometimes provides both parties, after years of living together, with that most gratifying of pleasures, a honeymoon without embarrassment. Rama and Sita were young and they had discovered that they were lovers. They were very happy.

This led to a second discovery. One day while Rama and Sita were strolling on Valmiki's terraces they came across the poet and his servant boy spreading dung on the ground. Rama recoiled from the sight and smell of this and walked away. Sita, following, said:

"But I suppose those vegetables he serves us wouldn't grow if he didn't, and they are certainly very good vegetables, especially as they don't cost us a single copper piece. Of course, Valmiki must be proud to have two princes to stay with him."

That evening, over their meal together, Rama said to Valmiki:

"I have been turning the matter over in my mind and it seems to me that for some months I have been living on other people's charity. When I left Ayoda my mind was too full of other things to think about money."

"Of course it was," said Luxmun, "but my mind's nearly always empty except when I'm fighting, so I brought along a little money myself. Still, that's all gone. But you were talking, brother. I am sorry I interrupted."

"Well," said Rama, "I think it would be for the best if I sent you, brother, to Ayoda to announce that since I am fully determined to stay away from the city until my father's pledge is redeemed, the Royal Council should send me some money for my expenses. What do you think, Valmiki? Is it a good plan?"

"No," said Valmiki. "You should send Luxmun with the

message that you are instantly returning. The Royal Council will pay you a great deal more to make you promise to stay away."

"But," said Rama, "I mean to stay away in any case."

"Then you can make the promise with a clear conscience, since you are sure to keep it, which is more than many people can say when they enter into a bargain."

The wisdom of this course being plain, Luxmun was sent on his errand. He returned a month later with a mule whose pack-sacks were heavy with gold.

Rama found it difficult to think of a graceful way of paying Valmiki for his hospitality, but Valmiki, being a man of genius and a writer, made it easy for him.

"I would not think of taking money for myself, but if you care to hire two gardeners for a year or so to cultivate my terraces, I shall be grateful," he said.

"I shall be pleased to do that," Rama replied. "I had thought of it myself but I was afraid you would not approve. I remember you saying one day that cultivating the soil was the one truly satisfactory occupation."

"I did," said Valmiki, smiling. "I still do. To make two ears grow where one grew before is a profound solace to my spirit. To watch a hired man do it would be an even profounder solace. I shall be able to devote more time to my poetry."

The matter thus settled, Valmiki asked Rama what he intended to do in the future. "You would be very welcome if you decided to stay in our hermitage," he said.

"The Gluttons are very courteous people," said Rama, "but I have never quite understood their principles."

"They have only one," Valmiki told him, "and that is to eat.

They can prove to you by exquisite metaphysical arguments that everything else is an illusion."

"I suppose they eat a lot?"

"Theoretically, they should," said Valmiki. "But people who can draw fine metaphysical distinctions rarely have enormous appetites. I was drawn to their company because I had heard that they spent more time eating than in arguing. If all profound thinkers did that how tranquil the world would be! Alas, my fellow hermits are no better than other men: they all put the world to rights after supper."

"Still, I should find that very interesting," said Rama. "I have thought things over carefully and it seems to me that it was wrong for me to try to renounce the world on the recommendation of a few self-seeking Brahmins. The proper thing for an intelligent person to do is to improve his mind. I cannot help feeling that what I have lacked is a proper education. I do not—for an instance—know anything about philosophy. But I should like to. After all, what can be better for a man than to study all the great thinkers that have gone before us? What could be more fitting than to learn all that the great sages have given to the world? Is there not an eight-fold path to salvation? There is, but I do not even know the names of two of the paths, much less all eight. And yet, is there anything more important than the salvation of my soul? No. How can I learn how to save it? By studying the treasures of esoteric knowledge of my forefathers. So I have decided to ask you if you will permit me to stay here with my brother and wife a little longer, and—although I hesitate to take up your time—to put me on the path to salvation."

"By all means stay," said Valmiki, "and you will not take up a great deal of my time."

"How many lessons do you think will be necessary?" asked Rama.

"One," said Valmiki. "Let us begin it under the carob tree at half past nine tomorrow morning. But this time be careful to sit in the shade."

Next morning, when they had again admired the view from the carob tree and selected each a comfortable root, Valmiki began (and ended) his instruction by telling Rama the tale of the Sage, the Cow, and the Studious Locust.

the tale
of the sage, the cow,
and
the studious
locust

There once (said Valmiki) was a locust who was born in a desert in Baluchistan. On the same day ten million other locusts were born, all of them with identical eyes, identical wings, identical legs, and the same thought in their very small brains which was: "I want something to eat."

This locust, however, was different. He had, it is true, the same large eyes as the other locusts, the same wings, the same slender legs, and his brain was no bigger nor his appetite smaller. He had, on the other hand, a touch of refinement.

When, one day, all the other locusts rose joyfully into the air to go to their first eating ground, he rose with them, but instead of making straight for the food like ten million others, he hung back a little. When the swarm hovered over a blossoming orchard and all the others clashed their jaws in joyous expectation, he looked down and said:

"How beautiful! The blossom is like . . ." But what the blossom was like he never discovered. While he searched for the right words, all the blossoms disappeared down the gullets of the other locusts. Sighing, he chose a leaf, and began to eat. As he munched, he savoured its sweet taste. Once or twice he cast hard looks at a locust in front of him who disturbed his pleasure by rending and bolting its food like one possessed. Hard looks having no effect, he tried another tactic:

"How delicious this leaf is," he said to his companion. "I think it must have been specially favoured by the morning sun. Try some."

The other locust stared for a moment at him with protuberant eyes. Then it said: "Eh?" The sensitive locust repeated his statement, in a pained voice with clear enunciation. But his companion was seized with a violent attack of hiccoughs and did not hear a word. It therefore asked "Eh?" once again.

"I said try some of this leaf," the locust repeated sharply.

"Oh," said the other and did. In a moment there was nothing of the leaf remaining, except a small square in which the sensitive locust was just able to stand.

"Er . . ." said his companion, eyeing this remaining patch. "Er . . . if you . . ."

The refined locust sniffed with disapproval, and delicately stepped onto the twig. As his companion devoured the last piece of the leaf in two snaps of its jaw, the sensitive locust averted his eyes. Unfortunately, wherever he looked he could see nothing but other locusts eating. He lost his appetite. This, in a locust, amounts to an extraordinary spiritual experience—indeed, it is often confused with one among human beings—and the locust felt a great desire to be on his own.

He therefore flew thoughtfully out of the orchard. As he did so he saw a party of men attack the very tree on which he had been sitting with long bamboo poles. They beat the locusts from the branches, and then swept them into a ditch. There, after a moment, they set fire to them by throwing oil-soaked brands among them. The locust watched a thousand of his companions die in less than a minute, with a most doleful sound of popping.

"What a dreadful fate I have escaped," said the sensitive

locust to himself. "How dismal to end one's life with a pop! See what gluttony leads one to! How lucky I am to have refined sensibilities! Is it possible that I should have been saved from such a horrid death for no purpose? Certainly not. It is clear that I am specially chosen. But what for? Ah! I do not know. I must be patient and humble and perhaps I shall discover."

So in patience and humility he sat on a tree that commanded a fine view of the orchard, and listened to the popping until the peasants ran out of oil. Thus, although he had not been able to finish his dinner, he early learned that the spiritual life has its own satisfactions.

Some time later in that afternoon when he was still sitting on his tree, but sleepily, he suddenly felt a violent blow on his back. He clutched at the twig beneath his legs, but immediately felt another blow, heavier than the first, which sent him reeling and tumbling through the air until he hit the hard ground at the foot of the tree with a shock which took away his senses. He awoke with a scream to find himself (as he thought) being burned alive. Within an inch of his nose was a wall of flame; the grass was burning all round him, and the heat of the ground was such that he had to keep hopping high in the air to prevent his legs from being burned to cinders.

It was borne in upon him that he, too, was going to end his life with a pop and that it was all a grave mistake. The owner of the orchard had plainly confounded him with his gluttonous companions and was burning him—a locust with a sense of re-finement and a remarkable spiritual experience—in the same bonfire as all the others.

The mere thought of this humiliation made him bound higher than ever before, and so great a hop did he execute that it carried him clear of the fire onto a raised pathway of trodden earth, and thus to safety. While he rested there, gathering his wits, one of the peasants spied him. Now this peasant owned the field on the other side of the embankment and this, so far, had escaped the locusts. The peasant, seeing a solitary locust about (as he imagined) to go into his field, raised a tremendous hullabaloo. All the other peasants came running, their long bamboo staves in their hands. When they understood what was the matter, they all set upon the locust, flailing their sticks and shouting.

The locust sprang along the path in a desperate effort to save his life. The bamboo staves slapped the earth all round with a report which deafened him, and raised clouds of dust which blinded him, so that it was pure chance that he escaped killing at the first onslaught. But he managed to leap a little ahead of his pursuers and for a while, hopping, bounding, fluttering, and rolling along the path he managed to elude their blows. But he was soon at the end of his strength. He staggered. A bamboo cane gave him a glancing blow, and he gave himself up for dead. The next, he thought, would surely kill him.

Then suddenly he felt himself taken up by the middle and raised high in the air. He was surrounded, he saw, by an enormous Hand. It smelled of sweet perfumes and was clean and smooth and the colour of sandalwood. Its fingers held him so gently that he felt no pain—only the exhilaration of being lifted so fast up into the sky. When the motion stopped he was not very surprised to find himself looking into a great, benign Face, with flowing white hair and an enormous beard.

"Do not be afraid," said the Face, but the words were very indistinct because across the mouth of the Face was a strip of linen. This was held in position by four tapes that, traversing the whiskers in four valleys, ended in loops that went over the ears.

"I'm not afraid," said the locust. "Am I dead?"

"You were very *nearly* killed," said the Face, mumbling through the strip of linen. "But nobody will hurt you now that I'm protecting you."

"No, I'm sure they won't," said the locust confidently. "I suppose you are one of the great gods. I knew that something - very special was coming my way, because I've just had what I might call a spiritual experience. It happened this way. I was—"

The Face immediately looked very weary.

"Yes, yes," it said. "That is most interesting, but perhaps you will tell me about it tomorrow morning when I feel fresher."

With that the great hand placed the locust next to the Face on a broad shoulder and the locust, observing the passing world in glimpses through the great white whiskers, saw that they were walking.

Soon they stopped, and the locust, holding apart two cable-like strands of white hair, saw a number of peasants. They were looking towards the Face, and some of them had their hands raised to their foreheads in adoration. The locust hoped these worshippers of this god could see him on the god's shoulder, and to make sure he trampled down a few more strands of hair so that their view of him would be unobstructed, and he gave way to a little fit of coughing.

When he saw that one or two of the peasants nudged one another and pointed to him, he was delighted. There was nothing to mar his happiness save the fact that the peasants' faces seemed much on a level with the Face that had rescued him. He had expected to be rather more elevated.

However, when the peasants laid bananas and fruits and flowers on the ground as an offering, and when the benign Face bent in acknowledgement, the locust bent his head as well, making his protruding eyes as benign as they would go.

After a while, a young boy gathered all the offerings and put them in a basket. Then the locust found that he was moving away at a walking pace as the Face left its adorers. Glancing back under one of the ears, he saw that the boy was following them, the basket of offerings on his head, at a respectful distance of twenty paces.

"They gave me all that fruit for sending away your companions," said the Face.

"Yes?" said the locust casually, for he did not much approve of being classed with the other insects. However, he could not resist a look at the orchard, which now lay behind them. As far as he could see through the thickets of hair, the locusts had left.

"They ought to be very grateful," said the locust, thinking of the peasants.

"They ought," agreed the Face. "But why to me?"

"Because you sent them away."

"I did?" said the Face. "As a locust yourself, how do you imagine I could send away a ravening swarm like that?"

"Because you are a god."

The Face chuckled behind its mask.

"If I were a god," it said, "you may rest assured I would not do anything so cruel and foolish as to make men with bellies and then make locusts to eat up all their food."

"Then you are not a god?"

"No."

"What are you?"

"I am trying to be a saint," said the Face.

"What is that?"

"It is a man who is so horrified at what God has made him that he wants to be something better," said the Face.

"And are you something better?" said the locust, clinging to a last hope that the Face be at least a demi-god.

"With God's help, I think I may become so," said the Face. "But you said," the locust pointed out, "that you didn't like what God had made you. Will He help you to change it?" "If He doesn't, I won't," said the saint. "That is very difficult to understand," said the locust. "It is quite impossible to understand," said the saint complacently. "I have thought about it for twenty-three years and I assure you it is stark, raving nonsense. Nevertheless, it is true. And so with God's help, I have sworn a vow never to take a life, not even of the smallest, humblest creature, such as you. That is why I wear a strip of linen across my mouth lest I should breathe in some innocent little flying thing. And that is why I rescued you." The saint walked on in silence for a while. Then he heard the locust sobbing. "What is wrong, little one?" he said. "I can't . . . can't explain," said the locust, great tears filling his eyes, so that they appeared to protrude more than ever. "In any case I couldn't make you understand." "Try," said the saint. "One of the things that I have learned because I have kept my vow is the language of animals. It was not very difficult. I learned all the sad words first and so I soon understood most of what they had to say. Still, I suppose that is the best way to learn any language quickly . . ." and in this fashion he talked half to himself and half to the locust, so that the little insect should have time to recover his self-possession. When he had done so, the locust said: "The fact is that only a few hours ago I had a spiritual experience. Then I saw all my companions being burned alive and I was saved—call it luck, call it a miracle. I don't know. But one thing I felt certain about—I was being saved for *something*. So I waited. Then I was chased along the path with bamboo sticks and suddenly I found myself lifted up to heaven. Or so I thought. I thought you were—well not the Great God of course, but still, perhaps one of the lesser ones. But . . ." said the locust, and a sob that had remained behind from his previous tears broke from him.

"I apologise for not being a god and for not being even one of the lesser ones," said the sage gravely.

"Now you are poking fun at me," said the locust.

"Not in the very least. My apology was more serious; I make it every morning at sunrise."

"Why?"

"Because one should always pray at sunrise, and that is a very suitable form of prayer for a human being."

"I see," said the locust, who did not see at all. "That is very interesting and I must try it. I suppose I'd better forget my spiritual experience," and the locust essayed, without success, a short laugh.

"Oh no," said the sage. "In any case you will not be able to forget it. I know, because I had one myself. It will change your whole life."

"How?"

"It will make you," said the sage, "either a great charlatan or a great saint."

"Oh," said the locust. "What is a *char-la-tan?*"

"A hypocrite, a deceiver, a sham, a fraud, a man who is as happy as the day is long," said the sage.

"Then, which are you," said the locust, gazing at the sage with his protuberant eyes, "a *char-la-tan* or a saint?"

"A good question," said the sage, ignoring the fact that it was also an impertinent one. "I have thought the matter over myself and I have come to the conclusion that it depends on the state of the weather."

While the locust felt that this mixture was far from inspiring he had to admit that its results were agreeable. They arrived at the place where the sage lived. The place was so remote that it was suitable only for a hermit; the situation was so beautiful that it was fit for a king. Here the sage lived without the pleasures of human society but in a most elegant manner, devoting his life to prayers and the cultivation of succulent vegetables.

The hermitage stood on a meadow bounded by the loop of a mountain stream. Forests rose in gentle slopes on all sides except one, and this side looked down a valley to the plain beyond. Small gardens, neatly stockaded and sited to catch the most favourable hours of sunshine, lined the curves of the stream, each garden devoted to the growing of something to eat. The hermitage was simply constructed of poles, straw mats, and plaited strips of bamboo. It had a verandah, a dining room, a bedroom, a room for reading, a room for nothing specific, a kitchen and outhouses, from one of which came the lowing of a cow.

"I shall put you with Comfort while I go and cook the dinner," said the sage, and took the locust to the outhouse from which the sound was coming. "Comfort," he explained, "is a cow whom I have taught to speak. By speaking I mean the language of human beings. She is called Comfort because that is what she reminds you of when you look at her and besides she never thinks of anything else. Have a quiet talk with her. Dinner will be ready in about half an hour. By the way, what do locusts eat for their evening meal?"

"I," said the locust, "eat practically nothing. A small leaf, to keep you company—that will do very well for me." At which the locust's stomach gave out a protesting noise. The locust blushed deeply, but was consoled when the sage showed no sign of having noticed.

Comfort, on the other hand, was plainly a cow that had never denied herself a single blade of grass. She was white. Her dewlap swung from her chin like a white curtain loaded with shot; her stomach struggled to be perfectly round, and, seen from some directions, managed to be so. Everything about her was fat except her tail, which looked as though it did not belong to her.

The sage patted her muzzle and explained in a few words how he had rescued the locust. When he said that the locust had narrowly escaped burning alive, the cow's great eyes filled with sympathetic tears. When the sage told her that the locust had been through a spiritual experience, she blew windily through her nose and shook her head in wonderment. When the sage said he must be off to see about dinner, she dribbled.

"Would you like to hear me say a few words in the human language?" she said when the sage had gone. The locust said that he would, and the cow, in a melodious bellow, said:

"*Good morning Your Highness, Sleep well my lady, Your Majesty is quite right, I bow to Your Eminence's opinion.*"

The locust was sitting on the half-door of the stall and the tremendous rumble made his ears sing. He did not, of course, understand a word that the cow had said, and when the buzzing in his ears had subsided he asked what they meant.

"I don't think they can be explained," said Comfort, looking down the broad expanse of her nose, "to anybody who has not moved in court circles," but in spite of this she explained at considerable length.

The locust gathered that when the sage had taught the cow to talk, the news of the miracle spread to the nearest city and a royal summons was issued that she be brought before the King. "I was received with every mark of respect," said the cow. "Her Highness—the King's daughter, you know—hung a garland round my neck with her own hands, an honour—so I was told—which is never conferred on people of lower rank than a cousin of the King. I was given a stall made of the most expensive wood and the food—I cannot possibly tell you of all the food that I was given. In the morning—"

But the locust begged her not to attempt so difficult a task: protesting winds were blowing through his abdomen.

"And you talked to all these important persons?" asked the locust.

Comfort replied: "Oh yes. Frequently."

"I should have died with embarrassment," said the locust. "I wouldn't have known what to say at all."

The cow said nothing, but merely lowered her eyelids and chewed her cud with what the locust found an irritating composure.

"I suppose the sage had given you plenty of instructions," said the locust.

"Oh, yes," said Comfort. "Some."

"What did he teach you?" asked the locust.

"It's a long time ago," said the cow, "and my memory is not very clear on the point. But I recall that he taught me a piece to say about 'How a wise man should act when his Duty would seem to conflict with his Destiny.'"

"What a fascinating subject," said the locust, the two knobs that were his eyes glowing. "That is just the sort of conversation that I have always longed to hear. Well, how does a wise man act when his Duty conflicts with his Destiny?"

"Eh?" said the cow. "Oh, well, he . . . follows his nose, I should say. Yes, follows his nose," she repeated, chewing rhythmically. "I can't remember if that's what the sage said—it was all a long time ago—but that's what I should say."

The locust looked a little disappointed, but he persisted.

"What else did the sage teach you?"

Comfort chewed until the locust began to think that she could not have heard the question. He was just about to repeat it when she said, swallowing heavily:

"There was a piece I was to use if any Brahmins came to talk. I recall that it began: 'Is the earth, which is supported on a tortoise, round or flat?' "

"How exciting!" said the locust. "And is it round, or is it flat?"

"Don't be silly," said the cow, beginning to show impatience, "of course it's flat. Just look at it. Flat as one of my pancakes."

"I am sorry if I am annoying you," said the locust stiffly. The cow, he could see, for all its experience of polished society, was still, at heart, vulgar.

"No, no," said the cow, chewing calmly again. "You're not annoying me. But to tell you the truth I never did talk about these things: not at court, I didn't. I chose my own subject and it went down very well. All the really important people were very pleased, although I must say that the sage was very annoyed. I think," she went on, "that living here all alone, the good man had got out of touch with the way that good society behaves."

"What was the subject that you chose?" asked the locust.

"I didn't really choose it. It just came," the cow replied. "In the give-and-take, you know, of my social life. But then perhaps you don't know." With which she chewed, more exasperatingly than ever.

"I don't know anything," said the locust. "That's why I'm asking." It was not the sort of reply that the locust would have made in his more collected moments, but the circular movement of Comfort's jaws was unnerving.

"Asking what?" said the cow.

"What you talked about," said the locust, in a manner which showed he was not to be fobbed off.

"Well, if you want to know," said the cow and, pausing lowered her eyelids. "The subjects always seemed to be . . ." She paused.

"Yes?" said the locust.

"Bulls," said the cow.

Neither of them said anything more for a while, and then the cow went on, in justification:

"I can see you agree with the sage. Well, I don't say it was the best topic from the point of view of improving the mind. I wouldn't have thought myself that it was really up to me—a cow, you know—to improve the minds of the royal circle: although in fairness I must tell you that that was just what the sage had in view when he sent me. All that I do see is that my recollections of—well, as I say—bulls—seemed to suit the court like a glove. The courtiers lined up to talk to me, and the Princess—well, at mealtimes Her Highness had to be dragged away by her ladies-in-waiting, who didn't want to go either. They'd all have eaten in my stall if court etiquette had not forbidden it. But of course there was the sage, getting more and more angry with me. Then there was the Chief Brahmin."

"Didn't he like your—your style?" said the locust, with a very keen look out of his enormous eyes.

"I can't say whether he did or whether he didn't," said the cow, opening her own eyes very wide. "He said that I was corrupting the manners of the court and I shouldn't be allowed to talk . . ."

"Ha!" said the locust, with open satisfaction.

". . . unless," the cow went on, "I said everything I was going to say to him, each morning, for his approval. He didn't approve, but how he listened!" said the cow, and munched with reminiscent pleasure on her cud.

"And then what happened?" said the locust.

"The sage came and took me away," said the cow with simplicity. "Her Royal Highness wept and she stormed and she even stamped her foot at the King. But he wasn't sorry to see me go. I think he felt I put him in the shade. Besides, he arranged for Her Royal Highness to be married straight away to put me out of her mind. But, do you know, on her wedding day she sent me—all the way to this hermitage by royal courier— a great big bunch of flowers, which I ate, and my, how delicious they werc!"

The cow ran her vast tongue round her mouth, and lowering her eyelids, shook her head at her happy memories. This was more than the locust could bear, and, excusing himself abruptly, he went in search of the sage to see if dinner was ready.

CHAPTER SEVEN

the tale
of the
studious locust
continued

It was ready, and it was a banquet. The sage
had piled leaves higher than his guest, even if his guest stood up
on his hind legs, and next to this he had laid out smaller heaps
of buds and tender shoots. For himself the hermit had set a
banana leaf heaped with rice, while around the leaf he had arranged a semi-circle of small bowls, each with a different curry.
A gleaming pot of bell metal was full of Comfort's milk, and
a wicker basket of fruit made the table's centrepiece. The locust
had punched a whole leaf full of semi-circular bites before he
remembered that he was a locust with a sense of refinement.
With reluctance, but an indomitable will, he stopped eating.
Only when the sage had begun a conversation did he resume,
and then delicately, a nibble here, a nibble there, as though
he ate not from hunger but politeness.

"Now tell me," said the sage, "what did you think of
Comfort?"

"Very well-meaning," said the locust, "but perhaps not very
brainy. She must have been a disappointment to you."

"No," said the sage. "I learned a great deal from her, and
I am most grateful."

"What did you learn?" asked the locust.

"Never to teach philosophy."

"To cows, of course."

"No," said the sage, "to courtiers. It has saved me from wasting a great deal of time."

The locust nibbled a last shoot, and then walked a pace or two away from the pile of food to show that he had finished. "I have something to ask of you," he said. "But I'm afraid that you'll think that a waste of time, too."

"I hope I shan't," said the sage, "but have you finished eating? You've taken very little. Perhaps I've picked the wrong kind of leaves?"

"They are delicious," said the locust.

"I always understood that locusts had large appetites," said the sage.

"They have," said the locust.

"Then aren't you hungry?"

"Yes," said the locust, and swivelling his large eyes full upon the sage, he said: "But my hunger is not for food: it is for wisdom."

The sage was suddenly taken with a fit of coughing. After it was over he wiped his eyes.

"Forgive me," he said, "I bit on a chilli. Please go on. You were saying that your hunger is for wisdom. So . . .?"

"So I would like you to teach me all those things that you tried to teach that foolish cow," said the locust passionately. "Ever since I was born I have felt that I am different from the other locusts—yes, superior to them—I'm not afraid to use the word. And now that I have had my spiritual experience I'm sure of it. Oh, I know that you are thinking that I will turn out no better than Comfort. I know that you think that after all your labours I'll just give way to my baser instincts and—"

"But you know you won't?" asked the sage.

The locust paused. He studied the sage's face. He thought that he detected a smile on the sage's lips, but it was difficult to be sure because at that moment the sage, having finished eating, slipped his mask back into place.

"Yes," said the locust. "I know I won't. And to help you believe me, I promise that every day that you teach me I shall eat no more than I have eaten today. You yourself have said that locusts have large appetites. This one has also got self-restraint. Four leaves, two buds, and a piece of stalk, every day that I have a lesson. Master, is it a bargain?"

"Little friend," said the sage, looking down at the locust over his mask with his dark brown eyes, "it is a bargain."

Now began a time of contentment for the strong-willed insect. The sage did not teach him to speak a human language: neither he nor the locust saw any purpose in so difficult a task if it were to end as it had done for the cow—but he taught him to read. The sage would prop the long palm-leaf books against some jars, and the locust would walk slowly in front of them spelling out the words that had been cut into them with a sliver of metal. Sometimes the sage would dip his finger into charcoal powder and rub it across the letters, blackening them and making them easier to read. Sometimes he would untie rolls of kidskin and the locust's round eyes would grow rounder still at the blaze of gold and vermilion on the inside of the leather, a meaningless splendour to him until he learned the trick of seeing the flat design as pictures. That learned, he went on many voyages into marvellous countries, saw many gods and kings, and philosophised over many beautiful women, all without leaving the floor of the room that had once no proper purpose, but which was now the locust's own.

From these simpler books he progressed to more profound studies. He learned that there were ten ways that a Brahmin may praise the gods on rising and only one way in which he

may defecate. After weeks of patient application he learned why
it was certain that the earth was supported by a tortoise, but
that nobody knew what supported the tortoise. He studied six
different ways of burying himself alive for twenty-one days and
not one reason why he should do any such thing. He read the
lives of the three great *rishis* who had devised fifty-eight flawless constitutions for the governing of a state and did not know
what to make of the fact that none of them had been asked to
govern anything bigger than the collection of mud huts immediately next to their hermitages. He read, with blushes, the
seventy-eight most delectable postures for the conduct of sexual
intercourse written by a sage who had castrated himself in order
to concentrate on his work, and he greatly approved of the nine
thousand verses in praise of chastity written by a team of
Brahmins at the request of a king who produced, in a reign of
thirty years, one hundred and ninety-three acknowledged children. He was delighted with a work on trigonometry which made
the measuring of landed property an easy matter and was sorry
that its author lived in a poorhouse. He read an epic poem in
one hundred books that praised the virtuous life, and six verses
of great wit and equal lubricity. When he found that he could
remember not a line of the first and could not forget a syllable
of the second, he was ashamed of himself until the sage confessed to a similar freakishness of memory. This led him to the
cultivation of good taste. Under the sage's instruction he learned
the principles of good painting in the books of a man who could
not draw, the art of good writing in a book which was unread-
able, and the essentials of good music from the analyses of a
man whose music nobody had ever sung. He studied history in
great detail and found that the reason why kings lost battles was
that the opposing kings had more brains and better troops; he
was instructed in the fact that the reason why states went

bankrupt was that their rulers spent more money than they had got; and after titanic studies he was satisfied that a thorough knowledge of the past could lead a profound scholar to predict the future course of history with great accuracy, provided that it did not turn out quite differently. He became, in a word, well educated.

He also became hungrier, and hungrier and hungrier. The sage, who found that keeping his side of the bargain was more exhausting than he had anticipated, hoped each day that the locust would not keep his. The sage spent what time he had to spare from instructing the insect in searching out the most tasty leaves and juiciest shoots, which he arranged in a tempting fashion in small heaps, one very close to the other, so that the locust might be led, unthinkingly, to go from one to the other and eat more than the agreed amount. This the locust did not do. He would divide out the piles and separate the exact quantity of food which the bargain allowed for, and, having eaten it slowly (but with a set expression), he would return immediately to his room and his studies.

But as he grew more famished he grew short-tempered. As his temper grew worse he felt the need to quarrel, which the sage, looking down at him with his great brown eyes, always refused to do. This drove the locust to seek the company of the cow. Comfort, if not of a quarrelling disposition, was fond of making downright statements and these gave the locust a chance to attack her sloth, her ignorance, her base yielding to the life of the senses, and her general failure to take the great opportunity that had once been offered to her, at the same time comparing her conduct with his own devotion to his studies, his austerity, and his rising above the temptations of the flesh. Then, for the hundredth time, he explained how he had been elevated above all common insects and animals by his spiritual experience.

The cow found this last very wearying, but she discovered by experiment that she could infuriate the locust to such a degree that he was deprived of words and went away. This she could do merely by slowly, rhythmically, and ostentatiously chewing.

One day the locust, thus enraged, flew away beyond the confines of the hermitage, not really knowing where he went, so plagued was he by hunger and so exhausted by study. He flew down the stream and into the broader reaches of the valley.

He returned that evening at dinnertime. The sage greeted him. The sage enquired how he had progressed in his studies. The sage asked solicitously if he did not feel unwell. To all these questions, the locust made no other reply than a loud hiccup.

The sage was mild, but terrible in his glance.

"Where have you been?" he said at last.

"The . . . fields," said the locust, and was once more shaken by a hiccup.

"To study, perhaps," said the sage, "the structure of newly growing leaves?"

"In a way," said the locust and, hanging his head, he hiccupped violently three times.

"Possibly," said the sage, "by eating them?"

"Possib—"said the locust, but could get no further, partly from the explosions of his hiccups but more from utter shame. He took one last look at the sage, but finding no hope in his venerable face, the blushing insect crawled to the door, and he flew away from the hermitage, never to return. The cow, observing his distracted flight, chewed with more contentment than ever.

CHAPTER EIGHT

the
fight
in the
glade

Thus warned, Rama still pursued wisdom,
but with moderation. He made the acquaintance of the other
Gluttons, among them a tall, spare, and venerable man called
Jabali, the founder of the Hermitage of the Gluttons, but
himself a man with a delicate stomach who lived largely upon
curdled milk. Of this, following his principles, he took more
than he really wanted, but it did him no harm.

Jabali's disposition was mild and kindly; the years he had
spent in meditation gave dignity to his bearing; his diet gave
sobriety to his conversation. He was immensely learned and
made light work of answering all of Rama's questions. The
advantage of the hermitage was that Rama had only to cross
over to a neighbouring hut to have it proved to him by another
hermit that all the answers were wrong.

Some months passed in this peaceful fashion. Rama was
contented, Sita dutiful, and Luxmun bored. Luxmun was sure,
as always, that whatever his brother did was right, but he was
disappointed to find that doing right did not include an occa-
sional fight. He had hoped to defend his brother from enemies,
and now, while the hermits split hairs, Luxmun longed to split
heads.

Rama rebuked him. Luxmun, disconsolate, went to talk over
his troubles with Sita. She had taken on the duties of running
Valmiki's hermitage (for Valmiki was now wholly absorbed
in his poetry) and Luxmun found her working with the boy in
the kitchen.

"Rama is angry with me," said Luxmun, "because I want
to do some fighting."

Sita stirred the rice, which was cooking in a large copper
bowl.

"Yes," she said. "He has told me. He says that if you kill a
man it's the surest way to lose your chance of becoming a real
philosopher."

"H'm," said Luxmun. "I know a surer way."

"Do you?" said Sita absently as she stirred the rice. "What
is it?"

"Let the other man kill you."

Sita smiled, then yawned, and then stifled the yawn. She
picked the rice grains off her wooden spoon to see if they were
each separate, as well-cooked rice grains should be.

"Well," she said, "there's not much danger of anyone wanting to kill you here."

"No," Luxman said, grumbling. "And even if some small
war should break out I can't see any of the soldiers troubling
to attack a lot of argumentative old men."

There, however, he was wrong.

Whenever the thought of another day in the hermitage had
grown unbearable to Luxman—with Valmiki muttering verses,
the hermits wagging disputatious fingers under one another's
noses, and Rama in a brown study—it was his habit to take his
spear and stride off into the surrounding forest, not caring

where he went but allowing the jungle paths to lead him, and turning back when the sun was halfway down, finding the hermitage by tracks, or the moss on the north side of trees, or by his hunter's instinct.

One day he had gone further than usual because his temper had been worse. He had spent the evening before in an attempt to persuade Rama to make a journey round the courts of neighbouring princes and to gain their aid in raising an army with which to return to Ayoda and claim his birthright. But Rama had argued that he was enjoying the only birthright that he cared to claim—namely, peace of mind and freedom to think. Luxmun had left him abruptly, not trusting his tongue.

Now he was walking through an open forest of smooth teak trees that stood, every so often, round small glades set with flowering shrubs. One such glade led, by means of a narrow path between two rows of bushes, to another and much larger glade that caused Luxmun to stand still in astonishment.

The glade was smooth and scattered with flowers. At one end rose a cupola of white marble supported by slender columns, also of marble, but marble of a yellow hue. Between these columns and hiding the interior ran a screen of filigreed metal, worked in a design of flowers and leaves and imaginary animals. Between the two front columns, the screen was taller to allow for two doors, also of filigree, one of which now stood open. The whole structure, though strongly built, was no larger than a tent and was clearly a summerhouse, as could be seen from the marble steps which led from the doorway into a stone pool filled with water. The glade and the cupola had the appearance of being cared for, but there was no sign of an occupant.

Luxmun, standing between the last of the bushes at the

end of the entrance path, called out. Some birds flew up, but
there was no answer. He called again and thought that he
heard, deep in the trees behind the cupola, an answering voice.
But a third call brought no reply, and Luxmun, advancing into
the glade, knelt down by the stone pool. He laid his spear aside
on the grass verge and began to drink, cupping his hands. But
the water lay well below the level of the stone edging, and he
could not easily bring it to his mouth. He lay flat and took off
his bronze helmet, the only sign of his calling that he wore,
since otherwise he was dressed in the loincloth and sandals of
a hunter.

As he dipped his helmet into the water he was struck a
heavy blow between his shoulder blades. He cried out with
pain, and loosened his grip on the helmet which fell into the
pool. Another blow, even heavier than the first, made him roll
over on his back, gasping.

A tall man clad in black armour stood over him. He was
holding a javelin close to its metal cap and he had swung it back
to give Luxmun yet another stroke. A helmet, of fine mail like
his metal jerkin, and lacquered black, came down low over his
forehead and carried a vertical bar that covered the man's nose.
The staff of the javelin fell upon Luxmun's ribs as the man
threw out his other hand in the contemptuous gesture used
when ordering inferiors to go away.

The man's armour proclaimed him a noble; Luxmun saw
that he had been mistaken for a forest huntsman of low caste
who would pollute the water by drinking from it. As the blows
fell on his sides and shoulders, Luxmun shouted: "My helmet!
Let me get my helmet!" for this would be proof of his rank.
The man laughed and swinging the javelin behind his head
poised himself for a final blow.

Luxmun, enraged, reached for the hilt of his hunting-knife,

at which the man brought down his javelin staff across Luxmun's fingers.

Luxmun rolled over in agony, and the man, still laughing, kicked him. Luxmun seized his spear and flinging it upwards with all his might struck the man in the black armour a blow upon his shoulder which, though turned aside by the mail coat, sent the man reeling backwards. His fingers still numb from the blow, Luxmun drew his hunting-knife, shouting: "I am Luxmun, Prince of Ayoda—defend yourself."

The man in black armour had a short warrior's dagger at his belt and this he drew, closing with his adversary as Luxmun rose from the ground. Luxmun seized his wrist and the man countered by taking a grip upon Luxmun's forearm of tremendous force.

They struggled in this fashion, their faces close together, for a few moments, and Luxmun knew that he was fighting a man of a strength such as he had never before experienced. But rage and anger gave Luxmun an advantage over the other, who had been surprised at the ferocity and boldness of the huntsman's assault upon him. Even so, the man in the black armour, straining his knife towards Luxmun's unprotected breast, suddenly scored the flesh so that Luxmun's blood spurted out over the man's forearm. Luxmun, exerting all his strength to save his life, forced the other man back a pace and then another. Thus stumbling and reeling, they drew near the cupola, Luxmun's bodily strength protecting him, but his numbed hand refusing to answer as he tried to drive his knife home.

The columns that held up the cupola stood on a plinth that projected some distance beyond their bases. Driven against this, the man in the black armour reeled heavily backwards, his shoulders pressing against the metal trellis. He slipped, gained his footing on the plinth, and eased his shoulders upwards

against the grille. But Luxmun pressed him with all his might
and in a moment the thin metal buckled and gave away. Both
men fell inwards under the cupola; the jagged points of the
broken metal tearing at the flesh of Luxmun's arms. As the man
in black armour fell he called out in a loud voice for aid; Luxmun heard answering shouts and the sound of men running in
the forest.

Luxmun shook himself free from the prostrate man. He
turned his back upon him, ran swiftly to the pool, and plunged
his arm into the water, searching for his helmet. The pool was
terraced in a series of steps that led down into the water and
Luxmun groped blindly. The man in black armour, still shouting, had got to his feet. A javelin struck the stone edge of the
pool beside Luxmun and bounded the full width of the water,
humming in the air. Luxmun leaned over further, and as another javelin passed over him, his fingers closed round his helmet. He rose, and flung it at his adversary's feet as a gage. Then,
seeing armed men at the further end of the clearing, he turned
and ran swiftly to the bush-lined path by which he had entered.
He struck out with his knife at a man who, breaking out of the
forest, tried to stop him, and felt his knife jar upon bone. The
man shouted in pain, and fell back. Luxmun, leaping between
the bushes, ran down the path across the smaller glade and so
made good his escape.

When Luxmun regained the hermitage, covered with blood,
the philosophers were very upset but Luxmun was serene. Rama
ran to him as soon as he saw him and supported him for the
last few yards to Valmiki's house (for Luxmun had no strength
left in his legs), but all the while Luxmun talked with calm
good humour about his fight, adding, now that his anger had
gone, a good deal of praise for the strength and agility of the

man in black armour. When Rama and the philosophers ex-
claimed at his wounds, Luxmun told them that he would not
have returned at all if his opponent had not lost his balance on
the plinth of the cupola.

Hearing this, Valmiki,, who had hurried from his room to
see what help he could be, asked Luxmun to describe the cupola
more clearly. Luxmun, resting now indoors, did so as best he
could while Sita bathed his wounds.

Valmiki looked grave when Luxmun had finished.

"You say," asked Valmiki, "that you threw him down on
his back?"

"Yes."

"That was bravely done," said Valmiki. "Nobody has defeated him since the day of his birth. You have made the most
implacable enemy in all India. Now you must rest: you have
been for a long walk," said Valmiki, "and if I am not mistaken
it is not yet finished. The name of your enemy is Ravan."

The hermits who had crowded anxiously into the room fell
silent and looked at one another in alarm. Then Sita took Luxmun to an inner room and the hermits left. As they walked past
the open window of his room, he heard the name Ravan several
times spoken in a low voice, and later its syllables tolled in his
dreams like a sombre bell.

He awoke to find Sita and Valmiki bending over him. Valmiki, with a gentle hand, was rubbing a salve into his wounds.
He had, he said, just made it from herbs in his garden, and it
was still warm from the fire. Beyond a pain where Ravan had
struck his hand, Luxmun felt no worse for his adventure, and
he was much refreshed by the sleep.

Valmiki left them. Sita, having seen that he needed nothing,
sat on a rush mat near the bed and opening a small box began
to prepare him a betel-nut to chew. She took the leaf, spread

lime on it with a spatula, powdered this with ground spices,
then folding the leaf, pinned the small bundle together with a
clove. Luxmun took it and chewed contentedly, savouring the
sharp, dry taste of the spices.

"He's a fine fellow, this Ravan," he said, seeking a chance
to talk about his fight.

"I know," said Sita. She began to prepare another leaf.

"Stands taller than me," said Luxmun.

"Yes," said Sita. "I know."

"As far as I could see, he's handsome in a fierce way."

"Yes," said Sita. "I think so, too. And he is not always fierce."

"I wonder who he is."

"He is a king. Not a big king; but still a king. He is the Lord
of Lanka."

"A *king*?" said Luxmun, sitting up with surprise. "But how
is it that you know so much about him?"

"He is in love with me," said Sita, and smiling, she offered
him a second leaf of spices. He refused it and insisted that she
explain.

"There's not very much to explain," said Sita, "I . . .
well, of course, I'm very happy to be here because my husband
is very happy to be here, but sometimes I do get tired of . . .
no, that's silly, because a wife can't get tired of doing what
pleases her husband. Still, sometimes I . . ." She stopped.
Luxmun continued for her:

"Sometimes you are so bored that for two betel leaves you'd
chase the next philosopher round the hermitage with a ladle,"
said Luxmun. "I understand that very well. What I always do
when I feel like that is to go for a very long walk."

"So do I," said Sita.

"I've never noticed."

"No," said Sita. "Of course not. Why should you? Though

I suppose—at least I hope—somebody would notice if I didn't come back," she said: but observing that she was growing wistful (a ruinous mood, in her view, for a princess in misfortune) she put the leaf of spices in her mouth and chewed upon it in a masculine fashion. "Well, then," she resumed, "I went for a long walk one day along the road to the south, and I came across a party of soldiers eating by the wayside. Their leader saw that I was alone. They were rough men, rougher than our soldiers back home. I was afraid. But he stood up and ordered his men to stand as well. He asked me if I was in any trouble. I said no. He said it was strange to see . . ." She hesitated.

"Yes?" said Luxmun. "Go on."

"To see a lady of noble birth walking alone, although how he could see that I was, I can't say, because I was dressed as I am now," and she looked sadly down at the stains on her sari. "I told him as much as was necessary. He made me rest and gave me something to drink—winc, I think it was. Then he, with about six soldiers walking behind, came back with me, but not all the way. He said that he would not cross the boundary of his kingdom, and that's how I found he was a king. Though, of course, he told me so when we met after that."

"You met him again?"

"By a small ruined shrine that has a pretty jacaranda tree," said Sita. "I should not have gone, but he talks so well and he never says, 'On the face of it what you say is true, but if you look deeper you'll see that you are mistaken,' like all these windbags here. Yes, I saw him again. Three times." She looked sideways at Luxmun and saw that he was frowning.

"Yes," she said, "he is indeed very strong and a good deal taller than you. I think it is quite wonderful that you managed to beat him." Looking up again she saw Luxmun no longer frowned, but beamed.

"A king, you say. Where is Lanka?"

"It's a town, he says. Not very big but with very thick walls. You go south along the road, through a great forest—that's why I've never been to see myself—and you come out on a plain and there it is," she replied. "I should like to see a town again, and hear the noise, and the temple gongs, and see the markets and the silks and the jewellers—just for five minutes."

"So should I," said Luxmun, and lay back on his couch, thinking not of silks and jewels but of a walled city whose king he, Luxmun, had already once defeated: a king to whom he had thrown a challenge.

The walls of Lanka rose straight from the plain. There was no moat, perhaps from lack of a river to divert. But the walls themselves, high, crenellated, and ponderously thick, stood in no need of any other defence than their strength. They hid all but the higher roofs of the town within and the walls, in their turn, lay half hidden behind slighter walls, cunningly disposed in lines and quadrants, to wear down the attacker before he could come within javelin cast of the main fortifications.

Luxmun surveyed them closely from the shelter of a small wood some distance away. He could go no nearer for fear of being recognised. Between his wood and the city there was nowhere to hide: all had been swept clear so that anyone approaching should be in full view of the watchtowers.

Luxmun turned back. He had satisfied himself that the man he had challenged was truly a king and the king of no mean city. To recover the helmet that Luxmun had thrown at Ravan's feet as a gage would need an army.

It had been a grim journey. He had set out upon it as soon as his wounds were healed, telling nobody of his intention. He had found the ruined temple, the place of Sita's meetings, but here he had left the road, and asking his way from a peasant in the fields, made a great circuit outside the boundaries of Ravan's small kingdom, lest he should fall in with soldiers. Then he had come upon a village, the shells of its huts still smoking, and bodies, covered with blood, waiting to be burned upon funeral pyres of their own beds and boxes. He was told that Ravan had crossed his boundary on a raiding expedition the day before. The headman had refused homage and had been cut down. Retiring from their foray, Ravan's soldiers had driven the cattle they had stolen over the bodies of the villagers they had killed on their way to their raid. When Luxmun expressed his horror, the villagers pointed to smoke on the horizon and told him that there they had done far worse, and killed more slowly. It was the season, they said, for Ravan to make war.

Luxmun returned to the hermitage, and told only Valmiki of what he had seen.

Valmiki said: "He is a cruel and bloodthirsty robber. Now that Rama has brought us gold, I think maybe he will come here. We should make fine sport for his soldiery."

"But not," said Luxmun, "before I have given them some sport of my own choosing."

sita's
rape

Ravan burned down the Hermitage of the Gluttons on the night of the next new moon.

His soldiers opened the attack in silence. They climbed trees in the surrounding woods and came up over the brow of the hills behind. Then they shot arrows tipped with burning pitch into the thatches of the semi-circle of huts.

Valmiki was the first to wake. Seeing the roof of the neighbouring house burning he shouted to wake Rama and the others. In answer there arose the bray of war trumpets and a pulsing howl, deliberately animal and thus doubly terrifying, as the soldiers streamed from the woods and down the hillsides, kneeling every so many paces to loose arrows into the conflagration.

As the first soldiers ran up the path that led to Valmiki's house, Rama came out from his room. An arrow struck the wall behind him and as he turned away to look at it he heard the animal-like cry, but close at hand. He turned back to see a tall soldier, grimacing with the effort of the war cry, standing not twelve feet away. His right arm was flung back ready to launch a short spear at the house. Rama, unarmed, stood irresolute. The man bellowed again but this time his cry rose to a scream. He stood for a moment, rigid, and then fell sideways. An arrow protruded from his left cheek.

"I can't expect such luck with the rest," said a calm voice

behind Rama, "so I suppose I'll have to use my head, and that's something I never like doing."

Rama turned to see Luxmun kneeling outside the doorway to his room; his bow was still trembling from the arrow which he had just loosed. He stooped, took another from where it lay by his knees, and sent it after the first, but a little higher, so that it fell among the fallen soldier's companions. These, hearing the unmistakable sound of a warrior's bow, fell back and turned their attention to more peaceable huts.

Valmiki came to the verandah, his arms round the woman and the boy who were his servants. Luxmun told Rama and the others to go into the room behind him. He did not move his stance, but allowed them to step past him as best they might while he sent arrow after arrow towards the great tree. Sita, behind him, handed the arrows to him as he needed them, stroking the feathers on the shaft into place as she did so.

When all were in shelter behind him Luxmun said:

"The house is as good as gone. Even if it doesn't catch fire they can still surround us. I can hold them here in front, but they'll come hopping down the terraces behind like a crew of monkeys. Brother, take the javelin you'll find next my bed and your bow; Sita, bring the rest of my arrows; Master Valmiki, get your poem or these barbarians will use it to fry their fish. I know soldiers. I am one. I shall bring the gold. All of you, go, please, to the carob tree on the terrace, lie down, and wait for me. Aha, you damned jackal," he ended, as evenly as he had spoken all along, and the shadow that he had thus addressed ran screaming into the darkness, tugging an arrow from its middle.

When they had obeyed him they could see, as they lay among the great roots of the carob, the sack of the hermitage. A half-circle of fires marked the huts. Here and there a naked or near-naked hermit lay sprawling on the earth. One had a spear through his belly pinning him to the ground. With horror Rama saw that the man's limbs still moved.

Then he saw the mild and venerable Jabali, he who had answered all his questions, driven naked with obscene thrusts and pricks of a spear towards the great tree. There he was made to bow down to the ground before a tall man in black armour who was taking no part in the sack, but who was directing it with shouts and encouragements to the soldiers.

"Who is that?" asked Rama, and Sita, staring fixedly at the man, said:

"Ravan."

Luxmun climbed the steps that led to the terrace, grunting with the effort of carrying the mule bag of gold. He warned Rama to watch the hill behind them, from which they were separated only by a low wall that was fully commanded by the slope of the hill. Then he returned down the steps for the second bag, refusing any help.

Rama watched the dark hill for a while, but a burst of laughter from below him drew his attention.

One of the soldiers by the tree was now performing a clumsy imitation of a male dancer and his companions with the help of their javelin points were forcing Jabali grotesquely to follow his movements as though he were a woman. When he tottered, they dragged him upright by his beard, tearing out the hair. The tall black figure of Ravan did not move during this savage game, but Ravan watched and did not stop them.

"They must be drugged with hashish," said Rama. Valmiki shook his head.

"Hashish takes a man out of himself," he said. "These have needed nothing. Perhaps a little wine, to make the blood run faster. Nothing else."

Luxmun returned to them with the second bag and himself took charge of watching the hill. Seeing, as he thought, a shadow move, he drew his bow, but the bowstring snapped under his fingers. He asked the boy to go down and get another, but the boy, trembling, could not move for fear. Valmiki said that he would go, but Sita forestalled him.

"If they attack, a woman will be no use here. I shall go and fetch it," she said, and when Rama protested she said that it would be safe for a while, since the soldiers were busy tormenting the old man. Before they could stop her, she had gone.

They began shouting under the tree and Rama saw that Jabali had fallen prone on the ground. A soldier was beating him with a spear butt, but Jabali did not move. Then the soldier reversed the spear and jabbed it repeatedly into the old man's shoulders. His victim began screaming.

Rama, maddened with rage, got up, shouted, and drawing his bow, shot an arrow. The light of the flames shone on his bronze figure, and flashed from the mounts of his great bow.

The arrow fell far short of the tree. But Rama's shout had been heard by the soldiers and they now stopped their torture of the philosopher and gazed up at the terrace.

Then Rama saw Sita walk across the space between the house and the tree, go up to the soldiers, pass among them, and bow to Ravan. The man in black armour bowed profoundly in his turn, and Sita and Ravan appeared to talk.

Jabali, bleeding, crawled away.

"They'll come at us now," said Luxmun.

But the soldiers did not. Some shouted; others loosed arrows up at the terrace, but wildly, as if jesting. Sita and Ravan still stood together.

Then a horse was brought from the woods beyond the

hermitage. Soldiers held it steady for Ravan to mount. When he had done so, he reached down his hand to Sita, who took it. Soldiers assisting her, she mounted the horse behind the man in black armour, and together they slowly rode away.

The soldiers, picking up their bows and lances, followed in a disorderly group. In a few minutes the watchers on the terrace could see no more sign of them.

Not daring to speak to one another Rama, Luxmun, and Valmiki went down and, in the light of the fires, they succoured the wounded and covered the terrible postures of the dead.

Forlorn, bleeding, with some wandering in their wits, the surviving hermits were shepherded away from the blackened hermitage by Valmiki and the princely brothers. Valmiki led them some miles to the town of a nobleman, a self-styled prince, with a tiny court and much pomp, or as much pomp as his annual tribute to protect himself from Ravan would allow.

Hearing Rama's name, he welcomed the fugitives. When they had rested in the ornate little palace for a day, Luxmun showed their host the gold that Ravan had not been able to find. Then he, speaking through the lips of the nobleman, showed Rama the only path that was honourably left to him. With his gold, he could rally the nobles, the rajas and the princes who had suffered for many years under the royal brigandage of Ravan, and lead them to their revenge on Lanka.

There was no gainsaying the nobleman's argument and, well grounded by Luxmun in Rama's way of thinking, he put his points well. Since Rama had not taken the saffron robe, he was still a prince, and a prince whose wife had been stolen by a petty, if formidable, raja. He must redress the injury, or forfeit his rank in the eyes of his equals, a thing which was not only a disgrace but a sin against the commandments of the gods.

The gold would start an alliance which would soon grow of its own accord into a great army. But great armies needed a leader, and the allies would fight among themselves if they were left to choose one from their own ranks. Rama, with Sita stolen, was the choice above all contention.

Rama bowed to this reasoning. Luxmun, well pleased with his work, instantly set out in Rama's name to the surrounding rajas and began his work of persuasion and bribery.

"But," said Rama again and again to Valmiki in the long weeks of waiting that followed, "she was *not* stolen. I saw what I saw. She went willingly on that blood-soaked monster's horse. I saw her. I say I saw her. What am I to think?"

It was plain enough from his looks and gestures that he had already made up his mind what he should think of her flight: and when Valmiki's servant told him that Sita had once said that she had met Ravan in a ruined temple, he did not attempt to hide the rage of jealousy which was eating at his heart.

He was sitting one hot night with Valmiki on a small terrace that the nobleman had built in imitation of the cool promenades of marble which greater princes had on palace roofs. He said to Valmiki:

"Everything that I set out to do when I left Ayoda has been brought to nothing. I am not a philosopher: I am a warring prince. I am not a hermit: I am living in a palace; and I am not chaste as the sages say one should be, but I am on fire with jealousy. I think continually night and day of what she may be doing, what I fear she must be doing, in Ravan's bed. But still, I have learned some few things, and I have grown more than a little wiser. Looking back, I see that this is due to your instruction. Have you anything to say that can cure a man of this base passion of jealousy?"

Valmiki thought, then smiled his deep smile until it grew into a grin.

"I have nothing to say about the passions of princes of royal blood. Such things are too great for me. But I do remember the advice that was given to four fishermen, and since it came from a god it should be worth considering."

"I shall be glad," said Rama, "to hear any advice that comes from a god. Tell me what it was."

So Valmiki, to lighten Rama's dark thoughts of Sita and Ravan, began the tale of the four jealous fishermen and their nocturnal adventures.

the
nocturnal
adventures
of the
four
jealous fishermen

There were once (said Valmiki) four fisher-men who led honest and simple lives and fished in the Rann of Kutch. Their names were as simple as their lives. They were called Luckyman, Stumbler, Quickly, and Shy. These were the names that the other fishermen called them by, and if they were neither ancient nor dignified names, they fitted. Luckyman was a handsome young fellow for whom everything went right. Stumbler was square and slow and was never sure of his feet or himself; Quickly was forty and knew all the tricks of fishing—it was a pleasure to watch the deft way he worked a boat; while Shy, the youngest, was shy.

They lived in a village which was built on a mud flat. It faced an inlet of the sea which was flatter than the mud and even more dull to look at. There was nothing whatever in the village or its surroundings to take the fishermen's minds off fishing, except their wives.

Now Luckyman, Stumbler, Quickly, and Shy all had wives of considerable beauty. It chanced that way; there was no design in it. Their wives had been chosen by their parents, and their parents had chosen the girls because their dowries were the best bargain going at the time. Luckyman, Stumbler, and Quickly had been married when they were seven, but Shy had been made to wait until he was twelve because he, by some freak, matured late. The dowries that Quickly and Stumbler received were much less than Luckyman's haul: while Stumbler's wife tippled. But in spite of these differences, in the matter of womanly attraction there was nothing to choose between them. Luckyman, Stumbler, and their two companions were all as proud of their wives as they were of *The Dancing Woman*.

This was their boat. They had built her themselves and she had cost most of the four dowries: but she was a beautiful boat, as sleek and quiet in flat water as a well-fed cow, and, when she got into the ocean, leaping to the waves so gracefully that she seemed to arch her back. She was black, with two painted eyes in her prow, a lateen sail, and a high red tiller. In front was a boom, bright yellow, from which they hung the iron basket that carried a fire. The fishes would come to look at the fire, and while Quickly steered the boat in a circle, Luckyman and Shy paid out the net and Stumbler watched that it did not foul. Then they would hit the sides of *The Dancing Woman* with sticks to frighten the fishes. An hour of this, and then all four would haul the net aboard, the fishes tumbling out of it, gleaming in the light of the fire like the money that the fishermen earned next morning.

But their lay their trouble. They had to fish at night. They launched *The Dancing Woman* at sunset and they did not turn her prow for home until the light began to whiten the sea. Then there was the selling to do. This called for a long cold trot across the mud flats with the baskets swinging from poles across their shoulders, then a haggle with the merchant, and much standing

around maybe for an hour shivering in the wind from the sunrise, while the merchant wrapped his woollen shawl about him
and beat them down till their toes were blue. After that came a
long trot back home to a sleepy wife blowing up the charcoal fire
to cook breakfast—a welcome sight, no doubt, but only if you
could be sure that she had slept on her own, as a good wife
should, all the previous night.

But could they be sure? This was the question that vexed
Luckyman and Stumbler, Quickly and, particularly, young Shy,
whose wife was the youngest of all and therefore the most tempting. When the boat was running well, when the fish broke the
nets with their weight, when even the merchant forebore to
screw them for the last rupee, neither Luckyman nor Stumbler,
Quickly nor Shy could be happy. This doubt prevented them.

Sometimes Luckyman would be staring down into the water
where the light made an emerald pit in the darkness, and he
would say:

"I wonder."

Then Quickly would begin to wonder, too; Stumbler would
hang his big square head and stick out his lower lip, wondering
slowly (for Stumbler had some difficulty in making his brain
work), while Shy would sit in the stern and blush, for he had
no difficulty in making his mind work whatever, especially on
such topics, being young and vigorous and very fond of his wife.

Of course they kept watch. They watched the lights of the
other fishermen's boats and if one turned homewards earlier than
the rest, instead of going to bed next morning they stayed
awake, red-eyed and irritable, and they would pester the villagers
until they had found out the reason, which, when they found it,
never satisfied them. But even then, there were days when the
fish shoals were on the run, and the fishermen had to chase them

for an hour or so before they settled round the light. *The Danc-ing Woman* would show her paces, and take them fast and far away from their companions. And then, when the others were out of sight, who could tell what they were doing? What was there to stop an amorous fisherman—even a boatload of four—creeping back to shore, and nobody the wiser? Besides, not all the villagers fished. Some of the young men were net-menders, a daytime job and very monotonous. If the young net-menders' thoughts were anything like their jokes, what woman could be be safe? Net-menders were Quickly's especial worry because one morning, after a shark had got among their tackle during the night, Quickly's wife had said:

"I'll take the nets to the mender's, Quickly. You rest your-self. You look tired."

Quickly's suspicions had been instantly aroused. It was not a wife's duty to take care of the nets, however solicitous for her husband she might be. He was not a man to dawdle in anything, and he could put two and two together faster than any man. He did, and his peace of mind was destroyed for a month. Stumbler was in a worse case. He could not put two and two together at all, and so he was driven to suspect everybody. Luckyman, who knew how to put things in a breezy manner, tried the device of joking with his wife about the cowherds—men, again, with little to occupy their minds during the long, hot day. His wife laughed long and heartily, and kissing him, dropped the matter and never raised it again—in all as unsatis-factory a state of affairs as could well be imagined.

Shy said nothing, but every time his wife raised her eyes in the presence of another man he was immediately sure that they both were laughing at him, for he was convinced that there was not a man in the village who could not make a better show at making love than he.

Such, in the small hours, by the light of the lamp reflected from the water, were the gloomy thoughts, night after night, of the four jealous friends. It was fortunate that *The Dancing Woman* was an intelligent and friendly craft. Otherwise many a time when her owners were sunk in reverie she would have got herself stuck on a mud flat. She kept them afloat; but she could not keep them fishing, and as the months wore on Luckyman, Stumbler, Quickly, and Shy caught less and less fish and grew more and more certain that someone was sleeping with their respective wives.

Now for many years it had been the custom of the four friends to stop at a temple on their way back from selling their fish and to give the Brahmin who looked after it a tenth part of the money they had made, as a devout offering. They would ask him to pray for success for their next catch, which he always did very heartily. Thinking about this one night at sea, Quickly, who was wondering whether they ought not to give up the practice now that their earnings were growing so small, was suddenly struck with an idea. The next morning, instead of handing the priest the money, Quickly kissed the hem of his robe and said: "Master, we are simple men but our souls are very troubled. We want you to help us." The Brahmin, who had not previously thought about the fishermen's souls—he had, after all, been asked to pray for fish—looked somewhat doubtful.

"I am not at all sure that it is proper for you to have troubled souls," he said, shaking his fat chops at them. "Whatever the bother is, you must submit to the will of the gods. They have planned everything that has ever happened in the universe and if you four fishermen don't happen to like it, well, that's a sad state of affairs, of course, but I doubt if the gods will alter their plans because of it."

Stumbler and Shy were abashed at this rebuke. Even Luckyman was a little out of countenance. But Quickly, once more kissing the hem of the Brahmin's robe, said:

"Master, we do not want the gods to alter the universe. We are only humble men, and if the gods have arranged that other men should sleep with our wives, we think that it is fine, but we would just like to know who is doing it."

"Oh?" said the Brahmin. "*Oh!* O-ho-ho-*ho*." For although he was aware that the things of this coarse and material world are all illusion, he had also discovered—during long, hot afternoons spent on his bed flat on his back—that some illusions are more interesting than others: and in the category of interesting ones came the wives of Stumbler, Luckyman, Shy, and Quickly.

"So *that* is what is troubling you," he went on. "Who d'you suspect? How did you find out? How long has it been going on? Does anybody know? Does anybody guess? Is it the same man or all four of your wives? Or a different one for each? When does it happen? What happens? Well if you're all going to sit there with all eight of your jaws clenched shut and not telling me a single fact you can't expect me to help. Answer me."

"Master," said Luckyman, "we will. But we were waiting for you to stop speaking."

"Well," said the Brahmin, sitting back on his large haunches, "I have stopped. Who d'you think it is?"

"The net-mender," said Quickly.

"The . . . what-do-you-call-him," said Stumbler as the Brahmin looked at him. The Brahmin clicked his tongue against his teeth impatiently and Luckyman supplied the word.

"That's right. The cowherd," said Stumbler. "I suspect the cowherd." Shy, flushing, said he suspected everybody, and Luckyman, seeing that the Brahmin was growing impatient again, said that he thought that the man in his case was the foreign fellow who came round selling wooden bracelets.

"Have you any proof?" asked the Brahmin.

"It's the way my wife talks," said Quickly.

"Eh? Proof?" said Stumbler. "Oh. *Proof.* No. No proof."

Shy said: "I'm sure it's somebody. I feel it in the pit of my stomach," while Luckyman turned the habits of the bracelet-seller over in his jealous mind and said: "Why should he always come just when the boats set out?"

All four had the feeling, now that they were faced up with the question, that their answers did not amount to very much.

But the Brahmin, it seemed, needed even less proof than they did.

"So you want me to ask the great god Shiva, who knows everything, to reveal the names of these scoundrels?" he said, and when they all nodded, he went on to be most affable and accommodating about the fee. They could pay when it was convenient, but they must promise faithfully to report all their suspicions and of course even the slightest actual fact every day as they passed the temple.

"But," said Quickly, "if the great god Shiva knows everything he'll know all that, too."

"If your fish," said the Brahmin rudely, "stink as much as your theology, I quite see that I shall never be paid."

It was true that none of the fishermen knew even the first principles of theology; but they knew one of its leading conclusions, which is that it is a very bad thing to contradict a priest. So they said they were sorry, promised to do what they were asked, and left.

Now in the Rann of Kutch (Valmiki went on) the great god Shiva was held to be one of the most powerful of all the gods. Every day from temples all over the land the god's ears were assailed by millions of prayers and his nose by the smell of seas of clarified butter. He had one additional eye in the middle of his forehead with which from time to time he reduced unfortunate human beings to a heap of ashes. He concerned himself with the potency of the organs of generation, a more amiable characteristic and one which accounted for a good number of the prayers and most of the butter.

He was deeply revered and very popular. The blessings of the other gods, such as wealth and good fortune, were erratic. The blessings of Shiva were children and these came to his worshippers with a frequency that spoke well of the god's concern for his devotees, and, as the priest explained, when they were male children (which everyone wanted) it was clearly the mercy of Shiva at work, and when they were not, it was as clearly due to the wickedness of the worshipper. In this way the god could do no wrong. In any case, he could do no wrong because he was a god and a god cannot do wrong by definition. However, any two arguments are better than one, even if neither is a very good one. Great, in any case, was the glory of Shiva, and his priests reflected it in their rotund faces which were like copper-coloured moons. No man who had received the favours of Shiva could be so ungrateful as to leave his priest unfeed, and no man who wanted them would be so unwise.

Thus the Brahmin in the village of the four jealous fishermen was able to take life easily. It added to his peace of mind that he did not believe that Shiva existed. After a lifetime of praying to the god, preaching about him, and offering him sacrifices, he had come to the conclusion that Shiva was a great deal of nonsense. Cautiously discussing this with fellow priests of a similar age he found that they had arrived at the same opinion themselves. But though they all thought Shiva an old wives' tale, they did not find that this hindered them in the discharge of their religious duties. No man can be at his best as a public figure if he feels that at any moment his superior will open an eye and burn him to ashes. "Nobody," as they reasoned—although strictly in private—"lives his life on the supposition that he might at any moment be struck by a thunderbolt. Nor can we. Nor need we. As far as common sense and a strict attention to the facts can show us, Shiva does not exist."

But he did. Not only did he exist, but he was often in the fishermen's own village; and not only was he often in the village, but he was fond of sitting outside his own temple.

On such occasions his third eye was kept tightly closed and it therefore appeared to be no more than a dignified wrinkle on a brow which was scored with the lines natural to a profound and benign philosopher. This is what Shiva would have passed for, except that his eyes were so bright and lively, and his glance so darting, that he had something of the look of a travelling charlatan lying in wait for a dupe. This impression the god increased by wearing the robes of a member of a religious community vowed to poverty. In this way he was able to sit, quite ignored, at the temple gate, save for worshippers who threw him a coin, but who immediately looked away in case (as was the habit of holy mendicants) he should ask for more.

It is Shiva's duty to destroy the earth: he may do it when he pleases, and what we call History is merely Shiva's procrastination. He was given this task by Brahma the Creator, a greater god even than Shiva; a somewhat profounder thinker but less sympathetic. Brahma made the world and peopled it with human beings. Having watched the result for several dispassionate millennia, he summoned Shiva (this was about eight hundred years after men had discovered the wheel) and said: "I can take all this to pieces again but it would be tedious and I am otherwise engaged. Destroy it or preserve it as you please." He then dismissed him with the toppling courtesies that pass between the all-powerful gods on the rare occasions of their meeting, and Shiva, after waiting a courteous century before looking at his gift, came down to earth, the first of many visits.

It was his habit to take a turn or two about the world, observing us, and then to seat himself upon a mountain preparatory to raising his third, apocalyptic eyelid. But he would consider us for a moment (no one knows, but it is said that he has spared us eleven times) and say: "I have noted that in the southeastern corner they have given up eating one another: who knows (save Brahma, who is otherwise engaged), they may even rise so high as to give up the habit of burying a living child in the foundations of their houses." So saying, he would quell the fluttering of his eyelashes and wait for another few centuries. Once more he would go here and there and finally seat himself on his mountain. Once more destruction would tremble in the balance of his lucid mind. He would say: "I have observed that in the westernmost areas they no longer found their houses in innocent blood: who knows (save Brahma, who may not be disturbed), whether in time they will give up founding their nations in it." And so, here we are today.

Thus it was no coincidence that Shiva sat outside the fishermen's temple, for he was attracted to human folly, and the prayers of the fishermen, reaching his ears even though garbled by the perfunctory Sanscrit of the Brahmin, nevertheless interested him profoundly. Having made it his business to find out the truth, he had discovered that the wife of Luckyman, the wife of Stumbler, the wife of Quickly, and the more newly-wedded wife of young Shy were all chaste and all virtuous and all respecters of their husbands' beds.

The Brahmin had discovered the same thing, and this is to his credit. His credit lies in the fact that he had less resources than the god. He could not make himself invisible, or pass through mud walls, or cross-question the village dogs. But he had another instrument. He was known as a man who was scandalised by other people's moral delinquencies. He was rewardingly shockable; his facial expressions of outrage were dramatic and exquisitely apt. He practised them daily. Therefore, every piece of scandal was tried on the Brahmin as a coin is rung on marble. But he had found that hint and fish as he might among the old women and the old men of the village, not a word out of place ever came his way about the wives of his four petitioners. So he concluded that they were faithful.

The Brahmin had sighed and dismissed the matter from his mind. If he was not wholly gratified at this evidence of upright living among his parishioners, it was not from any base motive. He was a man of balanced outlook: he admired the virtue of the women but doubted the enterprise of the village young men. But if he could dismiss the matter from his mind he could not get rid of the four jealous husbands from his temple.

They came regularly each morning and as regularly the Brahmin told them that Shiva had not deigned to give an answer. Finally he told them that in his opinion there never would be an answer. Possibly, he said, their wives were virtuous. They came again next day, all four this time as mute as Stumbler, but still determined upon an answer. Positively, the Brahmin said, their wives *were* virtuous. Since the god had not answered, there could be no doubt about it. He bid them goodbye and told them that they should be happy men.

They were nothing of the sort. They were jealous men; they had distrusted their wives, for months, and few things bind men together in comradeship more than being cuckolds. It is a silent communion, a wordless sympathy, and Luckyman, Stumbler, Quickly, and Shy felt it, every night: and they were not at all happy to think that they were going to lose it.

Again, they had been married for money. Their wives were beautiful but not aways interesting; or at least they had not been so before they were suspected. Now every one of their words was anxiously absorbing: none of their gestures was allowed to escape unnoticed; while in the marriage bed, the thought in the minds of the jealous fishermen that they might have been supplanted and—worse—surpassed, urged Luckyman and his three friends on to perform prodigies. This always has its interest for the performer, especially in retrospect. Previously, their usual conversation aboard *The Dancing Woman* had been about the admirable performance of their boat. For all save Shy, this now gave place to the discussion of things in which they could take a more vivid, though not less technical, pride. Shy did not take part in these conversations, but from no more shameful reason than his habitual modesty. He agreed with the others that a new interest had been added to their lives and regretted as much as they the risk of it being taken away.

Lastly, their jealousy had made them men of importance to themselves and—what with their temple comings and goings, their questions and veiled looks—men of mystery to the rest of the village.

Could it be that all this was built upon their own mistaken fancy? They turned the question over in their minds. Stumbler scratched his head, Luckyman looked gloomy, Shy wrung his fingers, but Quickly gave the answer: no. They went back to the temple and saw the Brahmin. It was a day in which Shiva was sitting outside his shrine, and the god heard their conversation as they came out.

Quickly was saying: "A silver net! Even if it is only as big as my hand, that will cost a great deal of money."

Stumbler kicked the stones unseeingly as he walked with his companions past the disguised god and muttered: "A silver man no bigger than . . . what is it . . .?"

"Your thumb," said Luckyman, "that'll be fifteen silver

pieces just for the metal. Then what is my bracelet going to cost, do you think? I'll have all the fiddle-faddle of decoration to pay for and . . ."

"And where shall I *get* a silver phallus?" said Shy. "How can I ask the silversmith to make one?"

"Still," said Quickly, "if it works . . ."

"If the god Shiva is pleased . . ." said Luckyman.

"And he tells us what we want to know," said Shy.

"You mean . . . ?" said Stumbler.

"The names of the men who are sleeping with our wives," said Luckyman, nodding.

"And you see," said Quickly, "that priest *does* think there's someone, for all he tried to put us off. Testing us, that's what he was doing. Very clever, these priests. Testing us, you see. But all the while he knew there was something in it, or else he wouldn't be putting poor men like us to the expense of these presents to the god, would he?"

"I wonder," said Stumbler, "what he'll do with them?"

"Who?" said Luckyman.

"The Lord Shiva," said Stumbler and swore as he stubbed his toe.

More the god could not hear, for they were too far away for the human ears which he had assumed when he disguised himself as a holy mendicant.

But he had heard enough to tell him that his priest was up to some rascality. The third eye in his forehead, which looked so like a quizzical wrinkle, moved slightly. The bark of a nearby willow shrivelled and gave off smoke.

The god rose. The god entered his own temple. The god greeted his own priest. His own priest waved a careless hand at his own god and went on with his task, which was pouring melted butter over the great stone *lingam*.

"And there's not a word of truth in the whole thing," said the Brahmin when he had explained the case to his visitor. "It is all their imagination. They stare into those fishing lights of theirs and addle their minds."

"Poor fellows," said the god and in his disguise as a holy mendicant he found it easy to throw a touch of mockery into his voice. "And now they'll be poorer than ever."

"Ah," said the Brahmin smiling across his broad face, "so you know about the silver votives?"

"Yes," said the god. His third eye moved very slightly, thus giving him an expression of worldly cynicism.

"I know what you must be thinking, but how else was I to get rid of them?" asked the Brahmin. "You won't believe me, but I hope, I do actually hope, they will not be such thundering fools as to have them made. But they will. I know it. And I shall have to take them. I see that you smile. Well, I don't blame you. But this is a small place and if I didn't take them I would lose all my influence. Still, simple tricks for small places, big tricks for big ones. I suppose," said the Brahmin with friendly envy, "that *you've* been to the holy city of Benares."

"I have," said the god.

"I've always wanted to go. Always," said the Brahmin sighing. "Conversation: that is what I miss so painfully here. Perhaps," he said facetiously, "a good long chat will be my heavenly reward."

"The conversation of the gods," said Shiva, "is very sparing."

"Ah, the gods!" said the Brahmin, slowly closing one eye, "the gods are very accommodating when it comes to things that they like. They like . . ."

"Holiness," said Shiva.

"For one thing," the Brahmin amiably agreed. "And for another—" he paused and then, reaching under the altar steps (which he could conveniently do because he was sitting on the bottom one), he groped about—"for another," he repeated, bringing out a gleaming brass container by its lid, "they like cold boiling fowl spiced with a little cardamon seed." He took off the lid and sniffed the odour of the food inside.

"The great and good God Shiva has a great partiality for boiled fowl offered by devout persons who are also good cooks, hasn't he?" The Brahmin, winking again, hospitably held out the brass receptacle to his guest.

"Yes," said Shiva, and took a piece of chicken. "This man," he had told himself only a moment before when he had almost determined to destroy him on the spot, "this man is a rascal and does not believe that I exist. But after all he is better than those others who are rascals and believe that I do." He thus ate the chicken with a tranquil mind, and with a sufficiently human palate to cast a silent blessing on the cook (forever after her chickens were plump, much to the envy of her neighbours).

When they had finished the chicken, they washed their fingers and gargled their throats at the well behind the temple, spitting out water to the north, the east, the west and south as ritual prescribed. They then sat in the shade of one of the buttresses and Shiva said:

"Now supposing there were a way of curing these four fishermen of their jealousy, would you use it?"

The Brahmin was picking his teeth.

"Yes, but there isn't."

"You mentioned Benares," said Shiva.

"Ah, Benares," said the Brahmin and sucked some chicken out of a cavity.

"When I was in Benares I was given a powder for use in just such a case as this," said Shiva. "The man who gave it to me is a very famous rishi. You take it with a little water and it enables you to be in two places at once, although you are visible only in one of them. By using it a man can go about his daily work and still be with his wife—unseen, of course, but seeing everything. Since you say that there is nothing to see, your fishermen should soon be cured."

Thus Shiva: and in saying these words he set philosophers a problem, in the solving of which heads may yet be broken and blood still flow. For the gods, by their essence, cannot lie. But Shiva lied. There was no sage in Benares who gave him the powder. There was no magic powder. It was only a little red earth which Shiva had quickly scooped up from the temple compound while the Brahmin had turned his back to clean his teeth. The god had put it in the small wallet that hung at his waist. Now, opening this leather bag, he showed the Brahmin the dust.

The Brahmin, smiling, shook his broad, round head from side to side.

"You forget," he said, "that this is not Benares. It is a little fishing village."

"I do not forget," said Shiva.

The Brahmin ignored him and went on:

"As the *guru* who taught me the elements of my job always said to anyone who was going to take up a cure of souls in an unknown village, 'My son, the smaller the place, the fewer the fools.'"

"That may be a remark showing worldly wisdom," said Shiva, "and it may also show rather more worldly wisdom than is fitting in a holy man, but it has nothing to do with this powder."

"It has everything to do with it," said the Brahmin. "In a little place like this a priest can't afford failures. If I were a priest in Benares or Ayoda and I gave this to some simpleton and—of course—it didn't work—how could it? Ha!—well, there would always be hundreds of other fools and temple-haunters to swear for the honour of their priest that it worked very well with a friend of their first cousin some ten years ago. But here—well, as my guru said, there aren't enough fools to go round. I should lose my credit."

"But if it did work, your credit would be increased," said Shiva, "wonderfully increased."

The Brahmin's broad mouth opened in a bellow of laughter. He struck Shiva on his knee.

"And so would yours, my good friend," he said, wiping his eyes, "in all the towns in which you've sold it. But I don't think you'll go back to find out if it has. Ho! Ho! Ho! That's where you foot-loose fellows have the advantage of us poor fixed priests. Onwards to holiness, eh? Never look back, eh? You never know who might be after you with a pitchfork!" With which he burst into more loud and friendly laughter. But suddenly he stopped.

"What is that?" he said, pointing with a thick finger. There was something half buried by the sand.

"I do not know," said Shiva.

The Brahmin prodded the sand and took the object up between his fingers. It was a small beetle of carved stone. The Brahmin held it up and looked covetously at it.

"Do you know what it is?" he said.

Shiva said: "No. The wallet belonged to a dead member of our order. He passed it me a few days ago." Thus simply did the god describe the miracle he had performed taking on the human form, the dress, and the wallet of a man who had fallen dead a moment before he did so.

"It's from Egypt," said the Brahmin. "It's a great bringer of good luck. A priest I knew had one and he discovered buried treasure."

"You believe in this Egyptian fable?" asked Shiva.

"I do and I don't. Well, then, yes I do."

"Would you like it?"

"Yes. Yes indeed," said the Brahmin, his eyes glittering.

"Would it not, do you think, be better to pray to the great god Shiva for anything that you may want? You are his priest."

The Brahmin grinned and shrugged his shoulders.

"You should know the answer to that," he said.

The great god paused. He thought of the millions of prayers that he ignored daily. A god is nothing if not magnanimous.

"I grant you your point," he said. "I shall give you this if you will do one thing."

The Brahmin closed his large hand over the amulet.

"Yes, yes. What?"

"Give the powder to the fishermen. Tell them what it is for and tell them that they must put as much as they can hold between finger and thumb in a jar of water and drink the water fasting."

"Is it a drug?"

"No more a drug," said Shiva, "than the common earth that is beneath our feet."

"Well, if you'll indulge my fancy, I'll indulge yours," said the Brahmin, opening his hand and gazing at the scarab.

"And now," said Shiva, "I must go."

"Onwards," said the Brahmin, "to holi—" But when he looked up from his amulet to wink, the god had gone.

the tale
of the
jealous fishermen
continued

The next night, four silent fishermen launched *The Dancing Woman*, silently lit the lamp, laid nets without a word, and sat down upon the thwarts to await the miracle.

Quickly was the first to break the silence.

"Is everybody here?" he said.

Luckyman looked at Stumbler, Stumbler at Shy, Shy at Quickly and then each checked the others.

"Yes."

"Yes."

"Yes."

"Well, then," said Quickly in a whisper, "is anybody anywhere else?"

None of the three dared answer, in such awe were they of the magic powder, but by the light of the lamp Quickly could see them slowly shake their heads.

"Nor me," he said, and sighed.

Then after a silence: "You all took it the right way," he asked anxiously, "and drank every drop?"

"Every drop," said Luckyman.

But Stumbler, lifting his heavy face, said: "Drop of what?"

"Water," said Quickly. "The water you had to put the powder in."

"Oh," said Stumbler. He groaned. "Did the priest say water? I forgot."

"Forgot?" said the other three in horror.

"I sprinkled it on my curry and rice," said Stumbler. "I wonder what'll happen to me now?" he added miserably.

"You won't be in the place you want to be," said Quickly in a threatening whisper. "You'll be in some deep, deep hole, miles underground, with devils pricking your bottom and serve you right for being a silly—"

"Sh!" said Luckyman. He held up his hand. The light from the brazier at the prow lit up one side of his brown figure and his handsome face.

"She's going to bed," said Luckyman. "She's loosening her hair. She's yawning."

Then the other three knew that it had happened to Luckyman first.

"Is she alone?" whispered Quickly. The sea was quiet and there was no noise save the tapping of the water on the side of *The Dancing Woman* as he waited for the answer.

"Quite alone," said Luckyman at last.

"Can you touch her?" said Stumbler.

There was another pause. Luckyman made no move except that he allowed his raised hand slowly to fall to his knee.

"I touched her," he said. "She felt it. But she brushed at her shoulder as though it was a fly."

"I can hardly believe it," said Quickly. "It seems such an impossible thing to . . ." His voice faded. Then, in a different tone, he said: "So that's where she hides the money she saves."

Then for a quarter of an hour neither Luckyman nor Quickly spoke. They would not answer Stumbler's questions. But from their eyes, their changing expressions, their little smiles and frowns, he knew that they were in *The Dancing Woman* but also at home with their wives.

"Has anything happened to you?" asked Shy at last.

"Nothing," said Stumbler. "Except I think I'm getting a stomach ache. What about you?"

"Me?" said Shy. "No. But, to tell the truth—it sounds foolish I know but . . ."

"So she drinks," said Stumbler suddenly in a mutter: and then, "I can't blame her. It can't be an easy life, living with me."

"Is she alone?" asked Shy. But Stumbler did not answer. Like the other two, he sat abstracted and silent on the thwarts of *The Dancing Woman*, there in the boat with Shy and yet not there at all.

Shy got up. He mended the fire, he eased the fishing tackle, he coiled a rope and he cursed himself for a fool. He alone of the four had not taken the powder. He had gone off by himself to put it in the jar of water, but then, thinking of peering unseen at his young wife, maybe in bed with her lover, he was overcome with embarrassment, and, hiding the powder in a tree, he had joined his braver companions on the beach.

But when the night's fishing had been done (after a fashion) and they were selling their catch to the merchant, Shy was glad that he had not taken the powder. His companions were all so abstracted, they all took so little interest in the bargaining, that the merchant straightway halved his usual price, complaining of a glut on the market. When the merchant named his figure Luckyman looked at him benignly and smiled a slow smile of pure pleasure. The merchant breathed heavily through his nose and plainly told himself he could have got away with a crueler price.

"They're right; I *am* a lucky man," said the smiling fisherman. He was seeing how the morning sun, falling on his wife's pillow, brought out all her beauty as she peacefully slept with her cheek upon her arm.

"You are," said the merchant. "And of course, I'm not going to take all the fish at that price. Only the big ones. For the little one's I can't go further than—"

He paused. He considered. He named the price and young Shy lost his temper. He lost it so thoroughly that for the first time in his life he spoke up for himself.

He attacked the merchant in a torrent of words. The merchant recoiled. The merchant waved his hands in a vain effort to calm him. Shy squeaked with rage. The merchant raised the price a rupee. Shy advanced upon him with a threatening gesture, and the merchant fell on his knees, raising, as he did so, the price by two rupees. Shy stood over him and dictated his own terms. As the merchant said afterwards, it was like being attacked by an abusive, swearing, red-eyed rabbit.

Luckyman, Stumbler, and Quickly observed all this with as much detachment as the market policemen who had been well bribed by the merchants to stay out of market-day quarrels.

When the merchant had paid and the money had been divided—the uninterested manner in which the bewitched three took their shining coins would have been a lesson to a saint—the four friends set out across the mud flats for home.

Shy was full of his victory. He went over his argument with the merchant step by step, greatly improving his phrases, stopping every so often for his friends' applause. But all Luckyman said was:

"You made so much noise I was afraid she'd hear and wake up. I didn't want her to do that. She looked so pretty. But of course you were two miles away."

All that Quickly would say was:

"I heard her murmur, 'I'll be late with Tu-Tu's breakfast.' At least I think she said Tu-Tu. That's what she calls me, you know. But just then you bawled something very rude at that man and I couldn't quite . . ."

All that Stumbler said was:

"She snores."

For a brief time of triumph, while they had been dividing up the money, poor Shy had thought of appointing himself the manager of their partnership. He had thought of declaring:

"Fellows, you go on watching your wives. Leave all the business to me. What do you say?"

But now that moment was past. As he walked along the road by the side of his distant-eyed and silent companions, ignored by them or, worse, considered a nuisance when he spoke, he felt lonely, forlorn, and out of the running. When Quickly, turning his eyes away from the horizon for a moment, asked him:

"You don't say anything about your own wife. Is everything all right?" Shy said: "It will be," and he left his friends at the entrance to the village, and went secretly to the tree in which he had put the powder.

It was still there. He tucked the packet into his loincloth and went home. Looking at his wife as she bent over the fire he thought once again how embarrassing it would be if he had to watch her in bed with her lover. He said:

"Rani, I want you to remember that whatever happens it is because I love you."

"Yes, yes," said Rani. "Eat your breakfast."

That evening, before he set out to join his friends for the night's fishing, he took the powder. When he met his companions he explained to them how the night before he did not have the benefit of the powder, and how, this night, he had

taken it. They said they were glad that he had changed his
mind. But they were soon to be very sorry.

That night Shy was the first to go home to his wife in spirit.
They had just laid the nets in a circle, and Shy was looking down
the black side of *The Dancing Woman*. He was watching the
light from the lamp caper and shiver in the water, when the
change began.

It started with the sounds of things. At night, the small noises
of the boat—the straining tackle, the footfalls on the planks—
were always echoing as though the sea were hollow. Shy was
fond of this vastness behind the noises and he missed it if he
stayed long ashore. The first thing that happened was that a
box seemed to close about his ears. The vastness went, the hollow sounds gave way to the padded sounds of dry land. Then
a flicker of light on the water below him stood still and became
a brass cooking pot. He recognised the cooking pot as one that
his wife always kept on the floor near her fireplace. Next, he
saw the fireplace, then the wall on either side of it, then four
walls, and he was home.

The fourth wall of the room was not of smoothed-down clay
like the other three. It was a curtain of strong cloth, once white
but grey now with the smoke from charcoal fires, and across it
danced angular figures of men and women, in rough imitation
of a village dance. His wife had made them and sewn them onto
the curtain in the first few months of their setting up house.
He had boasted round the village that he had married a beauty
and a houseproud woman at the same time—a rare thing, as
everybody said. But as the marriage wore on, she relied more
and more on her charms to please her husband and less on her
sense of art. Her choice was wise and pleased her husband; a
curtain is only a curtain, but in a woman there is infinite variety.

Yet her husband, in his more elevated moments, was still fond of the curtain. He looked at it now, recalling the happiness of their earlier first love. He had only to lift it, pass into the bedroom, to see if that love had been betrayed.

He hesitated. He remembered a game he had played as a child to settle prettier problems. He told over the figures, saying as he did so:

"I *am* a cuckold. No, I'm *not*. I *am* a cuckold. No, I'm *not*. I *am* a cuckold," and so on. But from the tail of his eye he sensed an ominous deficiency of figures. Like most shy men he was not, in the final test, a coward. He lifted the curtain.

Rani lay chaste and sleeping, their baby in her arms.

Just then there was a noise from the house next door, which belonged to Stumbler. Rani woke. Her great soft eyes looked straight at her husband. Seeing her thus, gracefully lying in the bed and looking at him, Shy was seized with desire. He thought passionately of taking her in his arms. He knew from the others that she would feel his touch, but he wondered, since he was invisible, whether she would altogether know what to make of it. While he hesitated, he heard voices in the next house. He listened, and Rani listened. Then Rani sank back into sleep, and Shy listened alone.

When Stumbler had moved in spirit from *The Dancing Woman* to his house, he was greeted by no shining pots or artistic curtains. There was not one child but eight. They fed in a circle sitting on mats on the floor. When they had done, it was his wife's custom to collect the metal platters and make a heap of them by the doorpost, a convenient place from which to take them to the well to be scoured and brought back, gleaming, to the house. Each time she made the pile, she saw them clean and bright, as they soon would be, and proudly ranged along the mud wall as they were in other women's houses. But

other women did not have eight children, nor Stumbler, nor
an exhausted feeling which had to be removed with sips of the
fermented sap of the palm tree. So each day the platters stayed
by the door, and here Stumbler, returning home in the spirit,
fell over them.

The noise woke the youngest child and an intelligent boy of
eight. The baby yelled ferociously, awakening (as we have seen)
the neighbour, but not its mother. This was the duty of the boy
of eight, who pulled her hair and slapped her cheeks until she,
groaning, sat up. When she heard the baby's squeals she rose,
pushed the hair from her face, and took the baby in her arms.

"Drunk or sober," said Stumbler to himself, "she's a good
mother."

The intelligent boy lit the lamp. His mother sat on the floor
and nursed the baby, pushing a sweetmeat into its mouth as frequently as it spat it out. Stumbler, pressed against the wall, saw
all this with a father's pride. The baby, during those moments
when it could free its mouth, was making a sound which (it
had been agreed between husband wife) meant that it wanted
Stumbler.

"Why isn't Dada home any nights?" asked the boy of eight.

"Because he is a fisherman," said the boy's mother. "And if
he didn't go out at night there'd be no money to buy you food."

"Why does he go to sleep in the daytime when he comes
home?" the boy next asked.

"Because he is very tired," said his mother. "Fishing is very
hard work."

"Will he always work?"

"No. One day he will give it up and be at home all night."

"When?"

"Before he trips over something and falls in the sea and gets
himself drowned," said his mother, "let us hope."

"When I grow up, shall I be a fisherman?" asked the boy, and Stumbler's eyes filled with fond tears.

"If you grow up to be as big a fool as your father," said the boy's mother, "I suppose you'll have to be."

In the still Indian night these words could be plainly heard by Shy and they brought his mind back to *The Dancing Woman*. He immediately found himself there. Seeing that the nets were straining their ropes, he called the attention of Quickly to them and together the four hauled in an early and enormous catch. For an hour, while the fish cascaded from the nets like wriggling pieces of metal, he did not think of his wife. Then he rested and mopped his forehead. He once more thought of Rani and on the instant was standing outside his house. He did not go in, but deliberately bringing his mind back to the re-markable catch of fish, he found himself, as he suspected that he would, back both in spirit and in body on *The Dancing Woman*.

While the four friends cleaned the nets of fish which had fixed themselves so firmly that they could not be shaken out, he explained his discovery of the way in which the powder worked. From their short grunts in reply he learned that they, too, had come upon the secret. For the rest of the night all four agreed to keep their minds off women and upon fish, for such a catch had not been known in these waters for twenty years. In their hearts they thanked the great god Shiva for thus mak-ing up their losses, and the god, who was particularly listening to these four of his devotees, heard. In reply, he put it into their hearts to make an offering that coming morning at his temple.

They were in magnificent fettle with the merchant. No longer distracted by being in two places at once, they drove him to offer a fair price: and the envious looks of the other fisher-men told the merchant that there would be no glut. He bought, and he paid, and he paid so much that Luckyman, Stumbler, Quickly, and Shy had to take off their turbans to make a bag to hold the money.

As they walked away each one said with great earnestness to the others that they should make an offering to the Brahmin: not only for his wonderful kindness in giving them the powder— and here they all clicked their teeth in astonishment at its properties—but also in acknowledgement of the god's new favours.

With the look of devoted and determined men, they marched up to the temple. The Brahmin, seeing them coming, cursed the mendicant and his powder, and tucking up his robes, he fled round the back of the temple into a nearby clump of tamarind trees to weather out what he feared would be the inevitable storm of disappointed protest. He wished that he had restrained himself from making a charge for the powder and promised himself that he would return the money. He was greatly surprised to find, on returning to the sanctuary when the coast was clear, four neat little piles of silver rupees laid out on the altar's lowest step.

Meanwhile the four fishermen made their way home in the best of spirits, filled with that most delectable of sentiments, the sense of having done a virtuous thing without particularly feeling the expense. In this happy mood Luckyman and Shy fell to the pleasant task of comparing the beauties of their respective wives when seen, by an invisible husband, as they lay sleeping.

Shy kept the conversation within modest bounds, but not so Luckyman. He drew such a picture of his wife that, as they came within sight of their homes, Shy's imagination was inflamed. On entering the house and being greeted by his Rani, Shy was not as overwhelmed by her beauty as was his custom. She seemed, he thought, a little dull in her looks. He asked her if she felt unwell, but she, with surprise, said:

"No, no, not in the least. Eat your breakfast."

From breakfast to their day bed, from day bed to suppertime, from the suppertime kiss and *The Dancing Woman* to watching Rani asleep again as he stood invisible by the curtain seemed for Shy a matter of a passing hour, his thoughts were so alluringly disturbed.

Even when he looked at Rani his thoughts wandered elsewhere—and so, of course, did his invisible body: such was the nature of the powder.

He found himself, that is to say, in Luckyman's bedroom, looking down at Luckyman's sleeping wife.

Luckyman had been pointed when he had described his wife and he had told the truth. Young Shy had seen few women save his wife for more than a few moments. Fishermen's manners did not allow staring at girls, and to stare at another man's wife as Shy was doing now would have been cause for complaint to the village headman and a fine. Shy gazed, secure and enraptured.

Then he cautiously looked round the room to see if Luckyman were present. Remembering that he would not see him if he were (would Luckyman see *him*? who knew? the powder was unpredictable) he even more cautiously thought of fish. As quick as his thought he was back in the boat. He noted with satisfaction that there was trouble with the tackle and that Luckyman was bent over it with every appearance of being there and nowhere else. Languorously allowing his thoughts to slide, Shy transferred himself to Luckyman's bedroom.

Luckyman's wife was called Silvermoon and she was a great dreamer of dreams. She had made something of a study of them, and she knew by heart some hundreds of rhymed jingles which helped in their interpretation. Silvermoon would even dream for other people: they had merely to give her something to hold in her hand which belonged to them and she would dream dreams symbolic of their future.

But that night Silvermoon had no need of jingles to interpret her strangest of strange dreams, and she was not, she felt sure, dreaming it on behalf of anybody else. The words whispered so passionately in her ear was meant for her alone; the invisible caresses were far from symbolic; and unlike her other dreams, it went on, deliciously, even when she had woken up. When it was over and she was alone again, she lay in bed, pondering. She was puzzled but not utterly at sea. Her visitor, she reflected (but in her own simple words) though lacking all flesh, was still plainly subject to its promptings.

As for Shy, he fled the house both elated and alarmed. His elation was only to be expected; his alarm was due to his peculiar circumstances. A lover must be prepared for a husband returning unexpectedly: there are windows, cupboards, and backdoors to help him. But there are no aids for a lover who must guard against a husband returning invisibly. For all Shy knew, Luckyman might have been in the room. But then, Shy reflected as he focussed his corporeal eyes on the details of *The Dancing Woman*, if he had been, for all *he* would know, his wife might have been having nothing more than a restless night. This, Shy decided, was the husband's problem. He was glad to find him still intent upon the trouble with the nets.

In fact the trouble with the nets had been such that Luckyman had been unable, all night, to summon up sufficient interest in his wife to get himself away. Stumbler had paid a fleeting and preoccupied visit home; Quickly had made a swift inspection. They were not less in love with their wives; but to a fisherman, when his net is entangled, nothing is more irrelevant than a woman.

The trouble was mastered just about dawn, and there being

no fish worth selling, Luckyman went straight home. He greeted Silvermoon and as usual asked her if she had had a good night. As usual she said that she had. She went on to say (and this was also customary) that she had dreamed the strangest dream.

Luckyman yawned. "Ya—ooo—ho—hum—what was it?" he asked. The question was as formal as it was polite; from long experience he knew that she would tell him, invited or not.

But she hesitated. She blushed.

Luckyman observed her blush. He put down the morsel of food that he was carrying to his mouth without tasting it. He repeated his question, this time without a yawn.

Silvermoon still hesitated, for she felt—she did not know why—that this was a dream that it would be wiser to leave untold. But when her husband pressed the question a third time, habit was too much for her, and she said:

"A prince came and made love to me."

"A prince? How did you know he was a Prince?"

"His skin was like silk," she said, "and . . . and . . ." Her usual flow of description was stemmed. "And . . . well, his skin was like silk."

"What did he look like?" asked Luckyman suspiciously.

"I don't know," said Silvermoon. "I didn't see him."

"You mean you couldn't see him because it was dark?" said Luckyman.

"It wasn't as dark as that—in my dream, I mean. He was— well, it was all a dream, of course—but he was—you couldn't see him."

"You mean he was like air?" Luckyman waved his hand in demonstration.

"That's right."

"Oh."

"Don't look so angry. It was only a dream," said Silvermoon, distressed by the cloud which had settled on her husband's face.

"Oh," he said again. "A dream, was it?" He lifted some food to his mouth and put it down once more without it reaching his lips. But so deep in thought was he that he chewed on nothing for a while.

"Listen," he said. "Say nothing about this to anyone. D'you understand? Nothing."

Silvermoon nodded, her eyes wide. An hour later when Luckyman was lying sleepless on his bed she was at the well. The other women, noticing her unusual silence, pressed her to talk. She refused. They pressed again. Fatally, she said:

"I have had a dream which my husband has forbidden me to tell to anyone."

By the time that the sun was in the zenith the whole village knew that Luckyman's wife had been visited by an invisible stranger with charms so extraordinary (including a skin like silk) that it was plain that he was either a god or a very handsome devil.

the tale
of the
jealous fishermen
concluded

That night *The Dancing Woman* was wrecked.

There was a bad omen of it in the evening. As Stumbler was leaving his house to go down to the beach, his wife, who had been incapable or unwilling to speak to him all day, pushed back her hair from her face and said:

"Have you heard the gossip?"

Stumbler said he had not.

"Silvermoon's dreamed she has a prince who makes love to her, only you can't see him."

Stumbler said he didn't understand. His wife ignored this remark, as one ignores a familiar mole on the face of one's husband or wife.

"I don't suppose I shall dream anything like that," she went on. "I shall just dream my usual dream about you."

"What is that?" said Stumbler fondly.

"You have fallen overboard and you are drowning and I am shouting on the bank, 'Swim!' because you are within ten feet of dry land. You keep shouting, 'What?' Then you drown."

"You shouldn't talk like that," said Stumbler. "It'll bring bad luck."

So it turned out. There was a light breeze blowing as they launched their boat but the night was very dark. Stumbler, made

gloomy by his wife's parting words, foretold bad weather. But
the others brushed his fears aside. They seemed very preoccupied, each with his own thoughts, and Stumbler feared that
it would be a night when little attention would be paid to fishing. For himself, now that his fears for his wife's chastity had
been set at rest, he had little interest left in women. Looking
round at this absorbed companions he envied their young
manhood.

They raised the lateen sail and *The Dancing Woman* jumped
away in a fashion which Stumbler, at the tiller, felt to be a little
too lively. The others noticed nothing. Luckyman and Quickly
were seated amidships. Shy was up at the prow dismantling the
fire basket (for with a breeze blowing it would be no use) and
fitting some other tackle.

Quickly said to Luckyman:

"Strange story, that about your wife's dream."

"Women's nonsense," said Luckyman. "I told her not to
tell anyone."

"Lover who can't be seen," said Quickly. "Sounds very like—"

But Shy interrupted him, turning back and speaking with a
new boldness.

"I've often wondered," he said, "but you know that I kept
that packet of powder overnight in a tree. Well, suppose—that's
what I say to myself—suppose somebody had found it, and
stolen some, thinking it was a medicine or—well, you know
what I mean."

"It's possible," said Quickly. "No way of finding out. A lover
you can't see, eh? That's a lover you can't catch, it seems
to me."

"Yes," said Shy decidedly, and turned back to his work.

Luckyman stared at Shy's back for a long moment.

"Skin of silk," he said, and spat on the floorboards.

Nothing more was said aboard the boat for the next hour. The breeze was too fresh for them to do anything but put on the big cone-shaped trawl net. This was soon done, and the fishermen chose their favourite positions in the boat to wait for the net to fill. By the light of the oil lamp that hung from the mast, Stumbler saw each of his companions fall into the abstracted and languid state that marked their spiritual departure to their wives. Stumbler shook his head and sighed. *The Dancing Woman*, it seemed to him, did the same in sympathy. The wind grew colder against his cheek. Stumbler tightened his hand on the tiller and began to form a sentence in his head that would make his companions aware of the danger that Stumbler felt in the air, under his hands, and in his seaman's bones.

Five minutes later the gale struck them. It was the rim of a cyclone. The tiller jarred in Stumbler's hand as thought it were grinding against rock: the lateen sail shook itself free of its ropes and streamed out before the wind like a banner: *The Dancing Woman* turned a drunken pirouette.

She was beyond Stumbler's managing. He could sail out a monsoon storm, but this wind was a sea terror that was new to him. He called desperately to Quickly to come and take the tiller. Quickly had sailed the Persian Gulf; Quickly had once sailed a dhow; Quickly could master *The Dancing Woman* now if anyone could; but Quickly sat on the thwarts, his head rolling with the boat, smiling vacantly into the storm as if into the face of a woman.

So with Luckyman and Shy. Stumbler, raising his voice above the wind, made them hear him; they rolled love-sick eyes at him and did not move. Then the tiller won its struggle with Stumbler's wrist: it broke free and wave after wave of foam-topped water came eagerly aboard. Stumbler called to his companions again and again but now he could not even see their

looks, for the lantern was gone and there was no light from
the sky: soon there was no sky at all, but only flying water.

With this peril as a goad, Stumbler rose above himself: he
strove, he wrestled, he sweated, he beat his skull, and at last he
managed to force his reluctant mind to think. He knew that if
his companions could be made truly aware of the danger in
which the boat stood (for now they moved about their tasks
like men of lead, too slowly and too late), they would give up
their dalliances, leave their wives in spirit as well as in body,
and save themselves. But how could this be done? Shouting and
shaking, even blows, were useless. Stumbler, drenched and dismayed, suddenly saw that he must go to their houses and, invisible appealing to the invisible, recall them.

He fixed his mind on his wife. Her charms were not easy
to visualise, although he loved her, and in a running sea whipped
by a gale, her allure had never been less. Obstinately, his mind
and his body both stayed in the boat. He whispered her name—
the same result. He thought of her when young—he had forgotten what she looked like. Half choked with salt water, he
imagined her dead to excite his emotions—his grief was inade-
quate to shift him an inch. Desperately he began to shout coarse
words into the wind and people the howling darkness with
images of gross delights they had known together but which
were never mentioned between them. At last, thanking the gods
that his wife was no lady, Stumbler heard the wind die and its
sound give way to his wife's snores. He threw her the hastiest
of glances as she lay surrounded by her children and, invisible
and dry, he sped away to Quickly's house.

He entered the bedroom. A single light burned in an alcove
in the mud wall, flickering in the wind which had already begun
to blow over the village, heralding the approach of the storm
that raged out at sea.

"Quickly," he whispered.

There was no reply. But Quickly's wife laughed softly and whispered and the coverlet of her bed humped itself in a manner for which she alone, a slim woman, could not possibly be responsible.

Stumbler went to the bed and seized where he judged Quickly's shoulder to be.

"Get up," he whispered. "It's me."

Quickly's wife giggled again.

"Go away," replied a male whisper from the bed. "Go away, you old fool."

"Not till you come with me, Quickly," said Stumbler.

"What's that you say, you wicked man?" said Quickly's wife tenderly.

"The boat's going down. You've got to save it," said Stumbler, shaking the coverlet furiously.

"Get Quickly," said the man underneath it.

"Aren't you Quickly?" said Stumbler, forgetting to whisper in his surprise.

"What is it?" said Quickly's wife sharply. "What is going on in my bed?" And the voice under the coverlet, answering Stumbler's question, said shakingly:

"No, I'm Shy."

"Then what are you doing in Quickly's bed?" shouted Stumbler.

"Well, what Quickly does," said the coverlet, falling back. "Anyway, don't shout so much; I'm getting up." But the last part of this statement was drowned by the loud screaming of Quickly's wife, her sense of propriety at last outraged.

"She'll wake the neighbours," said Shy and then consoled himself with the reflection that even if the neighbours came he could not be seen. At which the woman, as though able not only to hear his voice but also read his thoughts, put words to her screaming:

"Help, help, help! Shy is trying to—"

Shy clapped his hand over her mouth.

"Quick!" he said to Stumbler. "Into the street."

Once there, they paused for a moment to gather their wits, the woman calling tearfully upon her absent husband's name, evidence not only of her peril but of her faithfulness.

"But where *is* Quickly?" said Stumbler.

"I don't know," said Shy. "He wasn't there when I went in. I scouted around with my hands out."

At that moment the storm struck its first real blow at the village. A great gust of wind swept through the streets, and with it came the thatch of the house which stood next to Shy's.

"Is it a bad storm out there?" Shy shouted at Stumbler, and Stumbler nodded, forgetting that he was as invisible as the tearing wind.

"What did you say?" Shy shouted again and Stumbler said at the top of his voice:

"It's the worst I've ever seen. We *must* find Quickly."

The wind struck again and shook the roof of Shy's home.

"Rani!" he yelled. "I must warn her."

He began to run but it was unnecessary. No sooner had he thought of his wife, than he stood beside her bed.

The little lamp fluttered in the breeze and gave too fitful a light for him to see anything clearly.

"Rani!" he said. "There's a terrible storm blowing. Get up and go to the headman's house. It'll be safer because he's got a roof."

"Now you sound just like my husband," said Rani from the shadows. "He always worries so. Don't go yet, Your Royal Highness."

"Who's there?" demanded Shy, his voice rising.

A hand came from the bed. It felt Shy's calf.

"A skin," said a masculine and derisive voice, "like silk."

"What is the meaning of this," shouted Shy, his voice breaking into a boyish treble. "Luckyman! come out of my wife's bed!"

"The meaning is," said the voice of Luckyman, "that you and me is *quits*."

Rani wailed; the wind howled; and the invisible Shy swore in a fashion that surprised himself. Above the din came the voice of Stumbler:

"If you'd only all be quiet I could tell you where Quickly is. I've nearly worked it out but my brain won't go any more. Shy was with Quickly's wife—weren't you, Shy?—and here's Luckyman with yours—and mine's sleeping alone, the gods bless her, so Quickly must be—Oh, dear, it's gone again."

"Silvermoon!" roared Luckyman, and the thought of her striking all three at once, they were instantly in her bedroom.

The lamp was in a horn case. It burned steadily. They could see the coverlet over Silvermoon heave desperately.

"But I *must* go," said Quickly's voice protestingly. "Can't you hear the gale? I must go back to the *Dan*—My dear, I tell you I must go."

"Oh," said Silvermoon, embracing the top edge of the coverlet, "so soon? What does a little wind matter? We're quite safe and warm here. My other prince stayed much longer."

"I know, my dearest," pleaded the unseen Quickly. "But perhaps he wasn't a sailor prince. I am, you see, so I must—I must get back to my ship."

"You must," said Stumbler, "she's sinking."

"And by the gods," said Luckyman to the coverlet, "may you go down with her."

Thus at last, all four thinking of *The Dancing Woman,* they found themselves back aboard her.

Quickly seized the tiller. The others, knocked down continually by the incoming waves, said their prayers. Quickly tried to get her head round into the wind, but it was too late. With a great leap and a shudder that made the fishermen's teeth rattle in their heads, she went ashore on a bank of mud and lay broadside to the sea and wind.

Thus the four friends were high, but by no means dry, for the next six hours, when, the gale having blown itself out, they were rescued after heroic risks by one of the fishermen they had jealously suspected of seducing their wives.

One day some four weeks later Luckyman, Stumbler, Quickly, and Shy were going sadly towards the temple, each carrying a small bundle wrapped in a piece of cloth, when they met a holy man belonging to one of the mendicant orders. He looked venerable, and his forehead was heavily scored with lines made by deep thinking.

"Where are you going, my children?" said the great god Shiva.

"To the temple," said Quickly, and all four bowed to the holy man.

"What are you carrying?" asked Shiva and they showed him a small silver net, a small silver bracelet, a small silver model of a man, and a silver phallus.

"We are all very unfortunate men," said Quickly. "We were favoured by the great god Shiva but we forgot to make him the presents he asked for. So we lost our boat, and we must build another one, some day."

"Some day," echoed Luckyman dolefully.

"But when?" said Shy, while Stumbler groaned in misery.

"We have spent the last of our savings on these gifts," said Quickly. "We thought that it was our duty. May the great god smile on them."

The great god did.

"You are good people," he said, "and I think that you have a certain powder that makes you invisible."

All four hung their heads.

"Master," said Quickly, "the Brahmin has told you. Yes, we have."

"Then take back your gifts to your homes and sell them. The great god is satisfied with your willingness to make so great a sacrifice. Then go to the temple, tell the Brahmin of your adventures and give him all that remains of the powder. Do this, and I promise that you will prosper. Now I, who am a devotee of the great god, have a message from the god himself for you. Go down on your knees."

They obeyed, for the holy man spoke with awesome authority.

"When," he said, "in your new boat, you think of your wives on shore, you shall always say these words aloud to one another."

With that the great god went to each of them and whispered in their ears.

Then he dismissed them, with a blessing.

That afternoon the great god Shiva rose to his full height of seventy-five feet, frightening the animals of the village, who alone could see him in his giant splendour. He looked at the temple and saw through its walls as through glass. He looked at the Brahmin who was standing alone before the altar, the powder in his right hand, and Shiva saw through the priest as through still water. He looked at the Brahmin's soul and there he met an obstinate opacity, for Shiva, though a great god, was not Brahma himself.

The Brahmin spoke to himself and the god heard him. "How convincing they were with their story," the Brahmin mused. "Suppose it were true, after all. I would just take a little of this powder—in water, they said—and then Rani and Silvermoon would have another prince to bring them joy." He licked his lips. The god listened intently. He heard the Brahmin chuckle. The god's eye quivered. The butter on the stone lingam on the altar began gently to smoke. Then he heard the Brahmin snort:

"But nonsense, *nonsense*. What am I saying? It's all part of the game and if I start believing in my own hocus-pocus, why, I shall lose my self-respect."

With that he left the temple and threw the earth contemptuously on the ground beside the well, from where it had originally come. He then returned and, with a sceptical smile, began to intone the first of the evening prayers.

The great god retired to his mountain to think the matter out. But the more he considered the human soul—and particularly the Brahmin's—the more, in a godlike fashion, he grew confused. At last he gave the problem up.

"It is too deep for me," he said. "Brahma alone knows. It is a pity that he may not be disturbed."

So, during the long nights when the new *Dancing Woman* was out at sea and the four fishermen would start thinking of their wives on shore, one of them (and it was nearly always Stumbler) would say:

"Friends, remember the message."

Then the four men would repeat devoutly to one another:

"What is the use of being jealous? A wife is a woman; a woman is a woman; and a man cannot be in two places at once."

But Luckyman, Quickly, and young Shy would think for a moment of the time when they could.

Then they would all get on with their fishing, in a tranquil frame of mind.

BOOK THREE

the siege
of
lanka

CHAPTER ONE

a hanòbook
foR
RECRUItS

The war between the allies of Rama and the
King of Lanka is one of the most famous in the history of India.
Most of the leading generals on both sides won striking victories
and those that did not employed scribes to write their reminiscences, which were even more strikingly victorious.

Hostilities began in November. The first move was an exchange of ambassadors. Both embassies declared that they
abhorred war and wished for a just peace. The ambassadors of
Rama described a just peace as consisting in the return of Sita
to her rightful husband, the execution by plunging into molten
lead of Ravan, the demolition of one third of the houses of
Lanka, the razing of its walls, the imposition of a tax of one half
of the income of all the inhabitants for twenty years, and the
life imprisonment of all the Lankastrian generals.

These terms were rejected by all concerned but with special
vehemence by the generals, some of whom privately informed
the allied ambassadors that, while they could see reason in most
of the demands, they considered that the last clause spoiled the
whole affair. Ravan, in the name of his cheering people, denounced the offer as evidence of the barbarity and inhumanity
of the enemy. He in his turn proposed, as a lover of peace and
in the name of his people (who this time shook their heads at
his moderation) that a ten-year truce be proclaimed on condition that Rama gave his free consent to Sita's divorce and re-

215

marriage to him, Ravan, after which Rama was to be torn to pieces by wild horses as an enemy of humanity: further, the allied army was to return to their homes, leaving their weapons behind them; an indemnity equivalent to three times the cost of the war so far to Lanka was to be paid by the principal allies; all officers over the rank of sergeant-major were to do three years forced labour in Lanka, and all generals were to be imprisoned for life.

These terms were indignantly rejected by the allies as evidence of the Lankastrians' barbarity and inhumanity. The ambassadors on both sides returned. Rama's ambassadors, who had been led blindfold through the streets of Lanka and locked in an inner room during all the negotiations, informed him that the inside face of the walls of Lanka was crumbling and certain elements of the army ready to mutiny because of arrears of pay. Their report greatly heartened the troops and they were decorated for loyal service to the allied cause. The ambassadors of Ravan, who had been taken to a sealed tent in palanquins with boards nailed to the sides instead of curtains, reported that Rama had already quarrelled with two of the four principal rajas who were assisting him, one of the generals was permanently drunk, and several consignments of arms have proved to be boxes filled with old scrap iron and stones. Their reports greatly strengthened the belief of the Lankastrians that it would be a quick victory.

At the end of the war it was found that the reports of both embassies were substantially true. This was not extraordinary. While they were not magicians able to see through a blindfold, on the other hand they were old soldiers, who had been to the wars before.

Both sides now instructed their general staffs to draw up a plan of campaign.

The general staff of Rama and his allies met for several days
on end in a tent pitched in a location remote from the lines.
It was heavily guarded to prevent the escape of secrets. A local
milkmaid, gathering succulent weeds to feed her cow, contrived
(none knew how) to gather them within three feet of the tent.
She was arrested together with her whole family and (through
a fault in transmission of orders) the cow. She was suspended
upside down over a well by a frayed rope, her father was beaten
with ox whips, and the cow (through the fault of an over-zealous
corporal) kept under strict surveillance. They proved, however,
to know nothing of the plan which, after three days of deep
deliberation, the general staff had evolved.

This was the plan.

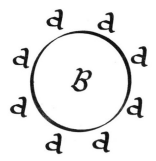

The circle represented the fortifications of Lanka, ignoring
small deviations in the course of the walls, to accommodate the
lie of the land. The letter A represented the disposition of the
armed forces of the allies. That is to say, the letters A represented the places where the forces were at the time of the
deliberations of the general staff. The letter B represented the
place where they ought to be at the end of the campaign. The
tactical manoeuvre which the generals had evolved consisted in
a movement, duly co-ordinated and begun at the most favour-

able moment, from the points A to the point B. In view of the intervention of the wall, the generals had decided that this manoeuvre, the only one militarily sound in the circumstances, called for more bows, more arrows, more scaling ladders, more movable turrets, more chariots, more sappers, more miners, and more money than they had at present got. This plan was laid before Rama, who, asking if they would also require more generals, was told that they had, fortunately, enough.

Shortly after the formulation of this master plan, a young soldier from the Nilgiri Hills was crawling among some bushes which surrounded the foot of the walls of Lanka in search of fennel, the taste of which in his curry he was inordinately fond. Having made his way for a considerable distance round the walls, he came across two outlying towers joined to each other and to the main fortifications by curtain walls. Observing no sentinels, he approached the curtain walls, which seemed to be broken in places and therefore a good place in which to find fennel. He did not find his herb, but he found something which interested him even more—the broken part of the wall constituted a breach ten feet wide that had been hastily repaired by piling the fallen stones loosely one upon the other. These had again fallen down in part, and it was possible for a man to walk through the gap. The young soldier being a hardy mountaineer who did not know what it was to be afraid, promptly walked through the gap. He found himself in long grass which, growing higher than his head, gave him excellent cover. Moving cautiously through this he came up to what should have been the main wall behind the outlying towers, but which was in fact merely a foundation two feet high, the wall itself having been destroyed, whether by an earthquake or by some previous enemy he could not tell, and which had never been rebuilt. He returned immediately to the camp with his news. After a brief court-martial he was condemned to death as a spy sent by the enemy to lure the allies into an ambush.

The unfortunate man appealed to Rama, who, in great perplexity, spoke to Valmiki, who had accompanied him to the field of war. Valmiki said:

"Either you must execute the soldier or you must execute your general staff. I recommend you kill the soldier. It is an accepted principle of warfare that when generals make mistakes it is the soldiers and not they who get killed for it."

Since there was no disputing this, Rama reluctantly confirmed the sentence, but mercifully commanded that, instead of being trampled to death by an elephant, the man should be strangled with a bowstring.

The generals, nevertheless, sent reconnoitring parties to spy out the breach, which they did with so much noise and alarm that the defenders of Lanka were made aware of their danger and immediately repaired the gap. The Lankastrian sergeant in charge of that section of the walls had previously reported their defenceless state, but his advice had gone unheeded in the press of business. This business consisted in drawing up their own tactical plan for the raising of the siege. It was based on the supposition that Lanka was now completely surrounded by an impenetrable ring of armed men. In view of this there was no possibility of help coming from outside and the only hope for Lanka was clearly to prepare for a long siege and to wear down the enemies' will to fight by the stubbornness of its resistance.

A married soldier impressed from a village some ten miles away, having been seized by an ungovernable desire to sleep with his wife, let himself down one night over the walls of Lanka, and with no more difficulty than having to lie still while an infrequent sentry passed, made his way safely through a gap in Rama's lines into his wife's arms. He, however, was too wise

to return. He stayed in his village until the battle was over and
for some fifty years afterwards. In this old age he was fond of
telling his grandchildren how he escaped the great slaughter of
the siege of Lanka. They listened to him politely but did not
hold him in any great esteem.

Preparations now began for the assault, but this was delayed
by an unforeseen event. The generals had set much store by a
mace which had been designed by an ironsmith who was married to a daughter of the senior general. This was unlike the
maces generally in use. It ingeniously employed the mo-
mentum which the wielder gave it in striking at his enemy to
lay low one, at least, of the soldiers on either side of the adversary. In addition to the normal spikes this mace had a heavy
iron ball attached to a chain which in turn was stapled to the
mace's top. Special exercises were decreed for the troops to learn
the use of this novel weapon. But on the first of these it was
discovered that the mace was too heavy to be lifted higher than
a man's navel.

The general who was the father-in-law of the inventor was
greatly chagrined, and although he could not be said to have
been wrong, since he was the senior general, he felt that he owed
it to his position to insist upon fresh and sturdier troops. A detachment of near-giants from the Carnatic was brought with all
possible speed to join the forces. These found no difficulty in
raising the mace but being men of an impetuous nature, not too
well endowed with intelligence, each exercise very nearly halved
their numbers since the balls struck their companions as frequently as they struck the stakes that represented the future
enemy. The general, however, was content. He pointed out that
the introduction of the new weapon had proved a stiffener of
the army's morale, since it gave such troops who neither used it

nor were near it confidence that, in the matter of inventive military science, they were the Lankastrians' superior.

The bustle of preparations was diversified by a comic incident—although tragic in its outcome for one participant—that caused much amusement in the ranks. An unknown apothecary waylaid every officer he could in an attempt to interest them in a black powder which, he said, when ignited, would explode with such force that, if placed in a suitable tube, it would raise a heavy projectile high enough in the air to go over the walls of Lanka and to descend destructively inside the city. This charlatan—or crackpot, for opinions about him among the generals were divided as to whether he was a swindler or a lunatic—became such a nuisance that the senior general finally ordered him out of the military lines. He was twice found peddling his black substance after this. On the second occasion he was bound and seated on a keg of his own powder, and a torch was applied to it. There was a deafening report, and although it was impossible to see if he had actually risen higher than the walls of Lanka, it was generally agreed, with much hilarity, that a part of him might well have done.

Valmiki, who witnessed this punishment, remarked to the senior general that the powder was certainly as effective as its inventor had claimed. At which the senior general clapped the poet on the back and said: "So it was; so it was. And it would be a damned effective weapon, if only we could get all the enemies' soldiers to *sit on the kegs*." This remark raised a general laugh against Valmiki, in which the poet, in so far as his grin grew even more marked, was seen to join.

the
challenge

The preparations for the fighting went on for three months, for there is no person more pacific than a military expert once fighting is inevitable. There are a thousand details to settle, innumerable exercises to perform; if an army marches on its belly, a general staff wins campaigns on its backside. When the later historians of this famous war speak of the allied army sitting down around the walls of Lanka, so far as the higher command was concerned, they do not speak metaphorically.

We must now return to Luxmun, who, as we know, was a more impetuous type of soldier.

It was Luxmun who had brought about the great alliance for the rescue of Sita. It had therefore been agreed by all the rajas and even by their staff officers that Luxmun should be given a post of high authority in the expedition. They had suggested this to Rama, who readily agreed. Rama would not have accepted, in any case, a different arrangement. He loved his brother, although he rarely spoke of his affection, and never (more importantly) thought about it. It follows that his love was a real one.

With very little debate Luxmun was given the post of Commandant of the Royal Guard, a name given to a body of some five hundred picked men whose duty was to guard the person and the standard of Rama in battle. Among the prerogatives of his rank were the right to fight from a battle-car, or chariot, the right to have his own bodyguard of ten men, and freedom to forage and loot as the fancy took him. These privileges pleased him: one other did not, and that was the right to a place in the planning conferences of the general staff. He begged to be excused from this duty but his brother insisted, saying that Luxmun as a prince of royal blood could not, with honour, refuse. Luxmun, as always, obeyed his brother, and went.

Rama was sometimes present, but not always. When he went he felt that he owed it to his position to speak. When he spoke the military men felt that they owed it to his dignity to listen. They also felt that they owed it to their own dignity never to follow any of his suggestions. Rama, noticing this, more and more frequently appointed Luxmun to represent him, with the duty of telling him what had taken place.

Luxmun was able to follow their tactical plans for the siege of Lanka, but he confessed that the general conversation of the warriors puzzled and dismayed him. Although Luxmun had done a great deal of fighting—rather more, he discovered, than some of the generals—they had only to begin discussing a past campaign and Luxmun was immediately lost.

"It's all flanks and wings, as though they were talking about a hawk catching a hare, instead of war," Luxmun complained to his brother. "When I mention something out of my own campaigns like hitting that big black mercenary on the head in the Battle of the Waterfalls—you remember?—and he wouldn't fall down although I hit him right square on his helmet with the spike of my mace—I've told you, haven't I?—so I hit him again—clang—and again—clang, clang—and he just grounded his spear and leaned on it—remember?—and there he was leaning stone-cold dead, leaning, you see—well, they look at me and make me feel crude. I don't understand all this business about the art of war."

"Neither do I," said Rama. "Let us go and ask Valmiki to explain it to us. Valmiki is certain to understand it because he knows everything."

Valmiki disclaimed the honour of knowing everything but admitted that he had made a study of the art of war.

They visited him in his pavilion, which was of saffron-coloured silk (Rama had chosen this unmartial colour for him to distinguish it from the tents of the warriors), and he invited them to seat themselves on the Sindhi rugs which lay three deep on the floor. Rama and Luxmun repeated what they had been saying to each other concerning the difficulties of strategy and tactics, and asked Valmiki to help them.

"I have never fought in a battle," said Valmiki, "and indeed I have never been near an army until now, but I have always been deeply interested in the theory of the matter. I have talked to the best authorities and I have recently had the advantage of listening at great length to the reminiscences of your general staff. I shall now explain to you military tactics.

"There are three theoretical ways of winning a battle. You can attack your enemy in the middle of his line and put him to flight. This is called crushing his centre and is considered rather jejune. Or, you can go round by his left side and roll up his forces while they are looking the other way. This is called turning his left flank and is considered highly ingenious. Or, again, as I scarcely need explain, you can do the same thing at the other end, which is called turning his right flank, and is considered equally clever."

"It sounds very simple," said Rama.

"So far," replied Valmiki. "But you must remember that

the opposing general will also be using tactics. That is to say, instead of obliging you by retreating, while you are crushing his left flank he may be crushing your left flank. In that case you must withdraw forces from your left and send them to your right. Observing this, the opposing general withdraws forces from his left and sends them to attack *your* left. Meantime a great deal of hullabaloo will have been going on in your centre. Things thus grow more complicated but not impossibly so."

"They would for me," said Luxmun, who had been tugging at his moustaches and frowning. "The trouble with me is that ever since I was a boy I have always got muddled about which was my right hand and which was my left—if I had to remember quickly, I mean."

"After a prolonged study of the descriptions of many famous battles," said Valmiki, "I have come to the conclusion that several generals have suffered from the same embarrassment."

"Wouldn't it be simpler," said Rama, "if each opposing general wrote his plan down and put it in a box? Somebody who is constitutionally impartial, like yourself, could open them and work things out and declare the winner."

"But that would be an impossible plan," said Valmiki shrugging his bowed shoulders and grinning, "because in that case the cleverest general would always win."

"What would be wrong with that?" said Rama.

"From the point of view of the stupider general, everything," said Valmiki.

"But the stupider general is bound to lose anyway," Rama protested.

"Oh, by no means," said Valmiki, his eyes glowing with amusement.

"I can vouch for that," said Luxmun. "Some of the orders

I've been given have to be heard to be believed. Still, I've usually come out on the right side."

"Among the best authorities on military tactics that I have consulted," Valmiki said, "have been the foot soldiers. What they have to say is very interesting, especially when you take it together with the descriptions of great battles that have been written in our chronicles. You will find that battles are not lost and won at all by turning flanks or crushing the centre or moving reserves. What happens is more simple. Among the decisive tactical events that I can recall at the moment I may mention the occasion when one general forgot that horses do not easily leap a thirty-foot ditch but customarily fall into the bottom of it. That blunder cost him half his cavalry and the whole campaign. Or there was the even simpler error when all the generals on one side forgot that their troops had not been paid, so as soon as the fighting began they went over to the other side. Then again there was the general who chose a site for his battle which was perfectly adapted to a most brilliant flanking movement which he had planned, except that he had not noticed that it was a bog. Nor must we forget the general who always made a point of sleeping soundly the night before a battle to set an example to his men. Unfortunately he set an example to the enemy, who stayed wide awake and won the battle between two and half past two in the night before it was supposed to be fought. Then there were battles which were lost because of the enemies' ruses. These ruses are the most interesting aspect of all for the thoughtful observer. They consist in such things as troops lying in the long grass and jumping up at the last moment, or pretending to run away so that the opposing forces run after them and straight into an ambush—tricks which might perhaps deceive a schoolchild once but which could not possibly deceive him a second time. Yet you will find if you study our histories that they have dumbfounded our military experts time and time again. Thus, my friends, you will see that tactics are by no means the deciding factor in warfare which, after all, is a chancy thing and the chanciest thing about it is the intelligence of your generals."

Rama thanked Valmiki for his instruction and told Luxmun to do the same. Luxmun obeyed, but with an abstracted air.

"What do you think?" said Luxmun when they had left the tent and were walking back to their own between the rows of gleaming pavilions, from each of which streamed pennants with the fighting symbol of its resident—lotuses done in silver thread, tigers in yellow silk from Peking, prodigious maces worked in gold, or delicately carved bows in padded embroidery, strung and with the arrow ready for discharge.

"About the art of war?" asked Rama. "Valmiki does not appear to think highly of generals, but then he does not think highly of anybody who sets himself up to know better than the rest of us. Besides, even if generals are as stupid as he says they are—and I don't doubt that he is right—he is not so light-minded as he tries to appear—still, I don't see what I can do about it."

"I think I do," said Luxmun, but Rama did not hear him, for at that moment there arose a great bellowing and trumpeting from some elephants that had just arrived in camp. They had been brought from the jungles of the south with enormous difficulty, and Rama hurried away to see them, eager to find out what use could be made of elephants in a siege. After diligent enquiries he discovered that nobody knew, but that there was a widespread impression among the more experienced officers that a few elephants were always a great comfort.

That night Luxmun gave a feast for some of his friends
among the Royal Guards. It was held in his pavilion and was a
very boisterous affair. Had anybody lifted the closed flap of the
inner tent to observe the jollity, he would have seen that instead
of ten soldiers sprawling around a drunken Luxmun at the
height of an orgy—which was what the noise suggested—there
were ten preoccupied men methodically singing songs, clanking brass dishes, and bursting into laughter at signals from an
efficient captain. And he would not have found Luxmun.

Rama's brother was, for the first time that he could remember, taking action without Rama's consent. Fearful that
his brother would discover his intention (for in spite of his
moustaches, Luxmun had no art in concealing his thoughts),
he had asked some of his friends to make the pretence of a
soldiers' party, from which, he was well aware, Rama would stay
away, such routs not being to his liking.

Luxmun meantime stole through the lines wrapped in his
cloak. Giving the password to one of his own men who was
on guard at a point opposite the city, he swore him to secrecy,
and then moved quickly out into the open space between
his own lines and the walls of Lanka.

These walls towered blackly above him. He drew near and
struggled to suppress the sound of his heavy breathing. He listened for some while to the tramp of the sentries, and judged
the passage of the nearest as he walked between two turrets.
When he was at the furthest end of his beat, Luxmun un-
wound a rope from his waist, to which was attached a grappling
hook. He swung it and it fell between the crenellations, which
were shaped like large leaves. The noise attracted the sentry,
who came running to the spot, calling his fellow guards. It was
not part of his design, but Luxmun, seeing the man's head
against the sky, loosed off an arrow at him and shouted an in-

sult. Then he retired out of range of their bows and strained his eyes in the darkness to watch what they did. The darkness was soon relieved by the light of torches. The sentry and, it seemed, some companions now began raining darts at the point where Luxmun had stood. They did not see the grappling iron for so long that Luxmun shouted and told them it was there. Then they saw it. They pulled at the rope and Luxmun heard them say there was nothing at the end of it. But in this they were mistaken. When they had pulled up the end of the rope they found a long, flat palm leaf into which a message had been cut with a stylus and rubbed with charcoal dust to make it easier to read. Luxmun gave them a last shout and told them to take it to their master Ravan.

When they had done so and Ravan, awakened, had sleepily put together the meaning of the symbols he found this message:

Ravan, King of Lanka. I, Luxmun, the brother-in-law of the Princess Sita, have come here to protect her honour. But now I am going back home because since I have seen your cowardice in not giving fight, I do not think my sister's honour is in any danger since you are not man enough to have attempted it.

LUXMUN, COMMANDER
OF THE ROYAL GUARD OF RAMA.

CHAPTER THREE

sinGle comBat

The next morning, two hours after the sun had risen, all the war trumpets of Lanka rang out from the battlements. These war trumpets of Lanka were not carried by men, like those of Rama and all other Indians. They were horns so long that they rested, fifteen feet away from the mouth of the trumpeter, on bronze stands wrought in the shape of slavering demons. They were grim to see; unseen, they were more terrible still.

Each trumpeter had a different note, but each had only one. When they spoke, twenty of them, from the walls of Lanka, it seemed as though a score of angry lions were roaring in a brazen cavern.

In Rama's army the morning bustle was stilled; men ceased their exercises and gathered in groups with their comrades. Rama and Valmiki came to the doors of their pavilions and gazed towards the city.

At the third sounding the commanders began to marshal their forces. The men moved quietly about their business but the animals—horses, elephants, camels, and mules—disturbed in their very bowels by the trumpets, grew restless and complained, their braying, bellowing, and long, high-pitched whinnies, making the nerves of their owners still more tense.

Rama spoke to the generals who were near him, and all predicted an attack. Rama called his armourer and went into his tent to prepare for battle. Soon his war chariot came to the pavilion door, shining with its bronze plates, the great quivers at the sides filled with arrows, its horses jingling their traces in a restless dance from hoof to hoof.

Then, armed cap-a-pie, riding in his chariot, Luxmun, his eyes gleaming, took out a body of the Royal Guard, all fully accoutred, as they had been since sunrise. He took up a position opposite the gates of the town but a quarter of a mile away and there in a short while Rama and his principal allied rajas and their officers joined him, each in his war chariot and ready for combat.

The trumpets of Lanka sounded again. The great doors of Lanka began to open. As the echoes of the trumpets died away the voices of Rama's officers could be heard putting their troops in readiness for the expected sally.

But only a single horseman rode through the half-opened gates.

His horse was a handsome bay. He was dressed not in the heavy panoply of war but in the light, fanciful armour of the court. His helmet was no more than a golden cap; light mail sparkling with jewels covered his chest, and his soft leather sandals rested lightly on his stirrups which lacked the shovel of bronze that in war protected his feet. He carried a lance from the point of which dangled a metal object that could not be clearly made out until he rode closer. Then it was seen to be a small perfume bottle. He rode with insolent unconcern right up to the ranks of chariots. He bore no sign or pennant to show that his mission was that of a herald, but his manner was sufficient to protect him.

He halted his horse directly in front of Rama, coolly surveyed him from head to foot, and then did the same with the principal allies. He moved slightly in his saddle, and looked at Luxmun, saying:

"I seek the brother of Rama."

Luxmun put up his hand to his moustaches and shook his shoulders till his armour rang.

"I am Luxmun."

The herald looked him over but gave no sign that he had heard him. Instead he moved his horse slowly away to the right, walking past the guard, past the company of archers that stood next it, until he came to a group of men armed with slings. Mingled with these were youths with bags slung round their shoulders who carried the smooth round stones that were the slingers' ammunition.

The herald reined in his horse. Choosing out a beardless boy who stood gaping in the front rank he bowed his head ironically and addressed him:

"My lord Luxmun: greetings."

The boy's jaw dropped further and he stared at the elegant herald wide-eyed.

"My master the serene and powerful Lord of Lanka, and descendant of the gods, Ravan, king, bids me tell you that he has received your message. He sends you his royal thanks."

Here the herald bowed his head again to the boy, who blinked his eyes at the dazzle from the herald's casque. The herald spoke again, loudly, so that his words carried far along the line of soldiers.

"In return he sends you this present."

The herald slowly lowered his lance until the point was level with the boy's head. The boy unthinkingly put out his hand to take the dangling perfume bottle, but the herald jerked the lance forward so that the boy fell back against the slingers behind him.

"It has been recommended by His Majesty's chief barber," declaimed the herald, "as the best recipe that is known for making the beard grow on the beardless chins of younger brothers. His Majesty's chief barber adds that the liquid must be well rubbed in. If, Luxmun, you do not know how this is done, my master, the serene and powerful Lord of Lanka, and descendant of the gods, Ravan, king and mighty warrior, will come here before these gates at noon tomorrow and do it for you."

He jerked the lance and the bottle fell to the ground at the boy's feet and the slingers scrambled to pick it up. The herald wheeled his horse and rode slowly back to where the real Luxmun stood in his chariot, flushing with anger. The herald again looked him over with deliberation, but this time there was a smile on his lips and a quizzical tilt about his eyebrows that showed plainly that he knew and had known who Luxmun was.

Luxmun did not move. The herald turned his horse towards the gates. His horse moved a pace forwards and then, as though the herald knew that the magnificence of his bearing would no longer protect him once he had turned his back, he kicked his horse's flanks and made for the gates at full gallop.

With this retreat of the herald, Luxmun, whose tongue had been bound by shame and rage, suddenly found words, a torrent of them, which he shouted at the fleeing horseman, accepting the challenge and offering to fight any high-born soldier in all Lanka, one by one, after he had killed Ravan. The whole watching army waved its approval and the horseman made the last few yards of his perilous withdrawal bent low over the neck of his horse, as darts, stones, and arrows fell around him. The missiles rattled on the great gates as they opened slightly to receive the horseman to safety and then closed, as, once more, the long trumpets sounded from the walls.

That evening Rama went to Valmiki's pavilion and sat wearily on the rugs. Valmiki served him with pomegranate juice.

"Thank you," said Rama. "I know only one thing as calming as pomegranate juice and that is to listen to your reprehensible opinions. The generals have objected to Luxmun fighting Ravan tomorrow."

"It is one of the things, like the ditch, which are not foreseen in the art of war," said Valmiki. "They will naturally object."

"They wanted me to stop him," said Rama.

"And what did you answer?"

"I said that it seemed to me that what they wanted me to do was not to stop him fighting tomorrow but to stop him sending the message that he delivered to Lanka last night. Once he had done that, nothing could prevent the rest."

"It is exactly the answer I would have made myself," said Valmiki.

"Yes, I fear so," said Rama, smiling. "I find that I have been infected with your way of thinking."

"You regret it?"

"No," said Rama and sighed. "But it does away with a lot of romance and speculation and fine speeches and wonderful despairing thoughts."

"I find it a little earthy myself," said Valmiki. "After all, it was very pleasant to be young."

"It was," said Rama. "It was."

A quarter of an hour short of noon the next day Rama, unarmed, received three priests in saffron robes from Lanka and pledged his honour as a prince that the rules of the combat should be observed: namely, that the contest being between princes of royal blood, it should take place in chariots, each prince to have his charioteer; that the contest should take place between the gates of Lanka to the one side, the standard of Rama to the other, a stone pillar to the left and a tree to the right, the space thus defined being a square some three hundred yards across: that each prince should be accompanied by three horsemen, of noble birth, who should take no part in the contest; that the contest should begin by the sounding of a conch shell by the horsemen of the challenging prince; should continue until one prince surrendered, or was killed, or fled the field; and should one die, then the other should forthwith take a white goat and kill it upon the altar of the god of war, to bear the guilt of the slaying.

The Brahmins retired into Lanka. Rama's army lined three sides of the square and there were men on every vantage point in the city, some even on the high pyramids of the temples within. The sky was a hard blue, and the heat of the day had already set the air at the bottom of the ramparts quivering.

Rama saw that on some of the rooftops in Lanka women had gathered. He searched among the tiny, bright-clothed figures, but whether Sita was among them he could not say, for they were too far off. He thought of his wife deliberately, and endeavoured to do so with tenderness: but he could not, for the picture of his brother lying in the dust beside his chariot supplanted all others, and Rama felt cold under the midday sun.

He went to speak to his brother, who stood patting his horses' necks and speaking to them. He took his brother's hand, but feeling his own tremble, he released him and left him without speaking. No sooner had he regained his position among his royal guards, than the great doors of Lanka opened.

The three noble horsemen came out at a gallop, riding in

great arcs before the chariot of Ravan. The chariot rumbled
out of the shadow of the gateway and tongues of flame seemed
to leap from it as its two black horses pulled it into the blaze
of the sun. The pole between the horses was of burnished
bronze, the chariot's high front behind the crouching charioteer
was of brass, polished and studded with square-cut nails, and
the wheels, spinning in the dust, made discs of light with their
metal sheaths.

The charioteer crouching on a foot-square platform at the
butt of the pole between the horses shouted, half stood, and
leaned back on the reins. The black horses reared in the air and
the chariot came to rest. Then all could see, standing upright,
with only one bare hand to steady him, the awesome figure of
the King of Lanka.

Tall as he was, he was made taller by his helm of black
iron with silver bosses across the front, and made terrible by the
iron strip that stretched from his forehead to his upper lip.
His body armour was black like his helmet, but a sash of gold
with a jewelled clasp hung loosely around his waist. His loin-
cloth, tight-folded between his legs, left his great thighs bare.
He rested upon his mace, a stout bar of iron that ended in a
spiked ball and which was bound to his wrist by a leather thong.

The noblemen reined in their horses behind him. The
charioteer crouched again over his pole and Ravan waited, upright and unmoving.

The chariot of Luxmun now came into the lists, at a slower
pace, for he had not the advantage of driving through a gateway but came from before his pavilion, his noblemen trotting
beside him. But his white horses, the golden ornaments of the
cedarwood chariot, and the silvery gleam of his body armour
and burnished iron cap gave him grace and ease. He took up his
station.

Ravan's three noblemen now rode to the centre of the field,

and Luxmun's supporters did likewise. They faced each other in two ranks, Ravan's men heavy, insolent, and swaggering: Luxmun's slighter in build and less certain of what they had to do.

There was an exchange of courtesies. One of Ravan's nobles raised a matter of the rules, but the watchers could not hear all that he said. The point was settled as the horses stamped and jingled their harnesses. The six horsemen galloped off the field to its edge and the last of Ravan's men turned in his saddle and put a conch shell to his lips. Its long, melancholy note echoed for a moment from the walls of Lanka, and then was lost in the shouts of the two charioteers.

To Rama, watching, it seemed as though the two chariots drove straight at each other. But as they were about to meet in the middle of the field, each charioteer turned his horses very slightly and the chariots passed each other, wheel all but touching wheel. Ravan and Luxmun swung their maces, and leaning over the sides of their war-cars, struck at each other. The impetus of his chariot and his mace betrayed Luxmun's judgment. His blow missed its mark and the end of his mace struck the wood of Ravan's chariot, splintering it and buckling its metal plates. At the same moment Luxmun felt a blow on his left shoulder that sent him reeling against his charioteer and deprived him, for a moment, of his sight. The charioteer held him up with his shoulder as he brought his horses round a tight circle. The chariots passed again and Luxmun, unable to gather his strength quickly enough, bent all his wits on parrying Ravan's next blow.

He swung himself into the position for striking a blow himself. Ravan, seeing this, was deceived into thinking that his first stroke had done Luxmun no harm. Had he known that Luxmun meant to parry and not strike, he would have changed his stance at the last moment. He did not. He struck downwards

and his mace fell upon that of Luxmun. The shock sent a great
wave of pain through his spine and his anger flared.

The chariots came together for the third time. Ravan swung
his mace, but his hot blood made his stroke clumsy. Luxmun,
his nerves steady, made as though to aim at Ravan's helmet,
but as the chariots passed each other, changed his stroke by a
great wrench of his wrist and brought it down upon Ravan's
breast and shoulder. The spikes drove home through the links
of the armour and the black lacquer turned red with Ravan's
blood.

Seeing this, a great shout came from Rama's army and Rama
rejoiced aloud.

But now the chariots did not draw so far apart. By the rules
of single combat they must now keep as close to each other as
they could, each man fighting continuously till the end of the
battle.

The three horsemen of Lanka rode forward: the three of
Rama did the same. The six stationed themselves at six points
that formed a rough ellipse. Within this, the chariots must
manoeuvre. The two chariots turned in a narrow radius and instantly it could be seen that Luxmun's car had the advantage.
It was lighter than Ravan's and more easily handled. The
chariots came close, withdrew and closed again, Ravan and Luxmun balancing on the balls of their feet and striking with their
maces at each approach.

To wild shouting from Rama's soldiers, Luxmun's strokes
again and again found their mark, and although the blows that
could be delivered in this twisting and turning phase of the
duel had not the force of the first tremendous strokes, they
wounded Ravan; when his chariot wheeled away it could be seen
that he was bowed with pain. He seized his charioteer's arm to
steady himself and he spoke to him.

The two chariots approached again. The dust rose in a great cloud around them: but it was not enough to hide what happened next. Luxmun's chariot came up, wheeled, and lay broadside to Ravan for a moment. Ravan's chariot feinted as though to turn as the rules demanded, but the charioteer, rising from his narrow platform, struck his horses with his whip and drove them straight into the flanks of the horses of his enemy. The bronze-shod pole shot at the terrified white horse like a spear. The horses whinnied with fear, jerked their reins from their driver's hand, and pounded the air with their forelegs. Luxmun's chariot reeled drunkenly. At that moment Ravan's horses were brought sharply up on their hindlegs and Ravan, leaning out of his war-car, struck Luxmun to the floor of his chariot with a single blow. As Luxmun's horses bolted away, he was flung out upon the ground, where he lay without moving.

The three noblemen from Rama's army galloped towards the witnesses from Lanka, shouting their protests. The men from Lanka hesitated: then a shower of missiles from Rama's roaring, cursing, and enraged army fell about them and, calling to their master, they put spurs to their horses and rode for the gate. Ravan's charioteer, whipping his horse, followed them. But his trick in driving at Luxmun's horses had strained his harness. It broke, and Ravan's chariot slewed in the dust.

Instantly the soldiers of the Royal Guard charged to capture Ravan, and the rest of the army in wild confusion began to follow them.

A mounted group of men from Lanka rode out from the gates, and laying about them with great ferocity, protected their king and, slowly retreating with him, took him at last safely within the gates, leaving many of their number dead on the plain.

Luxmun, coming to his senses, found his brother leaning over him. He saw his broken chariot and looked for his charioteer. He smiled when he saw that he was safe. He listened to the din of the battle that now raged at a hundred different points and he smiled more broadly.

"We're attacking?" he asked.

"Yes," said Rama. "There is no holding the men back."

"At last," said Luxmun; and then, "How very angry the generals will be with me."

For the next three days the siege of Lanka was waged by all branches of the army with the greatest confusion and high spirits. Attacks were launched and repulsed again and again, their leaders having no more plan than to outdo the next body of men in the line. Whenever, for reasons of exhaustion, there was a comparative orderliness, the generals seized it as a favourable moment to regain control. Things would go for an hour or so according to their carefully laid plans, but this did not, in the end, sensibly diminish the confusion.

Even the elephants played their part. They were led against the gates of Lanka in an abortive assault. Most of them, with the sagacity for which they are famous, surveyed the forces ranged along the walls on either side and returned to their stables at a fast trot. Three were killed by huge iron darts dropped from above. Their carcasses lay against the gates, affording extra defences for the Lankastrians.

But the confusion within the town seemed no less than that without. The defence slackened and in the morning of the fourth day since the combat it was decided in Rama's camp to make a full assault. The siege engines cast flaming balls of flax, a ram battered the gate, towers were wheeled towards the walls, and the messengers running between the generals ran so often that they fainted with exhaustion.

At last the gate gave. Rama, placing himself at the head of his guard, led the assault and entered upon his first taste of warfare, climbing over the carcasses of the elephants.

The fury of the assault, all the more terrifying for being virtually unplanned, dismayed the Lankastrians on the walls, who also had good reason to fear that all was not well behind them. They yielded. The gates fell. Rama, on foot, cut his way into the streets of the city. He had killed four running men before he discovered that it gave him a tremendous and bloodthirsty joy.

He performed prodigies as they fought their way to the Palace. He killed the single loyal guard outside the private chambers of the king with one thrust. He broke through the door with the aid of the closest of his own Royal Guard and found Ravan dead upon the floor. Ravan's eyes and tongue protruded. His fingers had been lopped off to get his rings. A heavy chest that had once contained treasure had been flung across his legs, breaking them. His chosen companions, the soldiers who had sacked the hermitage, had seen no reason to change their ways merely because their master had been defeated.

A eunuch crawling on the floor, offered to show Rama the room of Sita.

Rama went there at a run, and burst into the room. Sita stood by a couch, a short sword in her hand and a soldier jerking in his death agony at her feet.

She looked at Rama as he stood panting, his forearms covered in blood, and blood on his face. She looked at the sword in her hand.

"Let us go somewhere to clean ourselves of this filth," was her greeting to her husband, "and become human beings again."

But if a bath in Ravan's own bath could make Rama a human being again, nothing could make him an ordinary one. To kill one or more persons is always the shortest path to a rapid change in one's life; done at the wrong time, it results in the gallows; done at the right time, it leads to fame. Rama's killing had been in fact no more than a street fight. But his timing had been magnificent, as it so often is with those who seem born to lead. He became, overnight, a hero. It was said on all sides that he alone had been responsible for the capture of the city.

This credit really belonged to the soldier whom Sita had killed. He was a jealous cousin of Ravan's who had spread the rumour that the town had been betrayed and then, when he had helped to murder the King, had gone to capture Sita. He, however, now lay dead in a gutter into which his body had been kicked, while Rama sat on Ravan's ebony and silver throne. Rama's name rang throughout the land.

He had won a great victory; he was the master of a devoted army. There was nothing that was not in his power to do, if he wished it. Although it would seem wise to suspect such a man of the worst intentions, in practice the world tumbled over itself to think the best. Embassies arrived at Lanka daily, among them one from Ayoda announcing the death of his father the King. Rama kept the embassy waiting three days and then refused to discuss his return—for which they begged—on the ground that he was in mourning. He shut himself up, and it was given out that he was fasting and praying for the salvation of his father's soul.

He was, however, thinking of Sita. When he had appeared in the streets of Lanka, his soldiers shouted: "Long live Rama." When Sita had appeared, they cried: "There goes the whore."

In the cool of the evening Luxmun would sit on the paved roof of the palace, taking the air, and fretting at the time it took for his wounds to heal. There, soon after the coming of the embassy from Ayoda, Sita joined him. They sat silently for a while, listening to the noises of the city below.

"He won't see me," said Sita at last. "He won't even speak to me."

Luxmun blew his moustaches indignantly.

"If he hanged the next ruffian who shouted at you in the street, there'd soon be an end to it."

"An end to what?" said Sita.

"The—shouting," said Luxmun, and flushed deeply.

"Yes. That's what I thought you meant," said Sita. "You think it's true, don't you?"

"I don't think anything's true," said Luxmun violently. "Lies: all lies, and I'd like to see the man stand up to me and say it isn't when my shoulder's better."

"So you do think it's true," said Sita and looked away.

"What? I don't know what you're talking about."

"That I'm an unfaithful wife and I've slept with Ravan."

"You didn't do anything of the sort," said Luxmun. He struck his knee and winced with pain.

Sita said: "I did."

Luxmun said nothing for a long minute. Two drunken soldiers quarrelled near the palace and their obscenities came drifting up on the evening breeze.

"He made you, Sita. He forced you."

Sita shook her head: "Ravan was cruel and he was a monster when he went on his raids. But with women he was gentle. No; it was in the bargain, but he did not press me to keep it."

"Ah!" said Luxmun, "so there *was* a bargain. I thought so."

"Yes. I made up my mind when your bowstring snapped on the night they destroyed the hermitage. You looked round and I saw your face and I said to myself, 'Luxmun's getting ready to die.'"

"A soldier's always doing that, Sita."

"Not a good soldier. He only does it once, when he knows that there's no hope left. That's what you knew, then."

Luxmun nodded. "There was nothing to get our backs against," he said. "They only had to come down the hillside and they could have picked us off just as they pleased. So that's why you said you'd go and get the bowstring?"

"Yes. It wasn't very difficult to make up my mind, but I had no time to explain—especially to Rama. He never was an easy man to explain things to."

"He's changed," said Luxmun. "He's changed very much."

"Perhaps. Still, what *was* difficult was to cross that space in front of the house with the soldiers shooting everywhere. I kept telling myself that if nothing hit me it was a sign that what I was doing was right."

"Just what I'd have done myself," said Luxmun.

"Nothing hit me. When Ravan saw me he stopped the shooting. When he heard that I'd go with him if he'd stop the killing and torturing, he stopped that, too."

"You were very brave."

"Yes, I was, Luxmun. I'd have been a heroine. I meant to be. I meant to kill myself rather than keep my promise. I think I would have killed myself if he'd have come at me as I expected, all drunk and brutal. But I hadn't allowed for one thing."

"He played a trick on you, eh?"

"Yes, Luxmun. The oldest trick of them all. He just said that he loved me above everything in the world and that he would never force me to do anything I did not want. I was pleased at first. Then I was sorry for him. Then he kissed me. Then I wasn't a heroine any more."

"I see," said Luxmun. "Well, you could be sure a fool like me would let you down."

"You?"

"Of course. I had three chances to kill the swine—*three*. Once in the glade, once when he came to the hermitage right under my nose, and once more when I fought outside these walls. I failed each time. It's all my fault, and I know it."

Sita, hearing this, pulled her sari across her face: for the first time since the fall of the city, she wept and very bitterly.

Luxmun got up, watched Sita for a moment, and then left her.

When she next saw him, he came bursting into her room his face aglow, his extravagant moustaches in utter disarray.

"Quickly!" he said. "Dry your eyes! We're going to Rama."

"Have you seen him?"

"Seen him, talked to him, and given him a piece of my mind. What d'you think of that?"

"You?" said Sita incredulously. "*You* gave Rama a piece of your mind?"

"I have," said Luxmun and then, with awe at his own daring, he repeated: "I have. I felt I had to do something since I had failed you so badly. I found Rama with Valmiki. The moment I mentioned your name Rama turned his back on me. But I shouted a bit, and I made him listen to the whole story. Then I told him that if he didn't forgive you, I would pack up and leave him for good and go for a soldier in Persia or somewhere. 'And what's more,' I said, 'I shall be sorry I ever had you for a brother.' Stupid thing to say, wasn't it? But Rama turned quite pale. He took my hand and called himself a lot of names that I shan't repeat. And he said he was sorry. And he forgave you. So he should. He loves you, you know."

"Not only me," said Sita.

When she met Rama again they saluted each other gravely
and got down to business. This was quickly despatched. Rama
told her that he wished to go back to Ayoda and accept the
throne which was offered him. He had been turned over in his
mind the best way to allay the scandal. He had consulted Valmiki. On the poet's suggestion he had decided to award her, here
and now, the titles of First Queen and Most Faithful Wife.

When he had said this there was a moment's silence between
them. Then Sita smiled, and Rama smiled in return. After that,
they embraced. Later that night, lying side by side in what had
once been Ravan's bed of state, they agreed that during the
time that they had been apart they had both grown considerably
older; though not (they assured each other, embracing again) in
their looks.

the tale
of the
stone woman

The next day, somewhat late in the forenoon, Rama called the ambassadors from Ayoda into his presence and told them he had decided to return to his native city and to take up his inheritance.

The ambassadors prostrated themselves with shouts of joy, and for the first time in his life Rama heard himself addressed as "Your Majesty." At first it sounded well in his ears. In the course of the next hour he heard himself thus addressed some two hundred and fifty times as each of the ambassadors, unfortunately no longer prostrate, made him an eulogistic speech.

Rama listened with what he hoped was a kingly expression, but the pleasures of the night before had been fatiguing. Rama yawned, Rama nodded, and Rama fell soundly asleep.

An attendant touched his elbow and he awoke. The last of the ambassadors, observing that he once more had his monarch's attention, began his speech all over again.

"My poor father," said Rama to himself, thinking of King Dasa-ratha's nights in the seraglio, "how he must have suffered." And Rama, then and there, made up his mind that never, never, never would he follow in his father's footsteps.

Having made this good resolution, he set about finding a way in which he could keep it. He dismissed the ambassadors and, giving orders for his own departure, he retired to the inner courtyard of Ravan's palace to avoid the bustle and noise of packing, and to think.

He thought first that he would like to be known to history as Rama the Chaste, but he remembered Valmiki's tale of Kumar. He next thought that he might make a great study of the laws of his country and produce a code which would endure for a thousand years, the Code of Rama the Wise: but he remembered the locust and tempered his ambitions. He next thought of half a dozen ways that would help him to rise above his baser nature, but none of the six would have passed Valmiki's scrutiny.

"Yet," said Rama, pacing the courtyard, "even Valmiki says that he does not know everything. I feel that there must be some way in which a man can elevate his spirit which he has overlooked. Are we like animals, chained to our appetites? I cannot believe it."

At this moment an official of his retinue came into the courtyard and, bowing profoundly, asked if there was anything which His Majesty especially wished to preserve in Ravan's palace—any artistic object, furniture, statue, or so forth. If not, then, said the official, perhaps His Majesty would condescend to indicate at which hour the customary looting could begin.

Rama glanced round the ugly little courtyard, the lumpish statues, and the squat columns. He remembered with a shudder the gilt bedroom in which he had slept with Sita the night before.

"No," he said, "there is nothing. King Ravan's taste was even worse than that of my father." As he said this, a splendid and most elevated idea struck him, with which he was so enamoured that he forgot to set the hour for looting, with the result that Ravan's palace was stripped piecemeal and furtively, without joy, and without conflagration. For this reason, Rama was forever after known in Lanka as The Merciful.

Rama did not mention his splendid notion until the immense cavalcade of the court, the royal guard and the royal retainers had nearly completed its journey towards Ayoda. The city came into sight at twilight, and Rama gave orders that camp should be pitched for the night, so that his entry into his patrimony could take place in the full light of day.

A silken tent was put up for Rama and Sita, and by Rama's orders the front hangings were raised on ebony poles so that the city lay before them as they ate and drank. He summoned Valmiki to join him.

When Sita retired to rest from the fatigues of the day, Rama stayed and talked to Valmiki for some time, reviewing their experiences together and so passing on to what he would do in the future.

"Looking at the city of my birth again," he said, "brings back to me something of my youth—the time, that is, before I had the melancholy advantage of your wisdom. I think that there was something touching in my faith in the goodness of mankind, and in noble ideas. I regret that it is gone. But there is still something left. Your views of the general run of the world may be—indeed are—correct. But there are human spirits which rise above it and I think you are inclined to forget them—a strange thing, since you are a poet. I mean, of course, artists. These are the men who can elevate our spirits. These are the men who can show us a finer world than the one which you delineate. The wise man, it seems to me, will take refuge from the deficiencies of his fellow men by the cultivation of his sensibilities, his taste, his appreciation of the finest products of the human genius. This is what I mean to do. I shall beautify Ayoda with the most exquisite works of art that I can find. I shall raise harmonious buildings that will be a benison to the weary soul. And when the world becomes too much like what you say it is, I shall shut myself up in my cabinet and bury myself in beauty. In this way I shall not have held my early ideals quite in vain. I have given a great deal of thought to the matter, and I think that my solution is the wisest, perhaps the only one, for a sensible man. You are, I see," said Rama, "smiling. If I am wrong in my plans, please correct me."

"One does not correct kings," said Valmiki. "But Your Majesty's vision of the future reminded me of the experiences of one of the finest geniuses in creation of works of art that our country has ever known. But Your Majesty will have more important things to do from now on than to listen to my tales."

"I shall always be glad," said Rama, "to hear of the experiences of a genius, especially in the creative arts. Please tell me your tale."

"Well, then, as Your Majesty commands. But Rama," said Valmiki, taking Rama's hand and pressing it, "it must be the last. I am no courtier, and I have my poem to finish. I shall go with you into Ayoda—it is a long time since I have seen it—but then I shall ask your permission to leave."

"I shall give it very reluctantly," said Rama, and pressed Valmiki's hand in return. "But let me hear your tale, the last, if it must be so."

Valmiki drank deeply from his sherbet, looked into the crystal bowl for a moment, and then began the Tale of the Stone Woman.

Young Balan (said Valmiki) was a genius, but apart from that his parents and his friends had nothing against him. His father and all his friends were stonemasons. For ten years they had been engaged upon the building of a temple. This temple was in the shape of a small pyramid with a flat top and four sides. Each of the four sides was divided into eight layers and each of the eight layers had a hundred sculptures of gods, goddesses, devils, and attendants. The carvings were not very good because the stonemasons were not very talented: but the finished temple would have been harmonious, if rather dull, had it not been for Balan. When Balan had begun to carve he had tried to be as bad as his elders and betters. But although he shed many tears and was often thrashed, he was always the best carver of them all.

The stonemasons were, by and large, coarse men, very ready with their fists, and young Balan led a miserable life. Fortunately, the master mason could recognise genius when he saw it and when he saw it he knew what to do.

One day at sunset he told Balan to wait behind when the others went home, and in the twilight, standing in front of the small leopard which the boy had been carving, he spoke to the genius in this kindly manner:

"Balan, that is a very good leopard."

Balan looked up at him in surprise.

"Do you think so, sir?"

"I do. I think it is the best carving of a leopard I have ever seen."

"That you've *ever* seen, sir?" said Balan and tears of pleasure wetted his eyelashes.

"Yes, and I've seen more carving than most."

"Oh, yes, sir. You've seen everything."

"But I've never seen a leopard as good as that. Not anywhere. For instance, there are fifteen leopards already carved on this temple. Can you show me one as good as yours?"

Balan did not know what to answer. He assumed in any case that no answer was expected because the twilight was now so dim that neither his nor anybody else's carvings could be seen. But this did not trouble the master mason, who went on admiring

Balan's and disparaging the others as though it were broad day-light. The master mason was proud of being able to handle his men. He took trouble. He took so much trouble with Balan that at last the boy gained enough confidence to agree that his leopard, if not better, was certainly different, "because, sir," he explained, "I went to the palace gardens and looked at the leopard that the Prince has got in a cage there and I don't think the others have done that, or at least if they did, it was a long time ago. When leopards," he added politely, "might have been different."

"Different," said the master mason. "Different. That's the very word I have been looking for. Your leopard is different."

"Yes," said Balan, gaining even more confidence.

"So, of course, it spoils the design," said the master mason casually. "Of course it does and of course everybody says it does, and of course the Prince will say it does when he sees it and you'll get into trouble. People do not understand genius when they see it."

"No," said Balan, not quite so sure of himself.

"No," agreed the master mason, "so that's why tomorrow I'm going to take you off the outside and put you to work on a cor-ner of the walls inside where you can be as different as you like."

"Oh thank you, sir," said Balan, and he made to kiss the mas-ter mason's feet, but the man stopped him, patted his shoulder, and left. Balan, his pulse racing with pleasure, turned to his leopard. He stroked it fondly with the tips of his fingers. It was now quite dark.

So was the corner in which, next morning, he was put to work. It was one of the two corners which faced the altar. There-fore anybody who came into the temple in the right frame of mind would keep the back of his head towards it. When he left he would perhaps see it better, but only if he threw back his head and strained his eyes until they watered. The master mason led Balan to this corner, helped him up the bamboo scaffolding, gave him an oil lamp, and said:

"Now, my boy, I'm not going to try to tell a genius like you what you should carve on the stone there in front of you. You can carve exactly what you please. And if anybody tries to stop you, just you tell me and I'll have two words with him that he won't forget."

"Thank you," said Balan, and when his patron and protector had left him, he burst into tears. The violence of his weeping surprised him and he said aloud between his sobs:

"I didn't know that anybody could be so miserable as I am." In the next instant he told himself that he didn't know that anybody could be so frightened, for a voice that was neither human nor animal but more unpleasant than either had said mockingly in his ear:

"Ha!"

Balan knew that it was a devil and hastily began to pray.

"What's that you're muttering?" said the voice sharply and once more it came from the empty air next to Balan's ear.

"I'm praying that if you're a devil you'll go away," said Balan.

"I'm not a devil," said the voice. "Do you know what I really am?"

"No," whispered Balan.

"Guess," said the voice with a most unpleasant tone of mockery.

From the sound of the voice (which was all Balan had to go by) it seemed to Balan that he was being addressed by a very old and bronchial dog in the worst of tempers. But Balan thought it wiser not to say so. He therefore stayed silent, except for a single sob that remained from his storm of tears.

"Hold up your lamp, boy!"

Balan obeyed, trembling so much that the small flame was all but blown out. When it had steadied again, Balan saw that at the other end of the platform on which he stood sat an aged man who even in the flickering light of the lamp looked extremely dirty.

"Good morning, brother genius," the voice spoke in Balan's ear: but the lips of the old man moved with the words. Balan glanced to his right and back to the old man. "It's the echo from the shell," said the voice. "Fancy a young genius like you not guessing that," said the old man sarcastically and Balan saw that the corner near which he stood was carved into the shape of a large shell with ribs of the greatest delicacy.

"Come here," said the old man.

Balan cautiously edged his way along the platform.

"Look at that," said the old man, and taking the boy's wrists between fingers caked with dirt and stone dust, the old man drew the lamp towards the wall.

Balan saw what he took to be a growing flower and then beside it another, and then another. Balan touched them with his fingers and found that they were made of stone.

"One hundred and eighty-seven of them," said the old man. "One for every week that I've squatted up here like a monkey on a mango tree. I can do them with my eyes shut now. I don't even trouble to light my lamp. It saves the money that would go in oil. What d'you think of them? If you don't like 'em, don't tell me because I don't want to hear."

"But I do like them," said Balan. "They're wonderful. I wish I could carve like that."

"Well," said the old man, "since that son of a diseased she-buffalo has stuck you up here on this perch with me, you probably can."

An hour later, when the old man had told enough of his life

story to convince Balan that the master mason was a scoundrel, Balan said:

"I shall run away."

"I've done that," said the old man.

"I shall run away to another country."

"I've done that," said the old man.

"And when I get there I shall go to the first place where they're building and I shall take a bit of stone and carve it and then I shall say to the master mason, 'Give me some work.' "

"I've done that, too," said the old man.

"And what did they say?" asked Balan.

"They said that they didn't want any dirty foreigners teaching them their business."

"That was because they were ignorant," said Balan.

"Yes," replied the old man. "Then somebody on the top scaffold dropped a mallet and it hit me on the head. That was because they were ignorant, too."

"I see," said Balan. "So you came back here."

"I had to eat."

Balan sighed.

"And so have you," said the old man, "so you'd better get to work."

"What shall I carve?" said Balan.

"Anything you like," said the old man. "Nobody but me will ever see it."

"Well then, what would you like?" said Balan, for he had conceived a great respect for the old man, the flowers being so wonderfully well carved.

"Want to know?" said the old man, picking his ear and glancing at Balan out of the corner of his eye.

"Yes, master."

"I'd like a woman," said the old man and smacked his lips.

"You mean you'd like me to carve a woman?" said Balan.

"That's right. Never could do them myself. Do one standing on that shell. No. Sitting. No. Standing. Well, any way you like so long as she's a woman."

"I don't know that I can," said Balan. "I've only studied leopards. I don't think I've really looked at a woman."

"No?" said the old man, squeaking with surprise. "That's a funny thing. As for me, I don't think I've ever looked at anything else. I'll tell you what they look like. First," said the old man, and raising a grimy and descriptive finger, he catalogued their charms.

When he had done, Balan said:

"Well, sir, perhaps I'd better have a look for myself."

"Do," said the old man, croaking affably, "do. Mebbe you'll see something I've missed."

"I don't think so," said Balan, and edging away to his end of the scaffolding, he busied himself for the rest of the day taking measurements of the stones and chalking out a site for his carving.

That evening, and for many evening afterwards, he went to the well to study the women drawing water. Next morning, and for interminable mornings afterwards, he carved in his corner. The old man took so much interest in the progress of the work (although he was often impatient) that he brought his own lamp and oil, and all but gave up carving his flowers. Balan still thought him a great artist, but he had learned that if you wish to admire great artists it is better not to listen to their conversation, this being one of the reasons why great artists are admired much more when they are dead.

Balan had scarcely finished carving the last of the statue's toes when, one day towards the beginning of the rains, he and the old man were turned out of the temple. Their scaffold was torn down, and they were set to the ignominious task of seeing that there was not a single loose stone on the whole of the path from the doorway of the temple to the grand west portal of the Prince's palace. This was not because they had done anything wrong—nobody could recall what they had been doing—but because the Prince had decided to visit the temple and observe the progress of the work. This caused much anxious bustle because the Prince was a man of great taste who thought sufficiently highly of artists to cut off their heads when they were very bad; and when they were very good, to tell them so. This was considered most condescending on His Highness' part and every artist in the kingdom aimed to please him.

On the day of the visit, everybody who had taken any part in the building of the temple was assembled in front of it. In the first row were the Prince's counsellors and advisors, who had said that it was quite unnecessary to waste money building a temple but who, when the Prince had ordered work to start, had been broad-minded enough to raise no objection. Behind them came the Royal Suppliers, who had found stone (which was underneath their feet) and workmen (who daily stood in the middle of the market place in search of work). Behind these came the architects, of whom there were eight, each of whom had drawn up a design for the building and had had it turned down by the Prince, thus proving that the Prince was eight times as good as any architect in the kingdom. Behind these stood the master mason who had built the temple according to the Prince's instructions, save that he had put in a few tricks of the trade to ensure that it did not fall down: then, at a considerable distance, came the men who had built the temple, their sons, their relatives and friends: behind these stood Balan and the old man. Behind Balan and the old man was nobody because from so far away nothing could be seen at all.

When the Prince arrived the people in the front rows saw

a tall man without much hair on his head, who had thin but delicately shaped lips, a fine curved nose that was a little wrinkled up at the nostrils, and eyes that were half closed as though from insupportable weariness. He was dressed in the height of a foreign fashion that consisted of shawls draped around the upper part of his body, the whole elegantly caught in at the waist with a belt made of gold tissue sprinkled with little round pieces of looking-glass. The prince walked on gold sandals under a silk umbrella and the bystanders bowed to the ground and looked at him through their fingers.

The Prince tilted back his head and looked at the façade of the temple. It was forty-six feet high and it was carved with seven hundred figures.

The Prince said:

"Charming." He ran his eyes over the seven hundred figures and his expression was that of a man looking at a litter of puppies.

"Clumsy in places, but charming," he said.

Everybody took his fingers away from his eyes, straightened his back, looked at the forty-six-foot-high temple as though it were a litter of puppies and said: "It is charming."

Speaking to the man who bore his umbrella, the Prince said:

"It is not a masterpiece, but then, we did not expect masterpieces from our local talent." He then went inside and was immediately followed there by the Chief Brahmin and some seventy lesser Brahmins, all chanting.

The Prince's last remark had been spoken quietly and this caused confusion among the spectators. Some heard the word "masterpiece" and therefore gazed at the temple transfixed, drawing in little breaths of astonishment. Others heard the words, "We did not expect masterpieces from our local talent," and these were beaming upon the master mason: while others heard exactly what the Prince had said and therefore looked contemptuous and amused. Since this last is a striking and sobering expression, the others became aware of their mistake, and in due course everybody managed to look contemptuous and amused, except the stonemasons. Balan and the old man had no noteworthy expression on their faces at all because they had heard nothing and seen nothing except the tip of the Prince's honorific umbrella.

By the time that everybody outside had assumed the right expression, the priests inside had got well launched into the ritual of blessing the temple: a long affair in any circumstances, but particularly now, since the Chief Brahmin had the Prince at his mercy and the Prince, a year ago in the palace, had called him a prosy old fool. The Chief Brahmin therefore spun out the prayers and scattered the holy water with the deliberation of a man distributing the last remaining drink to a caravan lost in a desert. The Prince sat upon a carpet in a devout posture, and yawned.

The Prince looked up and round the hollow pyramid of the temple but could make out nothing, since the ritual lamps of the Brahmins scarcely carried beyond the altar. The Prince yawned again and began dressing himself in another foreign fashion, item by item, in his mind's eye. This was a favourite device of his to pass away the time, and in following it out, he began to play with his sash. The mirrors on the sash threw reflections. One of these fell straight on the face of the Chief Brahmin, putting his chanting out of beat in a manner which the Prince found amusing. The Prince now began to aim one of the mirrors with more accuracy, but the Chief Brahmin glancing at him as he did so, the Prince pretended to be throwing the reflection on the walls.

Thus, quiveringly alive in the beam of the mirror, Balan's statue burst upon the astonished Prince.

the tale
of the
stone woman
conclu∂e∂

When the ceremony was over the Prince
came out of the temple. His brows were drawn together, his
eyes flashed, and his lips were tight with anger. He spoke sharply
to a chamberlain, who spoke irritably to the front rank of the
crowd, who spoke furiously with one another. After a moment,
the master mason strode towards Balan and seized him by the
shoulder.

"This is the scoundrel," he said and gave Balan a vigorous
push. "This is the scoundrel who carved the woman. Beg pardon
at His Highness' feet and may he have mercy on you."

Balan could now see the Prince quite clearly, for the crowd
had parted to leave a lane for him. He saw not only the Prince,
but also the executioner who stood by his side.

The master mason gave him a second push and Balan ran
unsteadily down the lane until he reached the Prince, when he
flung himself face downwards in the dust a few inches from the
Prince's golden sandals. He heard the Prince's voice above him.

"Is this true?" the Prince said. "Is it true that you carved
the woman?"

Balan bobbed his head up and down in the dust.

"I mean the woman in the northeast corner," said the Prince.

Balan bobbed his head again.

"How old are you?"

"Eighteen, Sire."

"Did anybody help you?"

"No, Sire."

"It is a masterpiece. What is your name?"

Balan, lifting his mouth from the dust, told the Prince's shapely ankles his name.

"It is I who should be grovelling on the ground before you," said the Prince's voice. Balan lifted his eyes to the Prince's knees. The Prince went on: "However, in the circumstances, your present position is to be preferred. Look up." Balan did so. The Prince's expression was ferocious.

"Do not take any notice of the way I look," the Prince went on. "If they thought I liked your sculpture I would never have found out who did it. I should have been told it was done by the son of my superintendent of works, who has not enough talent to carve a pat of butter. Get down on the ground again."

Balan, his blood racing with pleasure, obeyed.

"I want to talk to you. Can you hear me?"

"Yes, Sire."

"When I tell you to get up, rise and follow the executioner. You understand?"

"Yes, Sire."

"Look as though you are going to have your head cut off."

"Yes, Sire."

Balan raised his eyes to the Prince's ankles again.

"Sire."

"What now?"

"How does a person look who's going to have his head cut off?"

"There speaks the true artist," said the Prince. "A person in these parts who is going to have his head cut off looks, if possible, even more stupid than he does in a normal circumstances.

I find it very disappointing. You would think that the prospect of being decapitated would sharpen their wits a little, but it doesn't. Now, be quiet and do as I told you. I cannot keep this expression any longer. It is making my face ache and I shall develop lines on my forehead. Rise!"

"He deserves it," said the crowd, as the Prince, his umbrella bearer, the executioner, and an expressionless but dusty Balan slowly walked away.

When they arrived at the palace, the Prince questioned Balan again, and in private, nor was he quite satisfied that Balan was the sculptor of the masterpiece until Balan had modeled a piece of clay into the shape of an animal. The animal that Balan chose to model was a leopard, and when the Prince had done admiring it, Balan explained how he had looked at the leopard in the palace gardens and carved what he saw.

"Do you always carve what you see?" asked the Prince.

"Always, Sire."

"Did you see that woman?"

Balan, thinking of the hours he had spent by the well, said: "Yes."

This answer put him into the most desperate peril, but not immediately. First the temple was surrounded by soldiers every evening: the soldiers built a platform inside the temple and for ten evenings in succession the Prince climbed the scaffolding, and while the officers of the army held flaming torches, the Prince gazed at the masterpiece.

He admired the lines, the planes, the pose, and the rhythm of Balan's sculpture until Balan's head swelled with pride and he stopped adding "Sire" to the end of every sentence when he spoke to His Highness. During these ten days Balan lived luxuriously in the palace and was given everything that he desired, except money.

Then on the eleventh day the Prince said to him:

"I have decided four things. First, I shall reward you with a gold chain, the title of Sculptor to the Court, and a suite of rooms in the west wing to be yours as long as you live."

Balan bowed, by no means to the ground, but respectfully.

"Second," said the Prince, "I have decided that these honours shall be showered on you on the day that you bring here before me the woman you studied as a model of your sculpture and," went on the Prince as Balan began to protest, "thirdly, I have decided to marry her: that is, if she is exactly, and in all respects, the same as your wonderful sculpture. Fourthly, if she is not, I shall cut off your head as an impostor, even if you carve me a whole menagerie of leopards. That is all. Have you anything to say?"

But Balan had nothing to say at all, for he lay at His Highness' feet insensible.

The Prince gave Balan seven days in which to produce the royal bride. A hundred times on each of those seven days Balan cursed his genius: although he spent hours at the well, he could find no one woman who looked like his sculpture. Some had the eyes, many had the mouth, a few had the bosom, and two had the hips. But short of cutting the women up and sticking them together again—which was what he had done in his mind's eye when he carved the statue—there was no way of meeting the Prince's demand.

On the sixth day he had chosen a girl in desperation and by denying the plain evidence of his eyes he had told himself that she would do. He had gone to the Prince with as much courage as he could muster and he had begun to say the woman's name: but the sight of the Prince's discriminating eyes, the sight of the Prince's fastidious nostrils, and the knowledge that in matters

of art the Prince was notoriously no fool had betrayed him. He
had backed out of His Highness' presence, confused, trembling,
and almost as bloodless as when he swooned away.

The Prince affected to notice nothing of all this. But when
Balan reached the door in his backward progress, the Prince
asked his chamberlain in a loud voice to tell him the date.

The rest of this sixth day of his allotted seven, Balan spent
in wandering through the town looking at women in a manner
so distracted that they drew their head-coverings more closely
about their faces and trotted rapidly away from his neighbour-
hood with indignant clatterings of their silver anklets. Thus
occupied, and scarcely knowing what path he took, he drew
near the temple in which his misfortune had begun. He was
seized with a great desire to tell his troubles to someone, and,
seeing the temple, he remembered the old man with dirty hands
who had been his partner on the scaffold. It seemed to Balan
that this old man was sufficiently obscure and friendless to be
safe with Balan's secret. He hurried towards the temple.

While nobody in the town knew just how Balan had contrived to escape (as it seemed) his fate, anybody with eyes could
see that Balan still carried his head on his shoulders. Besides,
he wore a court robe, a sure sign of the Prince's favour. Therefore, when the master mason saw Balan approaching the
temple, he scrambled down from his scaffold, ran towards him,
and made the young man a profound salutation.

"Ah," said Balan, with some irritation, "my old master. I was
looking for the man who used to work with me inside."

"His Highness wants him?" said the master mason, bowing
again.

"No," said Balan. "No, not at all. I—I wanted to discuss
something with him myself."

"Of course, of course," said the master mason. "Nothing

could be more natural. Unfortunately he has been sent away."
He bowed a third time and as he did so he could not help
admiring his own knowledge of how to handle men. Anybody
else, he reflected, would have made the mistake of treating Balan
as an old friend. But not the master mason.

"Is there any way in which I could help you?" said the
master mason.

"Yes," said Balan. "I've told you. I want to speak to the old
man. You can tell me where he is."

"Certainly, certainly," said the master mason. He permitted
himself just the least touch of familiarity. "His Highness was
very complimentary to me about the statue which took his
fancy. But of course I insisted that it was you who carved it,
not me."

"That was kind of you," said Balan, looking about him impatiently.

"It was no more than the truth. As I told His Highness, my
part in it was merely to guide your hand with my experience and
to encourage you to go on when the difficulties got too much
for you. His Highness—"

But at this moment Balan saw the old man sitting cross-
legged on the ground a hundred yards away, smoothing a large
stone with a chisel. He made his excuses very hurriedly to the
master mason, who, with all the breeding in the world, said that
he fully understood. He said that he hoped that Balan would
pay him a visit tomorrow.

At this word Balan went pale.

"Or the day after tomorrow," said the mason with great tact;
at which Balan said, seizing his hands emotionally:

"Oh yes. Yes, so do I. I do hope we shall meet the day after
tomorrow."

As the master mason watched Balan make his way towards

the old man, he smiled. There was no doubt, he told himself, that he knew how to handle men.

The old man had grown, if anything, dirtier since Balan had last seen him and his voice had become more cracked. When Balan had seated himself beside him (for the old man gave him no greeting) the old man said:

"They don't let me work inside any more. Know why?"

"No."

"Because they think the smell of me might annoy your fancy friend."

"You mean His Highness?"

The old man, for an answer, sent chips from the stone flying in Balan's direction.

"So they put me on this," he croaked. "To what," he said, "do I owe my promotion? Your pull at court, I suppose?" The old man spat. Balan with tears in his eyes said:

"Don't be angry with me. And I haven't got any pull at court. In fact, I'm in dreadful trouble."

The old man glanced at his face and then, laying down his chisel, said:

"Tell me, my boy."

"How long have you got to find her?" asked the old man, when Balan had finished.

"Till tomorrow morning," said Balan, and he stared at the old man with wide-open eyes, picturing the morning, the executioner, his sword, and his own head rolling across the Prince's marble floor.

"Well, that's plenty of time," said the old man. "I know she's in the village because I saw her on the road not an hour ago. Fancy little chit," said the old man with a salacious grin.

"If you go now you'll catch her by the well, I shouldn't wonder."

"Catch who?" asked Balan.

"The woman you're looking for."

"But she doesn't exist," said Balan.

"Oho yes she does," said the old man. "She's the one we all call Lotus Blossom."

"*Lotus* Blossom?" said Balan in a shocked voice, for she was the town's most notorious young woman.

"Yes," said the old man. "Though she's pretty well in full bloom by now, eh?" He chuckled enormously at his own joke until he had to stop for a fit of coughing.

"But she's nothing like my statue," said Balan.

"Look," said the old man, wagging a dirty finger at him. "You're maybe a genius but you don't know anything about life."

"That's true."

"Whereas me," said the old man, "I *am* a genius and I know a sight too much about life. So just you go and tell Lotus Blossom to have a talk with me and after that you take her to the Prince. It'll be all right, I promise you."

"But what a gamble," said Balan, almost crying with anxiety.

"Better a gamble than a dead certainty," said the old man and he made a chopping gesture with his unwashed hand that made Balan's blood stand still in his veins.

Balan went to the well. He did not have to search for Lotus Blossom. The difficulty for any well-dressed young man in her vicinity was to avoid her. She cast Balan a languorous look and walked past him in a provocative manner. Balan coughed. She stopped. He looked furtively to left and right and delivered his message.

Lotus Blossom listened. Balan asked her if she had understood. She lowered her eyelids slowly looking sideways up at him. In her usual daily run this expression spoke volumes. Balan, in the circumstances, found it uninformative. But she sinuously walked away and since she was going, however loiteringly, in the direction of the temple, Balan took it that she had grasped his message. He looked after her and sighed. She was not even the same height as his statue.

In the cool of the evening Balan presented Lotus Blossom to the Prince. His knees shook but he managed to keep control of his voice as he told the Prince of his final success in finding his model. He waved his hand towards Lotus Blossom, who stood beside him swathed from head to foot in innumerable gauzes.

"Unveil," the Prince commanded.

"Highness," said Balan, "the lady requests that she be seen by the same light as you saw my statue: namely, she asks for lamps and a darkened room."

"Aesthetically," said the Prince, "there is much to be said for such a course. Come, my dear," he said, endeavouring to pierce with his eager eye the wrappings about her, "let us go to an inner apartment."

Curving rhythmically, Lotus Blossom followed the Prince into a small but restfully appointed room in which the Prince had his day bed.

Attendents drew the curtains; servants brought lamps. When they were lit, the Prince clapped his hands and everyone save Lotus Blossom and the Prince withdrew.

"Come, my dear," said the Prince and drew her down onto the bed. As she slowly sank into a sitting position, Lotus Blossom deftly dropped an aromatic pastille into the nearest lamp.

The Prince remembered his reputation. He made some remarks about sculpture, but they were perfunctory. "Now, my dear," he said.

Lotus Blossom leaned towards him, kissed him, lowered her eyelids, and lengthily unveiled.

As Balan knew, there were innumerable differences between her torso and that of his statue. The Prince passed them over, noting only one. He observed, with rapturous delight, that Lotus Blossom was by no means made of stone.

Balan waited in an agony of suspense until the Prince sent out for an elaborate supper for two. Balan waited on till midnight, more puzzled than anxious, until the Prince sent out for sherbets and his sleeping gown. Then Balan went to bed and slept until next morning, but with some very bad dreams. A knock on his door brought him bounding out of bed, his fingers feeling his throat. The door opened to admit a gigantic Negro slave bearing a scimitar.

Its hilt was incrusted with precious stones. Turning this rich hilt towards Balan, the Negro slave thrust it into Balan's trembling hands. A bustle at the door heralded a court official who, out of breath with running, read from a vellum scroll the announcement that His Highness had raised Balan, at six o'clock that very morning, from the rank of Sculptor to the Court to the rank of Sculptor Extraordinary, with the right to bear arms, the rank of a nobleman, and a pension for life.

Once more, Balan fainted dead away.

Some weeks later Balan and the old man were taking their ease in the garden enclosure of Balan's palace suite. The old man was now Advisory Assistant to the Sculptor Extraordinary and he, too, had a pension. He also had an official robe of white damask, in which, despite a thorough scrubbing by the palace attendants, he managed to look dirtier than ever.

"How did you know," asked Balan, "that His Highness' celebrated good taste for artistic things had—well—its other side?"

"How?" said the old man. "I'll tell you something, and see that you always bear it in mind. Art is long, my boy, but a touch of Mother Nature goes a dam' sight further."

"Yes," said Balan, and remained silent until it was time to go to an official reception.

He scarcely touched a chisel again till the day of his death forty years later, for he was too busy being an officially acknowledged genius.

the oRdeal
of
chastity

During the whole length of the festivities which greeted Rama's return to Ayoda (with his army accompanying him to add conviction to the citizens' rejoicings) Sita's title of Most Faithful Wife had the desired effect of repressing gossip. Barat met his brother a mile from the gates, dressed in plain white, and in a lengthy speech insisted that he accepted the throne only as a regent. Rama and he went on together in the same chariot and the acclamations of the citizens were frantic. Flowers were rained upon Sita, and some of them fell upon Valmiki, who rode in her train disguised as a royal tutor, for he feared his enemies, the Brahmins, even under royal protection.

At the gateway the procession was witnessed by a stately if coarse-featured lady who was dressed for travelling, and whose sumptuous caravan waited in a side alley. This was Mantara, once a nurse, then the Lady Mantara, and now a rich old woman with a safe conduct from the clement Rama.

When she heard the citizens near her shout Sita's new title, she said:

"Most faithful, eh? When I was a girl, a woman who'd lived in the house of another man had a little test to pass before she was called that. Some of 'em passed it, I don't deny, or so it's said. But most of them were done to a turn."

The citizens laughed, and Mantara, the procession over, called her camels and went on her way, wicked, malicious, exposed, disgraced, and the owner of a small fortune in state jewels. Thus nemesis, if not bankruptcy, overtakes the wrongdoer in the end.

The rejoicings lasted three days. At the end of this period the citizens, reluctant to return to the daily round, looked about them for other entertainment. It was then that the words of Mantara bore fruit. The citizens, in a loyal address to their beloved ruler, asked that he put his wife on a pile of inflammable wood and ignite it. If she was burned it would prove that she had been unchaste. If she was not burned—and they were loyally sure she would not be—it would prove that she was chaste. The Brahmins, to a man, applauded the idea which, they said, had the sanction of religion and ancient custom.

Rama received the address in full state. In the days before his exile he would have been enraged, horrified, and indignant. He would have denounced the custom as barbarous and the citizens as ghouls. Now he dismissed them with little gifts, and sent for Valmiki.

Valmiki, in turn, sent for the King's astrologer.

The King's astrologer listened to Valmiki and said that it could certainly be done but the matter would take time. He would have to make experiments, first with an unchaste woman and then with a chaste one. In these matters one had to proceed step by step. He would need apparatus.

Rama, who was present, had progressed sufficiently in the art of government to tell the astrologer that his apparatus was ready and waiting. Striking a gong, he called for someone to lead the astrologer to his new laboratory. The astrologer was less surprised than Rama had hoped when after a moment the two torturers, grown rather fatter but no less menacing, stood ready in the doorway.

The astrologer sighed and turned to Valmiki.

"It is called Egyptian Fire," he said. "It is used by the priests of Anubis to produce miracles. I can make enough of it for your purpose in twenty-four hours."

The next day but one the great square in front of the temple was packed with citizens standing shoulder to shoulder, so many that the soldiers could barely keep them clear of the pyre which had been built in the middle. It was an immense platform of wood, with two wall-like heaps of lighter wood running its entire length, leaving between them a narrow pathway.

At noon Rama took up his station on the temple steps under the royal umbrella. At five minutes past noon, chanting was begun by a choir of Brahmins of hymns in praise of chastity, and Rama noticed that one of the best-received by the crowd (which joined in) was that written by Kumar.

At half past twelve Sita came out, dressed in white and surrounded by weeping ladies-in-waiting. Bowing to Rama, she stood in prayer for a moment. Then she mounted the pyre amidst a great silence. As she reached the top, men put torches to the lower levels of the wood, which blazed instantly. Sita now began to walk slowly through the narrow corridor, and this burst into a furious flame and smoke of the most vivid colours. She was immediately lost to sight.

The citizens groaned but whether because Sita was, it seemed, unchaste, or whether because they were going to be cheated of seeing her burned to a cinder, they themselves could not have said.

Then, after a considerable interval, Sita emerged, soiled in places by soot, but otherwise unharmed. As the citizens caught their breath, white doves descended out of the sky and flew around Sita's head.

The enthusiasm of the people knew no bounds except those of the spear butts of the soldiers who plied them manfully on anybody who approached too near the now historic pyre of chastity.

Drinking cooling sherbet in the palace afterwards, Rama said to Sita:

"I hope you were not frightened."

"A little," said Sita, but without agitation. "There was more smoke than I expected from what you told me about the Egyptian Fire."

"You need not have been alarmed," said Rama, "I had fifty guards with buckets of water hidden behind the temple in case of accidents. But the astrologer did very well. I must reward him. Altogether, it was most impressive."

"Still," said Valmiki, "the fire was only a conjurer's trick. The doves, now, which were my contribution, raised the whole thing to a poetic level."

envoy

The next morning, very early so that they might part unobserved, Rama and Valmiki rode to the main gate of Ayoda. Two guards, discreetly armed beneath their cloaks, rode with them, a bag of gold at each of their saddlebows, the King's gift to his mentor.

The gates had been closed the previous night. The two guards rode forward to awaken the gatekeeper. Rama and Valmiki reined in their horses and waited.

A tipsy citizen who had been spending the night in an unsavoury quarter of the town came lurching round a corner. Seeing two well-dressed gentlemen on horseback, he pulled himself together, wished them a dignified good morning, and went on his way, unsteady in his walk, but with an expression of profound respectability.

Rama and Valmiki watched him go and then smiled at each other.

The gates opened.

Rama said:

"Now we must part. I shall miss you greatly. I lay awake last night remembering the time we have spent together. I made up my mind to ask you a question. You have shown me how many things are illusion. But in your way of looking at the world, is there anything that you believe is real?

Valmiki said:

"Certainly, Rama. There are three things which are real: God, human folly, and laughter. Since the first two pass our comprehension, we must do what we can with the third. And now, we both have work to do. We must say goodbye."

The two men leaned from their horses and for a moment embraced.

Then Rama rode back to the palace to govern Ayoda, and Valmiki, his guards on either side of him, rode through the gate towards a place of tranquillity in which to finish his story.

THE END